High Density

FREYA BARKER

HIGH DENSITY

Copyright © 2025 Freya Barker

All rights reserved.

No part of this publication may be reproduced, distributed, or transmitted in any form or by any means, including photocopying, recording, or by other electronic or mechanical methods, without the prior written permission of the author or publisher, except in the case of brief quotations embodied in used critical reviews and certain other non-commercial uses as permitted by copyright law. For permission requests, write to the author, mentioning in the subject line: "Reproduction Request" at the following address: freyabarker.writes@gmail.com

This book is a work of fiction and any resemblance to any place, person or persons, living or dead, any event, occurrence, or incident is purely coincidental. The characters, places, and story lines are created and thought up from the author's imagination or are used fictitiously.

9781988733968

Cover Design: Freya Barker

Editing: Karen Hrdlicka

Proofing: Joanne Thompson

Cover Image: Jean Woodfin—JW Photography

Cover Model: Brandon Thyfault

FREYA BARKER

Since taking over the veterinary clinic in Libby, Montana last year, Janey Richards has been burning the candle at both ends. She's grateful she is busy, but there has barely been any time to build a life outside of work. To help pay down her debt faster, she agrees to take on responsibility for the livestock at Libby's annual rodeo, but perhaps she should've thought twice about the added stress.
Although, her personal life is definitely looking up.

JD Watike never thought he'd end up following in his father's footsteps, but he's found his stride these past six years as a member of the High Mountain Trackers team. He enjoys the simplicity of small-town living, which has only gotten more interesting since Doc Richards appeared on the scene.
Spending most of the past year patiently observing from a distance, the time feels right for him to make his move.
Or at least to clear up some misunderstandings.

The opportunity presents itself sooner than expected, when the pretty veterinarian stumbles onto some serious criminal activity at the Libby Roundup, and a young woman

One

JANEY

There is nothing as pretty as a spring sunset in these mountains.

Golds and purples streak the sky and reflect off the peaks; almost too much abundance for the eye to take in.

The first few months after taking over Doc Evans's clinic last year, any time I'd get called out around sunset, I would stop to take pictures. I must have hundreds of them eating up memory in my phone, but none of them even come close to reflecting the depth of colors nature provides.

Tonight, however, I can't afford to slow down.

I just got home and was looking forward to the leftover lasagna in my fridge, after driving all around the county to administer spring vaccinations, when I got an urgent call from Lucy at Hart Horse Rescue. One of their horses is in distress with what appears to be colic.

It's not an uncommon ailment, but it's painful for the animal, and can be dangerous if it involves a twist in the bowel. That's why proper diagnosis is key. If the horse is simply impacted, the treatment is pain control, mild exercise, and hydration, but if we're dealing with an intestinal torsion, surgery will be needed. Of course, that would require transporting the horse to the nearest equine hospital, which would be Ponderosa in Kalispell, since I don't have the facility or the equipment.

When I turn onto the property, I can see the lights are already on at the barn. I don't bother stopping at the house first and drive straight through, parking my truck right by the barn doors. I have everything I need, including my portable ultrasound, in the back. My truck has a cover on the bed, so I can keep my stuff dry and secure back there.

Bo, Lucy's husband, is already opening the barn door for me.

"Need me to grab anything?" he asks.

I hold up my field bag. "For now, this is all I need."

I follow him to a stall that is bathed in light from a flood lamp clamped to a post. Inside, Lucy is trying to coax a dark bay mare to get up on all fours. She's currently sitting on her hind end like a dog would and looks to be in obvious distress, her eyes wild and nipping at her own side.

"Okay, let's get her to her feet first," I order, dropping my bag in a corner before turning to Bo. "We'll need a long strap or a rope."

While he goes in search, I find my stethoscope and try to get a heart rate, which isn't an easy feat with the horse crazy with pain and sitting in this position.

"How long has she been like this?"

Lucy blows a long strand of blond hair out of her eyes.

"She didn't eat today, and she looked restless this afternoon, so I came back to check on her after dinner and she was in obvious pain, which is when I called you. I tried to

2

get her to drink, walked her around a bit in the meantime, and was just about to try some water again when she plopped down like this."

I do a quick check for dehydration by pressing on her gums to see how long it takes for the small capillaries to refill.

"She's definitely dehydrated," I confirm, just as Bo walks into the stall with a long cargo strap. "That's perfect. Let's double it up and slide it under her hips."

It takes a bit of doing, but we manage.

"Lucy, if you grab both sides of her halter and pull at the same time. On three. One, two..."

On three, I put all of my one hundred and ninety-two pounds into the effort. This is one of those rare times where I'm grateful to be of a heftier variety. I'm not short at five foot eight, and the pounds are distributed well on my body, but I'm more than aware there are quite a few too many of them.

Luckily, because of the work I do, I am fit and strong, and I eat pretty healthy most of the time. Still, whenever I'm weighed at my doctor's office, I am sternly reminded that at my age it wouldn't take much to slip from simply over-weight into obese territory.

God, how I dread that stupid BMI scale. How can you use one single standard for the endless variety of human beings there are? It's numbers, and they don't take into account genetics, metabolic speed, health issues, mobility, and I could list an endless number of individual circum-stances that should be taken into account when looking at what constitutes a healthy weight for a particular individual.

That's not even the worst part; any health complaints you might have are so readily linked to that number on the scale. We're supposed to believe that losing weight is the be-all end-all of every conceivable ailment.

I call bullshit. I've never been a small girl, I grew up on a ranch, was put to work from the time I was seven- or eight-years-old, and am generally fit as a fiddle. I've always been comfortable in my skin, and I'm not about to let some arbitrary number on a scale invented by some random Belgian mathematician make me feel bad. The man wasn't even a physician, for Pete's sake.

"Good girl, Starla. Good girl," Lucy soothes the horse when we have her standing on trembling legs.

Now that she's upright, it's easier for me to listen to her gut sounds. There appears to be some increased activity.

"I'm going to do a quick rectal exam, and after that I'll probably use a nasogastric tube to see if there is a buildup of fluids in her stomach. Are you okay with me giving a sedative now? Spare her any more discomfort?"

I prefer getting consent before administering any medications, especially sedatives or anesthetics, because they always come with risks.

"Whatever you need to do, Doc."

Once the sedation starts taking effect, I quickly don a disposable long-sleeve glove with shoulder protection, and set to the fun task of rooting around the poor animal's gut.

"I can feel an impaction," I report, retrieving my arm and disposing of the glove.

Luckily, there is no fluid build-up in her stomach, but I leave the tube in to hydrate her. With the help of the portable ultrasound, I confirm there isn't anything else going on aside from the impacted stool she has trouble moving.

The fluids will help, as will the pain medication I give her, and after waiting to see the first signs of improvement, I leave Starla in Lucy's good care. Nature will have to take its course.

Bo walks me to my truck.

"Thanks for coming out, Doc."

"No problem. Call me if there's any change for the worse. I'll check in tomorrow to see how she is."

I smile and wave as I pull away from the barn, but as soon as I'm out of sight, I grimace with hunger pains. My stomach feels like it's eating itself.

Rather than driving all the way home to get to my left-over lasagna, I pull into the first place I come across I know has food; Foxy's Bar. It's less than two miles from the rescue. I've grabbed something here once before, so I know it promises greasy bar food.

Just what the doctor ordered.

It's not crazy busy, just a couple of bikers sitting at the bar, a few locals playing pool, and only two tables occupied with families.

"Find yourself a spot," I'm told by a waitress toting a tray full of drinks to one of the tables.

I grab a table near the back. I'm not up for socializing and plan to dine and dash; I'm exhausted.

"What can I get you?" the waitress asks when she finds me.

"What is fast? Food-wise," I quickly clarify.

"Five minutes for a pulled pork sandwich and fries."

"Sold," I tell her with a grin. "And half a pint of what-ever pale ale or lager you have on draft."

"Coming right up," she promises, before walking straight through what I assume is the door to the kitchen.

As I watch her disappear to the back, I can feel a rush of cool air when someone opens the front door. When I turn around, I'm unexpectedly met by a familiar pair of dark-brown eyes locked on me.

~

JD

"Are you heading out, son?"

I turn around to find Thomas sitting on the porch.

Thomas is my boss Jonas's father and old as dirt. I swear he spends most of his days out here on the porch just so he doesn't miss a damn thing that goes on at the High Meadow ranch. He's in his nineties and may be frail, but his mind is still sharp as a tack.

My ma runs the ranch house here at High Meadow, and she and Thomas have a special bond. They bicker like siblings, but everyone can see they adore each other. For Ma —who grew up in the foster system—Thomas is more of a father figure.

The old man sits on the porch and doles out his wisdom to anyone passing by—whether you want it or not—and is about as subtle as a two-by-four between the eyes. My mother doesn't mince words either, so in that respect they're peas in a pod.

"Yeah, it's been a long day."

We rode out early this morning to take a herd to pastures close to the ranch's boundary lines, where they'll graze for the summer months. Unfortunately, when we got there, we found a lot of the fences damaged and ended up spending the rest of the day fixing those.

By the time we got back it was almost dark. Dan went straight home, but Jackson and I grabbed some dinner here.

"I heard," Thomas shares. "What do you reckon messed up those fences?"

"Not sure. Looked like a bunch of elk or something plowed through, but some of the lumber was already rotting, so it needed repairs anyway."

"Herd secure?"

"Yup. They're all set for the summer."

The storm door creaks when Alex, Jonas's wife and Jackson's mother, pokes her head outside.

"Are you gonna come in tonight, Pops, or are you planning to sleep on the porch?"

He huffs and flips back the throw blanket that is covering his spindly legs.

"Hold yer horses," he grumbles, hoisting himself to his feet.

I move to his side and grab him firmly by his elbow when he wobbles a little as he begins to shuffle to the door.

"Weren't you on your way home?" he snaps ungraciously, even as he puts most of his weight on me.

I grin and catch the amused twinkle in Alex's eyes as she patiently waits with the door propped open.

"I'm leaving right now," I tell him as I hand him off to Alex, who leads him inside. "See ya in the morning."

The old man doesn't turn around but lifts his free hand and waves as he shuffles down the hallway. I close the front door and head over to my truck.

I imagine it's not fun getting so old your body won't move the way you want it to anymore, and you need help with the most basic things. Still, I'd rather have a sound mind in a decrepit body, than the other way around. My grandpa on my father's side had vascular dementia, and he became a person we didn't recognize anymore. I know the prospect scares my pa, even though the disease itself isn't necessarily hereditary, the risk factors to developing it can be.

Up until last year, when Jackson—Alex's son and my friend—tried to finish the job himself, after nearly losing his life at enemy hands in a military operation overseas, I hardly ever gave thought to my own mortality. But that shook me up. Since then, I've tried to exercise a little more awareness, a little more consideration, and definitely more appreciation in my day-to-day life.

Like this old 1974 Ford F-100 I fixed up over the winter. It had been sitting in my parents' barn since my grandpa died over a decade ago. It was the first and the last vehicle he ever bought new, and he kept that truck in mint condition for as long as he could. He left me that truck in his will, and I never once looked at it.

Pa put it in the barn and kept it there all those years, maybe hoping I'd want it one day. He never said anything— Pa doesn't talk much anyway—but he joined me in that barn and worked with me to get the truck roadworthy.

She's old, there's a tear in the bench seat on the driver's side I still want to fix, and it could use some rust treatment and a new paint job, but her engine is in prime shape, and I've come to love every imperfection.

I turn right to get to my place—a trailer parked on a patch of land bordering Libby Creek—and pass Foxy's Bar. I used to stop in there all the time, but I haven't been there in months. It does decent business on the weekends and during the summer months when the RV park is full, but it's fairly quiet tonight. Not many vehicles in the parking lot.

Wait, is that Doc Richards's truck?

My foot is already slamming on the brakes before my mind processes the information.

Janey Richards. I don't think the woman likes me much, which is a shame, because she sure as hell has my eye. Just last week she lashed out at me when she was at the ranch dropping off a litter of puppies. I still don't fucking know what I said wrong, but the snap of fire in her eyes sure got my blood going.

I pull my truck in beside hers and without giving it a second thought, head inside.

That may have been a mistake.

My eyes zoom in on Janey the moment I walk through the door, and I see the surprise in hers when she recognizes me. I start walking toward her table, when I hear a squeal and see a flash of movement from the corner of my eye.

I turn in time to see Britt running in my direction. I barely have a chance to react when she launches herself at me, wrapping her arms around my neck and her legs around my hips. My hands automatically go to her ass to keep her from falling.

"Hey, handsome! I missed you."

Then her mouth is on mine, and I realize I should've stopped outside and thought this through.

Two

"Morning, Doc."

Logan is already feeding the patients when I walk into the clinic.

Although, clinic is a big word for what once was simply a barn.

Doc Evans—my predecessor—converted half of it into a clinic space with a waiting room, an office, bathroom, examination room, and a combined surgical and recovery room. The other half is still a barn of sorts, and it's where we keep any overnight *guests*. The old tack room barely holds the full-sized bed we sometimes use when a patient needs closer monitoring.

Logan slept there last night, keeping an eye on a pet goat that was brought in yesterday with a perforated gut. I did the best I could fixing him, but the shard of glass that had pierced his bowel had done quite a bit of damage. Miraculously, the animal came through surgery, but we have to monitor him closely for any signs of infection.

"Morning, Logan. How is our patient?"

"Hanging in."

I poke my head over the stall door and notice the animal is still pretty lethargic.

"Any sign of fever?"

Logan shakes his head, his floppy blond hair hanging in his eyes. He is one of my assistants, at least he is for the summer until he returns to college in Bozeman, where he is a third-year veterinary student.

"Not so far."

"Good. Let's hope he perks up a little over the next twenty-four hours."

It had been my recommendation to euthanize the animal, given the damage done and the questionable chance for recovery. Surgery would be expensive, and I ended up having to resect a substantial portion of his small intestines. Best-case scenario is the goat will need a special diet for the remainder of his life, or else he'll have ongoing digestive problems. However, the owners insisted I do whatever possible to save the goat, since their nine-year-old daughter is very attached to him.

Hey, I wasn't going to argue with them, but I won't stand by and watch any animal suffer unnecessarily. If he starts going downhill, I will strongly urge them to put him down.

"How did he end up with glass in his bowels anyway?" Logan wants to know.

I'm curious myself. I know there's a preconceived notion out there that goats will eat anything, and I guess some of them eat weird stuff, but I can't see one picking up a piece of glass and eating it. Unless, it was stuck inside food of some kind.

"I asked the owners to look around his pen, see if there are any broken light bulbs, make sure there is nothing in his feed, but I haven't heard anything yet."

"I don't think that glass came from a broken lightbulb, it was too thick for that."

He probably has a point. It was more the thickness of a clear bottle or a mason jar.

I do a quick check on our one other patient; a shepherd mix found on the side of the highway, probably hit by a car. She's not microchipped and I don't know her. I had Frankie —my full-time assistant—contact the other two small animal clinics in town to see if they were familiar with the dog, but no one knows who she is.

It's possible she was actually tossed from a car. It wouldn't be the first time that's happened. For whatever reason, some idiot owners think that's a valid solution when they can no longer keep the animal, instead of dropping it off at a rescue or even a clinic like mine. I don't run a rescue, but I wouldn't turn my back on an animal. Most people here in Libby know that.

She seems to be a sweetheart. Her tail is wagging when I sit down in the straw with her. The poor thing looks like she was dragged a ways, with deep abrasions along one side of her body. She also suffered a broken hind leg, some cracked ribs, and a fractured orbital bone. She must be in quite a bit of pain but still manages to be loving to anyone who gives her attention.

"Do we have a name for her yet?" Logan asks, hanging over the stall door.

"I don't know. What does she look like to you?"

"How about Ginger? She's got a bit of a reddish coat," he suggests.

"Yeah, we can call her Ginger. Do you like that name, girl?"

Her tail wags even faster at my voice.

"Let's see how she does eating, and maybe after try to coax her into a little walk outside."

"Will do."

I get up and brush the straw off my butt, when my phone buzzes in my pocket. It's the High Meadow Ranch number.

"Doc Richards."

I use Doc, a title I inherited the first time I showed up at the ranch and it stuck. I don't mind it, doctor seems so stuffy, and Janey is too easy to dismiss, especially for some of these ranchers who are more set in their ways. Doc seems to hold the perfect balance, it's casual, but the title still affords me some professional respect, albeit reluctantly in some cases.

"Doc, it's Alex at High Meadow. Sunny, that paint mare you saw a few weeks ago, is in labor, but she's struggling. Looks like the foal is wanting to come backward but one leg is folded forward."

Shit. That's a tricky presentation.

Only thing worse would be if the foal was a full breech with both legs forward. As it is, I'm going to have to try and move that stubborn leg backward without damaging the uterus. Once we have both legs, we can help the mare deliver quickly. Any time the back end comes first, there is a risk of the foal dying. The umbilical cord is compressed between the foal and the birth canal, cutting off oxygen to the foal. It's imperative it is delivered immediately, with or without the mare's help.

"On my way. Keep her on her feet and moving. Hopefully, it'll keep her from straining."

"Difficult delivery?" Logan asks, having guessed at the problem.

"Backward presentation with one leg breech," I tell him. "Sorry, kid, you're gonna have to hold down the fort. Frankie will be here in half an hour to give you a hand."

I know he'd love to come—and it would be good experience for him—but I have open clinic this morning and someone has to be here. He'll be able to handle most of the complaints that walk in.

I rush to toss any supplies I might need in the back of my truck and jump behind the wheel. Time is critical. But even as I'm peeling out onto the road, I find myself wondering if I'll bump into JD at the ranch. I haven't seen him since that awkward scene at Foxy's a couple of weeks ago.

It sure looked like he was coming straight for my table when the waitress bolted out of the kitchen and jumped into his arms, practically mauling him on the spot. He was quick to pluck her off him, setting her back on her feet, and he didn't seem too pleased with that course of events, but he did change direction. Instead of heading my way, he veered off to sit at the bar.

At that point, I turned away, and tried to put JD out of my mind. The man is as aggravating as he is attractive, or maybe I find him aggravating because he's attractive. In my experience, men who are that good-looking tend to be cocky, arrogant, and often players.

That last encounter did little to prove me wrong.

"Come on, girl, keep moving," I urge the pretty little paint, who keeps wanting to lay down.

When I walked into the barn earlier, Alex was trying to manage this mare by herself.

It's quiet at the ranch, Jonas and Sully are on day two of a three-day trip to Billings for a livestock auction, while Fletch, Jackson, and my father are on a search for a missing hiker. Dan is sticking close to home since Sloane is on bedrest with only five more weeks until her due date.

This time I volunteered to help Alex keep an eye on things here. Sunny isn't the only mare about to pop, there are two others who are getting close. Maybe I wanted to stick around because of the possibility we'd need to call Doc in. I haven't seen her since that disaster at Foxy's after I finally worked up the balls to approach her. I should've explained what she witnessed right on the spot, but I didn't, and there really hasn't been an opportunity since.

Staying behind appears to have paid off, as I watch her stride into the barn, all business. She's already wearing coveralls—probably wise, since birthing can be a messy business —and her hair is in two braids with a bandana tied around her head. Her eyes are focused on the mare, and she barely even acknowledges me as she puts down her bag and starts rummaging through it.

She works with a singular focus, which is one of the things that drew me to her in the first place. The animals are her first and main concern, and she has a bedside manner many a physician could learn from when dealing with their human patients.

"Did her water break?" she asks when she rounds the mare.

I notice she's looking at the dark wet spot running down the horse's legs.

"No. She had the shits and made a mess of herself. I rinsed her down."

Her eyes briefly flash my way before I get a mumbled, "Thanks."

Then she hands me the horse's tail to keep it out of her way.

"Alex is just up at the house grabbing a thermos of coffee for us," I share.

She barely nods, already easing her gloved right arm into the mare's birth canal.

"Hold her tight," she warns, her cheek pressed against Sunny's butt.

I can see the concentration on her face as she closes her eyes and frowns. The mare shifts uncomfortably, the invasion of her body not exactly a pleasant one.

"Hush, girl, you'll feel better soon," I mumble at Sunny.

The poor mare is grunting, her eyes are wild and every muscle in her body is trembling. She's in obvious distress.

Over her head I catch Alex walking into the barn.

"Morning," she greets.

"I'm going to try and move the second leg back," Doc announces without bothering to return pleasantries. "But I can't have her moving on me or I could damage her uterus. JD, I need you to brace her against the wall and use your body weight to keep her there, but glove up first, because as soon as I have the leg back, I need your help getting this baby out. Alex, if you'll take her head and keep it still."

The urgency in her voice has us jumping into action, and

the next ten minutes it's all-hands-on-deck. I end up on my ass in the stall, the slippery foal between my legs as I rub her roughly with handfuls of straw to stimulate her to breathe.

"How is she doing?" Doc asks, as she keeps a close eye on the mare, who is barely able to stay on her legs.

"Nothing yet," I report.

"Clean her nose, keep one nostril covered and blow puffs in the other," she orders. "We need to get some air in those lungs."

"I can do it," Alex offers, but I wave her off.

"I've got this."

I whip my shirt over my head, wipe as much of the mess off the foal's nose as I can, cover one nostril, and fit my mouth over the other. I'm really gonna need that coffee after this.

"Easy puffs," Doc warns. "Watch her chest move."

It only ends up taking a few before the little foal takes over breathing by herself.

"Good job."

When I look up at Janey, she's wearing a big smile aimed at me. Fuck if that doesn't make me feel like a million bucks. Worth the ruined shirt and the mouthful of gunk.

"Now I'm going to need some help back here again. Poor mom has a prolapsed uterus we need to get back into place."

Making sure the foal is okay by herself, I get to my feet and toss my dirty shirt on the other side of the stall door. Then I go see what Doc wants me to do.

"I need you to keep this elevated while I get things ready. We can't let it hang down, or it could cause tearing." She's holding up a substantial mass of bloody tissue in her hands. "But first wash your hands. Then grab one of the green sterile sheets from the bottom of my kit and bring it to me."

As I'm washing up at the sink, Bo comes strolling in. He stops in his tracks when he catches sight of me.

"Whoa."

"Not mine," I assure him when I see him scanning my body for injury. "Sunny had a messy delivery."

"You don't say. Giving Doc a hand, are ya? Flashing some skin in the process?"

Bo is our resident comedian. A good guy, but he sure loves to poke fun at people.

"Shut up and wash your hands," I grumble, bending over to rummage through Doc's bag for the sterile sheet. "You can give us a hand."

Bo—a former surgical nurse—does as asked. "Poor baby's got a prolapse," he establishes when he pokes his head into the stall. "Morning, ladies."

Armed with the green sheet, I motion for Bo to stand on Doc's other side, before reaching between her and the horse's back end to hand Bo two corners of the sheet. Holding on to my own two corners, we lift the sheet like a hammock underneath the inverted uterus Doc is holding.

"Perfect," she mumbles, when she's able to remove her hands.

"What did she have?" Bo asks, while Doc gets herself cleaned up.

"Little filly," Alex fills him in.

"Pretty markings," he points out.

The little one has a completely white mask, with chestnut on her stomach and legs, as well as framing every patch of white on her body. Her eyes are the kind of pale blue you know is going to stick. She'll be a beauty.

Doc sidles up to me, a roll of bandages in her hands, the rough fabric of her coveralls brushes my bare skin causing goosebumps to rise up.

"Don't move," she warns me. "I'll just work around you."

She gets even closer as she tries to wrap up the mare's tail to keep it out of the way. I close my eyes and groan on the inside, my body all too aware of her proximity. A soft deep chuckle has me snap my eyes open, only to find Bo's amused look aimed at me. When I narrow my eyes on him, it only makes him chuckle more.

Asshole.

The entire process of waiting for sedation to take effect, making sure the uterus is cleaned, and slowly massaging it back into the mare's abdominal cavity, feels like it takes hours. By the time I can let go of the sheet and help clean up, my arms feel like lead and my resistance is almost nonexistent.

So when Janey approaches the sink where I'm washing up—her coveralls hanging down from the waist, revealing her strong upper body in nothing more than a white tank top—the last string of resistance breaks.

"We need to talk."

Her eyes snap wide open.

"We do?"

"Damn right."

Three

"Breakfast."

I look over my shoulder to find Alex behind me.

I was just stripping out of my coveralls at the back of my truck, and loading everything up.

It was a good morning, difficult, but with the best possible outcome. Thank God for all the help, otherwise it could've ended up with a totally different result. Everyone stepped up, but I was particularly impressed with JD, and not just because of that smooth, sculpted chest he was flashing.

As if his good looks weren't intimidating enough, that chest only emphasized it. Not only do I suspect he is years too young for me, but I know for a fact he's well out of my league in the looks department.

Still, when he announced we needed to talk, I folded like a cheap suit instead of telling him where to shove it. Then he stalked out of the barn, leaving me standing there like an idiot. So I quickly washed up, and rushed to pack up my things, hoping to be out of here before he returned.

"I can't," I tell Alex.

"Yeah, you can. You haven't even had the coffee I brought into the barn. Besides, Ama will have a shit fit if you take off before eating something."

"I have clinic this morning," I insist.

"Then grab something for on the go. It'll take you five minutes."

The walk-in clinic opened an hour ago, five minutes won't make a big difference.

"Okay. I'll drive the truck over."

Since my business here is usually at the barn, I park my truck there and not by the house. In fact, I don't think I've actually ever been inside the house. The outside is beautiful —all natural stone and wood—so I imagine the inside will be spectacular as well.

I pull the truck into an empty spot next to JD's old pickup and walk up to the porch, where Alex is waiting for me. She leads the way into the house, where the smell of bacon and fresh coffee greet me. We walk through a hallway, past a set of stairs leading up to a large, open kitchen. The entire back of the house is one open living space, with a large dining space in front of massive picture windows in the middle, and a comfortable seating area with a big stone fire-place on the far side.

Ama glances up when we walk in and points her spatula at a seat at the huge kitchen island.

"Sit."

She is not someone to mess with, from what I under-stand. I've been told she's waved the scepter at the ranch house since long before Alex came along, even though she doesn't live here. At the time, I guess it was just Jonas and his men living here, but over the years more women came along, as they all seemed to have found their significant others.

Now there are only a couple of single men left, one of whom is sitting at the dining table, reading a newspaper over breakfast; Thomas Harvey, Alex's father-in-law. I wave at him as I take my seat.

"How do you take your coffee?" Ama asks, her tone begging no argument.

"Cream and sugar, please," I return politely.

I mumble, "Thank you," when she sets a large mug in front of me.

I feel Alex's eyes on me and when I glance over, the older woman wears a little smirk on her face. I'm sure she knew exactly what she was doing when she invited me in. From what I've seen from a distance, Ama is a little intimidating, and I don't really want to get on her bad side. Therefore, I don't argue when she piles a plate high with waffles, scrambled eggs, home fries, and bacon, and slides it in front of me.

"Eat up."

"Ma, she's not a dog," I hear a familiar voice snap behind me.

"No, but she works as hard as you boys do and needs her fuel just the same. She just doesn't have someone looking out for her like you do."

Undeterred by his mother's stern expression, JD rounds the kitchen island and bends down to kiss her cheek. His thick, short black hair is wet and he's wearing a clean shirt. Looks like he had a quick shower. I could probably use one too, but mine's going to have to wait.

Ama waves her spatula again. "Sit," she orders him, and he complies with a grin, taking the stool next to mine. In no time he has a hot coffee and a steaming plate of food in front of him too.

"Well, don't let it get cold."

Right.

I dig in and, having worked up a healthy appetite, manage to finish about three-quarters of what had been piled on my plate. But the five minutes I was going to spend have already turned into twenty, and I really need to get back to the clinic.

"This was delicious. Thank you. But I really should get going," I announce, resolutely getting to my feet.

I grab my mug and plate, and carry them over to the sink.

"See how easy that is?" I hear Ama say.

When I turn around, I see she has her eyes fixed on her son, who is grinning at her with a mouthful of food, but wisely keeps it shut.

"These boys," she continues with a headshake. "And I bet you left the wet towels on the bathroom floor as well. I already pity the woman who decides to take you on."

"Don't worry, Ma. For the right woman I may even put my dirty socks in the hamper."

Alex snickers, and I don't know why I'm suddenly blushing like a schoolgirl, but I'm instantly in a rush to get out of here.

"Thanks again. Have a good day." I throw in an awkward little wave and beeline it to the front door.

I barely make it to my truck when I hear heavy boots coming down the porch steps after me.

"I thought we were going to talk?" JD points out as he catches up with me.

"I have to get back to the clinic. I probably have a waiting room full."

I'm already climbing in behind the wheel, but he's holding on to my door.

"Okay, but I'd still like to talk to you," he insists. "How about dinner?"

"I don't know if I'll have time," I sputter.

He snorts. "You're gonna have to eat at some point. I'll pick you up at seven."

This is not a good idea, Janey.

But I'm so eager to get out of here, when I open my mouth, "Fine," comes shooting out.

As an afterthought, I add, "Unless I'm called out."

He leans in, fixing those dark, brooding eyes on me.

"See you at seven."

~

JD

"Nice."

The quarter horse Jonas backs out of the trailer is a beauty; dapple gray with a white mane and tail. He carries both his tail and his head high, dancing on his feet as he takes in his new surroundings.

"Yeah, he's a looker," Jonas confirms. "Spirited too, and already a big boy, even though he still has a good year—maybe two—before he's done growing."

Based on that, I'm guessing he's two and a half, at most, three years old. Horses are generally at full height at between four to five years of age.

Sully takes the lead from Jonas and starts walking the new stallion—who dances sideways alongside him—to the stables.

"He'll make some pretty babies," I observe.

"Let's hope he produces," my boss states. "I want Doc over here checking him out as soon as possible."

"Doc was just here this morning. Sunny went into labor and the foal was stuck backward."

At Jonas's look of concern, I immediately clarify, "Both are fine, but it took some doing. They're both still in one of the birthing stalls. The mare had a prolapse Doc managed to get back in place, but she was gonna check in again in the morning."

Jonas nods. "Call her. See if she can have a look at the new load then too." He points at the large trailer. "Picked up a couple of draft-quarter crosses, solid trail horses. Help me unload them?"

Most of the team's horses are that crossbreed, mainly because they're strong, sure-footed, and reliable, all of which are traits we need when we're out in the field. We want to be able to keep our focus on what's around us, rather than on trying to keep our horse controlled. Sure, it's fun from time to time to ride one with a bit more spunk, more spirit, but for work strong and steady does the job.

"We'll put these guys in the small paddock behind the barn for now."

By the time we've unloaded the three horses, and I've made sure they have some fresh hay and a filled water trough, it's already closing in on six thirty. I need to get home and grab another quick shower before I go pick up Janey.

"Taking off without dinner?"

Ma is just helping Thomas inside from his rocker on the porch when she catches me heading for my truck.

"I'll grab something. See you tomorrow," I quickly add as I jump behind the wheel.

If I don't get out of here right now, I know Ma will give me the third degree. As it is, I can see her watching me back out of my spot, her eyes narrowed in speculation. The woman has a sixth sense, she always knows when something is up. I never could lie worth shit to her, she always found a way to pick the truth out of me. She can be relentless.

As is evident two minutes later, when I pull onto the road and my phone notifies me I have a message. A quick glance shows it's Ma.

Don't forget your sister is visiting this weekend, in case you were hoping to make other plans.

Like I could've forgotten, she's been reminding me Una is coming up from California at least once a day for weeks. Ma doesn't know I probably talk to my sister more than she does, and I'd like to keep it that way.

Una is a little over four years younger than me. Growing up, I took my role as her protector pretty seriously, it was engrained by my father I had to look out for her. But that ended up taking on a different meaning than what he'd intended as we got older.

Una had a turbulent adolescence, facing off with my more traditional parents—especially Ma—constantly. My sister was struggling with her identity, something I'd become aware of, but our parents were oblivious to. Things became so strained between my parents and sister, that the moment she graduated high school, she packed her stuff and hit the road.

She landed in California where she ended up becoming

a wildland firefighter with the CCC, the California Conservation Corps. She's stationed out of San Luis Obispo and, from what I can gather, is happy there.

She rarely comes home though, maybe once or twice a year, and my parents have never been to visit her. I carefully suggested it a few times to both Una and our parents, but was shut down quickly with one excuse or another. They're civil to each other, but it's like they're still locked in a stand-off, with Ma and Una equally stubborn.

Unfortunately, I know for Una it's more than stubbornness keeping her away, but it's not my story to tell and a secret I'll take to my grave. Still, I'm not keen on being stuck in the middle, which is what it feels like on those rare occasions my family is together.

The moment I pull up to my trailer, I force thoughts of my family out of my head, and focus on getting cleaned up in record time.

With barely a minute to spare, I walk up to the door of the modest, single-story house set back from the road. I've been here before when Doc Evans was still living here, but I never realized how isolated this property is. Janey has a few neighbors, but they're not exactly within shouting distance since the house and clinic sit on a couple of acres. It's not like she can easily hop off her porch and knock on a neighbor's door for help. I should ask her about security.

But when I hear her footsteps approach, and the door opens to reveal Janey, every noble thought dissipates, only to be replaced with mostly indecent ones. It's the hair; dark and shiny, hanging loose in generous waves skimming her shoulders. I don't think I've ever seen her without braids or a ponytail, and I immediately want to sink my hands in those thick tresses.

The jean jacket and cowboy boots are familiar, but the

blue floral, flowy sundress underneath is also very different. Unexpected and very feminine, yet still Janey. She looks gorgeous. I'd like to think she dressed up for me, but I haven't seen that much of her outside of work, so I wouldn't really know if this is more the norm than the exception. Either way, I'm glad I thought to put on my dark jeans, good boots, and a navy dress shirt.

"Ready?" I ask when I'm finally able to peel my tongue off the roof of my mouth.

"Sure, let me grab my keys."

I notice her purse is a small, crossbody bag the size of a wallet, which can't house more than her phone, maybe a tube of lip balm, and now her house keys. She's clearly not a fussy woman, which suits me just fine.

As I open the passenger side door of my truck for her, she turns to face me.

"So where are we going?"

Fuck.

Maybe I should've planned this better.

Four

I was seriously tempted to pretend I got called out before he got here.

Especially after that call this afternoon, adding even more to my already substantial workload.

But then I caught myself.

It's not like invitations to dinner are a weekly occurrence. On the rare occasion I do eat out, it's by myself. I've been too busy for much of a social life since moving here last year. Hell, I haven't even started on any of the projects I had hoped to tackle in the house. The place was built in 1976, and I want to bet nothing much has changed since then. Not even the olive-colored appliances.

All that to say, I don't get out much, so why not enjoy when the opportunity presents itself? Even if it's just over dinner because I have to eat sometime.

So, instead of bailing, I had a quick shower, blow-dried my hair, left it loose, and put on one of the two dresses I own. I even put on some mascara, even though it had almost dried up in the tube I found in the back of the bathroom vanity drawer. I made an effort.

Not that I should have bothered, since he barely even seems to notice.

Of course, *he* is handsome as hell. He always is, but the dark navy of his jeans and shirt enhance his good looks even more. Still, he appears a bit distracted, and even though he said our destination is a surprise, I'm starting to wonder if he even knows.

"Is everything okay?" I ask cautiously as he drives us into town.

"Fine. Why?"

I shrug my shoulders. "I don't know, you seem a little... preoccupied?"

His grin is a little shy as he shakes his head.

"Nah. I'm just trying to figure out where the hell to take you."

I knew it.

"You don't *have* to take me anywhere," flies out of my mouth.

To be honest, I am pretty annoyed. Why the hell would he insist I have dinner with him, when it's apparently a chore?

"But I want to," he responds immediately, looking rather startled. "Otherwise, I wouldn't have asked."

Fair point, I guess. However, I'm starting to think staying home with a grilled cheese sandwich and a bowl of leftover squash soup in front of the TV might've been the better choice. Clearly, I'm out of practice socializing and at this point appear to be embarrassing myself.

I let my eyes drift out the side window, but I'm not really seeing the landscape passing by.

"Janey," he says in a low voice. "There's a new Mexican food truck parked by the Libby station I've heard great things about. I was thinking we could pick up some food there and head across the street to the Riverview Park to eat it. But then you opened the door looking gorgeous in that dress, and I realized you deserve better than a food truck and the park."

That's probably the most I've ever heard him say at once, but what sticks out is that final comment about me looking gorgeous. I'm instantly blushing like a schoolgirl again. Maybe it's hormones? Am I perimenopausal? At thirty-eight?

"I like the park," I tell him. "Mexican food by the water sounds perfect."

"Are you sure? I was going to find you a fancy restaurant."

That makes me snicker. "Me? I'm a simple country girl, JD. I grew up on a farm and still spend most of my days covered in animal guck; a fancy restaurant is no place for me. I'd probably use the wrong fork or something. A food truck and the park is more my speed."

I get a rare flash of strong white teeth between a pair of smiling, full lips, and suddenly my eyes are glued to his mouth.

"Good to know."

When I snap my eyes up, I catch him watching me before he turns his attention back to the road.

With our orders in hand—two soft beef tacos with Mexican slaw for me, a pair of burritos for JD, and a couple of drinks—we aim for the pavilion on the water's edge, which currently looks to be vacant. We sit down at one of the few picnic tables under the shelter.

"This is really good," I mumble around a mouthful of my taco.

The beef has a nice kick, which works really well with the crisp fresh taste of the slaw. Thank God for the stack of napkins the guy stuffed in the bag, because the juices are dripping down my chin. Perhaps not the most flattering food to choose under the circumstances, but I was hungry. Besides, JD seems to be suffering the same fate, his food no less messy.

He hums his agreement.

While we eat, I watch a couple of guys backing their truck with a fishing boat on the trailer up to the boat launch on the other side of the pavilion. One of them seems to recognize JD and calls his name. JD turns around and yells back a greeting.

"Friend of yours?"

"Not really. Played darts with him a time or two at Foxy's, but that's it."

I shove the last bite of taco in my mouth and wash it down with my bottle of water. Then I notice JD is already finished.

"About Foxy's..." he picks up, as if he was waiting for me to be done. "When I saw you there a few weeks ago, I was actually on my way over to your table but I was interrupted."

I had a suspicion him wanting to talk to me might have something to do with that awkward encounter. Bringing up the subject feels just as awkward, and I don't really know what to say, so I keep my mouth shut.

"Britt...she's just a friend."

I'm not good at keeping a straight face, and I can feel my eyebrows shoot up in my hairline. Or, apparently, at keeping my thoughts to myself.

"Does she know that?"

JD chuckles at that. "Guess that's fair. Uh...I thought we were friends...who hooked up a time or two, but when I noticed it might've been more to her, I tried to do the right thing. She wasn't really good at taking no for an answer, so for a while I stopped going in there."

"You know what?" I stop him, my hands up defensively. "I'm not sure why you're telling me this, it's really none of my business."

He's quiet for a moment, looking down on his folded hands in front of him on the table.

"What if I told you the only reason I pulled into the parking lot that night was because I saw your truck parked there?" he finally asks, glancing up from under his heavy eyebrows.

"I...my truck?" I echo stupidly.

My heart is almost painfully bumping around in my chest, and I'm suddenly mildly nauseated. Mostly because I'm not quite sure what is happening here, and it's making me a little nervous.

"Yeah, I didn't think, I just marched in there, hoping to catch you alone. But, clearly, that didn't go the way I'd hoped."

I shake my head to stop the swirling thoughts.

"What had you hoped for?" I manage to force out.

It earns me a small, upward tilt of those lush lips.

"A chance for a quiet talk without a bunch of nosy witnesses at all times."

Then he leans forward over the table, and I'm frozen in place, afraid to even blink.

"I like you, Janey. I'd like a chance to get to know you better."

JD

I take a swig of my water and sit back, giving my words a few beats to sink in with her.

My mouth is dry from talking more than is normal for me.

I've laid out my cards, and all I can do now is wait to see how she takes it.

"Okay, well...uh..." she stammers, before settling on, "what do you want to know? I'm not that interesting."

I beg to differ. Even though this is the part I suck at—small talk, the bane of my existence—I meant what I said, I want to learn all about her.

"Do you ride?" is the first thing out of my mouth.

She seems a little surprised at the question, but then smiles. Her smile is generous and I notice how her face changes: fine lines spread from the corners of her eyes, and a small dimple appears on her left cheek. I've only seen her smile a handful of times and always at a distance. Having that smile aimed at me feels like a gift.

"Love it. I used to try to get out as much as I could when I was still in Eureka, but I haven't had the time since I came here." She tilts her head slightly as she narrows her eyes on me. "Why that question?"

I have to think about that for a moment before answering.

"Looking for common ground, I guess. I like riding. Feeling connected with my horse and the land. It's peaceful, nourishing. Healing, even."

She nods at my words. "I know. I'd hoped moving here

would help the world slow down a little, allowing for more downtime so I could enjoy more of all the things I love to do." She shrugs. "But these days I'm all work and no play, I'm afraid."

"I'd like to change that," I offer.

She scoffs at that.

"You're gonna have to talk to Phil Jericho first. He called just before you picked me up, it looks like any spare time I might've had in the coming weeks is going to be taken up."

"Libby Roundup?"

"You've got it in one."

Phil Jericho is a former champion bull rider. A Libby native who hit it big on the rodeo circuit before returning home and getting involved in local politics. He's on the city council for his second term and is getting primed to run for mayor in next year's elections.

He's also the organizer for the Libby Roundup, an annual, open entry, amateur rodeo he's been putting on for the past couple of years. The Roundup is supposed to promote the development of local talent and also act as a warm-up for the much larger, pro-circuit Kootenai River Stampede, which lands in town at the end of July.

The Libby Roundup—which takes place earlier in the month on the Fourth of July weekend, and is combined with a festival on the rodeo grounds at J. Neils Memorial Park—has gained in popularity these last few years. People apparently find it highly entertaining to watch neighbors and friends getting thrown and bucked off when they try their hand at the broncs or the bulls. The surrounding festival is a draw as well, with livestock auctions, an artisan market, a beer tent, a fair, and nightly fireworks.

Something to do for the whole family, and Jericho has smartly engrained himself into the fabric of Libby. He's well-liked and almost ensured a victory at the next election. Personally, I don't like him. The man loves himself too much.

"What does he want from you?"

Janey sighs heavily.

"He wants me to cover the rodeo. Mackey Livestock, who supply the bulls and broncs, normally brings their own vet. But, apparently, there was a complaint about animal cruelty at an event they supplied last weekend that has Mackey under close scrutiny."

"And Jericho doesn't have time to change suppliers, so he wants you to take responsibility for the animals' well-being," I guess.

"Pretty much," she confirms. "And since Mackey is trucking them in early next week already, I'm going to be swamped." She chuckles at herself. "If that's even possible, given how swamped I already am."

"Have you thought about getting someone else in?"

She eyes me speculatively.

"You mean like another vet? I wish. I sank a lot of money into buying the clinic just last year, and I'm gonna need at least another year or two of hacking it alone before I can even think about taking someone on. I'm lucky to have a third-year veterinary student helping out for the summer, and for the moment I can only afford him and my assistant, Frankie. They keep the clinic going as best they can when I'm out and about."

Wow. Clearly this takes up a large chunk of her brain space, and I can see why it would.

Not that I have any insight into what it takes to run a business. After college, I worked for four years as a game warden in Flathead County before returning to Libby and joining the High Mountain Trackers. I love what I do and doing a good job is all I have to worry about. I know what my pay is every two weeks, and I live simple with little overhead, so I can save up for a rainy day. I like it that way.

"Can you pass on it?"

"I should," she says, sounding a little defeated. "But I really can't afford to. His offer is very generous, and it would mean being able to afford an extra pair of hands sooner rather than later."

"Damned if you do, damned if you don't," I mutter.

"Exactly," she agrees. "And since I'd like to have some space in my life for fun stuff before I'm too old and decrepit to enjoy it, my time is fast becoming limited."

"Oh, come on. We're not that old yet," I mock her gently.

"No? Maybe not, but time flies. Hell, it feels like yesterday I left my parents' farm to go off to college, and that was almost two decades ago."

She turns her head to look at the Kootenai River flowing by, seemingly lost in thought.

Two decades?

I'd pegged her at around my age—I had my thirty-fourth birthday last month—but I guess she's a little older. She doesn't look it, and besides, it doesn't matter a lick to me, but I get the sense it may matter to her.

Either way, this doesn't seem a good time to draw attention to it, so I should probably steer the conversation away from the topic of age. But Janey beats me to it.

"I'm sorry I've been chewing your ear off with my issues. Whatever it was you had in mind, I'm sure it wasn't listening to me complain. Can you tell I don't get out much? I haven't even asked about you."

She laughs a bit self-consciously as she rips a napkin into tiny strips. I cover her restless hands with mine.

"Don't do that," I gently admonish her. "When I said I wanted to learn about you, this is what I meant; the things that occupy your life. I appreciate you sharing."

It earns me a genuine smile.

"And I appreciate you listening. I have to admit, you're a bit of a surprise. Not what I was expecting."

"Now you have me curious."

Instead of clarifying, she slips her hands out from under mine and stands up.

"Ah, I'm afraid it'll have to wait for another time. I have a few overnight patients at the clinic, and Logan is waiting for me to relieve him."

I get up as well, and gather up the remains of our dinner to toss into the garbage can at the edge of the park.

"I can wait," I assure her. "As long as I know there *will* be another time."

She doesn't say anything, but I catch her smiling from the corner of my eye as we head back to my truck.

The drive to her place is silent, but I'm enjoying that too. Most people get restless in silence and try to fill it with inane chatter. It's rare you find someone who is comfortable simply enjoying time and space with you.

"Home or clinic?" I ask when her driveway splits in two different directions.

"Home, please. I have to get out of this dress and into some muck-about clothes."

I veer left and pull up in front of the house, putting the truck in park as I try to find the right way to share what's on my mind. I'm just going to lay it out there. That seemed to work the first time.

"For the record; I like the hair and the dress, you look very pretty like this, but you're no less beautiful in jeans and braids. I'm saying this because I like spending time with you, and I'll take any time you've got available, even if it's a few minutes for a quick coffee when you're running from one place to the next."

The soft smile on her face when she turns to me conveys direct honesty works for her.

"Thank you, and I'd like that." She hesitates briefly before adding, "Goodnight," and slipping out of the vehicle.

She's already halfway to the front door when I catch up with her to walk her the rest of the way.

"Night, Janey."

She glances at me over her shoulder as she opens her door, and sends another smile.

"Night," she echoes, before disappearing inside.

As I drive away from the house, I wonder if I missed an opportunity to kiss her. I've been thinking of little else tonight, and for a moment there it seemed like she might be open to the idea, but I don't want her to think I'm only after one thing. So, I'm going to take things slow.

I'll kiss her next time.

Five

JD

"You were seventeen at the time."

I shrug at my father's comment.

"So? I remember being pretty good at it."

"You gave your ma sleepless nights, and she made sure I wasn't getting rest either because I'd encouraged you. That's all I remember," he grumbles, shaking his head.

I bite off a grin. I recall that too. She'd been pissed when she found out a few of my buddies and I had signed up for the Indian horse relay at a rodeo outside of Kalispell. Because I was underage, I needed a parent's signature and had talked Pa into signing off.

But I learned my lesson at seventeen, after ending up with three cracked ribs when I got trampled in the horse exchange, and have no intention of signing up for the relay again, but it's fun to jerk Pa around a bit. He overheard me asking Jonas for a couple of days off during the rodeo and he poked his nose in.

We're up near the Swede Mountain Lookout, looking for a young woman who—according to friends—had planned to come up here for a hike yesterday morning and hasn't been heard of since. The game warden found her vehicle was still parked by the tower, so we were called out for a search.

The tower is pretty rough to get to. The six miles of dirt road zigzagging up the mountain was a bit much for our trucks to haul the horse trailers all the way up. So we set up a staging area in a clearing a couple of miles down and are doing the rest on horseback.

My father is riding beside me and every so often I can feel his eyes on me, until I finally put him out of his misery.

"Relax, Pa. I have no intention of entering any relay or rodeo."

"Asshole," he mumbles, but I can see the relief on his face. "I swear, with your sister coming this weekend, your ma is already strung out enough. This might'a sent her over the edge."

Right. Una's visit.

"When is she getting in?" I ask.

"Sometime tomorrow afternoon."

Well, I hope like hell we've found this woman by then, because Ma and Una alone for any length of time could be explosive.

I love my sister, and I wish I'd see her more, but I'm always walking on eggshells on those rare occasions she does visit. She, in turn, doesn't understand how I could've moved back to Libby, but I don't have the same relationship with our parents she does.

Una was always outspoken and rebellious, while I tended to be quieter and more reserved. I was no angel by any stretch of the imagination, but most of the time I'd fly under the radar, while my sister was like a lightning rod, drawing all the attention her way. I guess I take after my father, but Una is the spitting image of Ma, who is also fiery and feisty, and they clash.

We were raised to respect our elders and honor traditional values, but I guess that created different expectations for Una than it did for me. I'm a man, and although Ma would love to see me with a family—something she reminds me of from time to time—it's quite acceptable for me to be single and independent. I'm still the proverbial hunter and gatherer, so it doesn't take away from my worth as a man.

It's not so simple for my sister, whose traditional values would be very much wrapped up in family and home, something she balked against from the time she was an adolescent. At almost thirty, she's built her own life, set her own standards, and created her own values, but sadly those don't line up with traditional expectations and that creates constant tension.

Regrettably, until there is transparency, there can't be understanding, and until there is understanding, there can't be peace. Oddly enough, I think if there ever was to be an honest discussion, Ma would be the more receptive one, whereas our father would struggle with the truth.

Unfortunately, I will be the one left on the hot seat, having had knowledge but not sharing it would be considered a lie, at best, but—given my mother's penchant for the dramatic—more likely seen as a betrayal.

"So, if you're not planning to enter, why the fuck do you need time off during the amateur rodeo?" Pa circles back to the original subject. "Why not hold out a few weeks until the pros come to town?"

I chuckle at his inability to leave it alone. I'm about to

tell him I prefer the smaller crowds, when Jackson pipes up behind us.

"Because the pros bring their own veterinarian."

I twist around in my saddle to find Jackson looking smug he called me out. I have no idea how he came by the knowledge, it's not like there's been a public announcement or anything since I saw her.

"I took the pups in for their shots yesterday morning," he's already explaining. "I overheard Doc talking to her assistant about it."

"About what?" Pa asks.

"Doc Richards is working the Libby Roundup this year," Jackson readily volunteers.

I shake my head and turn to face forward again, but I can feel my father's eyes on me.

"I see," he mumbles, but I don't have to see him to hear the grin in his voice.

Fuck.

"You're gonna tell Ma, aren't you?"

"Damn right I am. It'll be a good distraction for her this weekend when your sister is here."

Great. I'm not even sure which is worse, being hounded about Janey, or getting sucked into Ma's ongoing conflict with Una.

Either way, it looks like it'll be a shitty weekend.

Maybe I should take on an extra shift at the ranch.

"Is that what I think it is?"

Dan points at a couple of rocks up ahead, a scrap of pink, lacy material just visible tucked in between. Immediately the hair on my neck stands up.

"It's gotta be hers," I confirm, closing in on them.

Since there is no real assigned hiking trail to follow, we split up in two pairs, and have taken the most likely routes Maggie Aldridge might've chosen. Dan and I have been following this game trail for the past almost two hours. There were some signs she might've come this way, we found some fresh tracks and even a partial boot print, but that looked to be too big for a woman and the tracks could've been left by a large animal, and I was just starting to wonder if we should maybe turn around.

I dismount and loop Santiago's reins around the saddle horn. He won't go anywhere while I explore on foot. I'm careful to stick to dry or at least needle-covered ground, so I don't inadvertently trample all over a potential crime scene.

Abandoned panties may not be that unusual in favored teenage hangouts, along with condoms and empty beer cans, but we're way off the beaten track here. Finding those panties screams foul play to me.

"Stay put," I tell Dan, as I make my way to those rocks, dreading what I might find.

Scanning the undergrowth on this side of the boulders, I search for anything that looks out of place. I spot the cuff of a hiking boot when I'm about ten feet away.

"Boot," I call out to Dan. "Two feet to the right of that rock," I point out.

"I see it."

A few moments later, I'm able to look behind the rocks, and my chest squeezes when I catch sight of an outstretched hand, the fingers far too relaxed. I force myself to keep moving forward, I need to know if this is now a recovery instead of a rescue.

She's dead, I'd stake my life on it.

I'm not law enforcement anymore, but my training

takes over as I take in every detail of the scene. She's spread-eagled, both arms flung out over her head, and her legs are open, one cocked at the knee. Her shirt and bra are shoved up over her breasts, and a pair of discarded jeans are crumpled at the base of the rocks on this side. She's still wearing a sock on one foot.

There is no visible blood anywhere, but when I approach her, I can tell her eyes are open.

Unfortunately, she's not seeing anything. Not anymore.

~

Janey

My brain has been scrambled for days.

I'm trying to get ahead of the game, so when I'm expected at the rodeo grounds on Monday to meet with Phil Jericho and Mackey Livestock, I can be focused on the job at hand.

In addition, I've been boning up on my knowledge of rodeo, which is surprisingly thin, as I've come to discover.

All I know is I've always had a vague distaste for rodeo, despite it being a pretty standard part of living here in the Northwest. I hated it as an idealistic teenager, but that has mellowed some with age and exposure, although I'm still rooting for the animals.

I'm not sure if that makes me more or less qualified for this job. Either way the job is mine, and I'd do well to study what I'm getting into so I don't make a fool of myself.

So, I've been doing a lot of reading and researching when I haven't been working these past days. There hasn't been a lot of sleep, but at least I know now what types of injuries to look for in the different events, and have studied up on signs to look out for.

Hopefully it's enough to keep me from looking incompetent. I don't normally lack in confidence when it comes to my work, but I'm already burning the candle at both ends and I guess I'm worn a little thin. The prospect of adding more to my plate has me dreading the upcoming week of activities.

But I asked Logan to assist me at the rodeo, and he seems excited enough for both of us. He's been working a lot already, taking most of the nightshifts when we have overnight patients, but he seems to enjoy it. Who am I to argue? I'm no longer that young, or that driven.

I watch as Logan leads Daisy, the potbelly pig, through the door separating the clinic from the barn. The animal was brought into the clinic earlier this afternoon with labored breathing. Pigs are notorious for respiratory issues, and this one seems to have developed a serious case of pneumonia. She had her first shot of amoxycillin but will need several more tomorrow and over the coming weekend, which is why we're keeping her here.

"Go home, Frankie," I tell the assistant I inherited from Doc Evans.

I'm not sure what I would've done without her this past year. A Libby native, she knows just about everyone, which has proven helpful at times. She's also handy with the animals, friendly with their owners, and knows how to manage a schedule. I'm not kidding when I say she's been indispensable.

"I'll just finish this," she says, pointing at a stack of filing.

"It'll wait until tomorrow. And remember, I don't want to see you here this weekend either. Get rested up, because next week is going to be a test of endurance for all of us."

"You get some rest too, and don't forget to eat."

I've probably got at least a decade on her, but that doesn't stop her from trying to mother me. Honestly, I probably need it. The last time I sat down for a proper meal was when JD took me for Mexican earlier in the week. Since then, it's been PB&J sandwiches, canned soup, and frozen pizza. I enjoy cooking but haven't had the energy.

As Frankie heads out to her car, I look down at Ginger, who is doing a lot better and has taken to hanging out in the clinic during the day. The last few nights I've been taking her home with me.

"What do you say, girl? Ready to go home and get some grub?"

Her tail thuds on the linoleum floor in response.

I turn off the lights, grab the stack of printouts I plan on studying over the weekend, and hold the door open for Ginger. She hobbles to the grass where she has a quick pee while I lock up the clinic. Every day she gets around a little better on her three good legs. She sometimes tries to put weight on the casted leg, but it's painful. Good thing, since she really shouldn't be putting weight on that leg at all.

As soon as I open the door at my place, she slips past me and makes a beeline for the dog bed I put next to the couch. Even that short walk from the clinic here tired her out, and by the time I've showered and changed into something more comfortable, she's already snoring.

I'm in the kitchen, checking my pantry to see what I could throw together for dinner, when my doorbell lets out a garbled ring. Something else on my list of things to replace. It's rare to have someone at my door, especially at this hour, so I'm a little apprehensive when I peek outside.

"I took a chance," JD says, looking a bit sheepish as he stands on my porch, holding up a brown paper bag.

I dart a glance down at my ratty sleep pants and old concert shirt and am about to blow him off, when I notice a haunted look in his eyes, and strain on his face.

"I'm not dressing up, but you're welcome to come inside," I tell him instead.

The moment I step aside to let him in, I hear Ginger's low growl.

"It's okay, girl," I coo, slipping ahead while he kicks off his boots. I crouch next to her, assuring her with my voice and my touch. "He's a friend."

"Who is this?"

I glance over my shoulder to see him standing right behind me.

"Ginger. At least that's what we call her. I don't know who she belongs to. She was brought in by a Good Samaritan who found her on the side of the road, injured. No collar, no microchip, and no record with any of the other vets either."

Despite looking at JD with obvious distrust, she starts furiously sniffing the air.

"She smells the brisket," he rumbles.

"Brisket?"

My mouth is already watering before the smell of smoky barbecue hits my nostrils.

"Like I said, I took a chance. Picked up dinner at The Smoking Gun in town. Figured if you'd already eaten, it'd probably keep for tomorrow."

"Good thing I haven't eaten yet then."

I get to my feet and take the paper bag from his hands and am about to head to the kitchen when he stops me.

"Hold on." He reaches inside the bag and comes up

with a chunk of meat. "Peace offering," he adds by way of explanation.

I continue to the kitchen, set the food down on the counter, and pull down a couple of plates. When I turn around, I see JD crouched down a few feet from Ginger's bed, sitting perfectly still as he holds out the piece of brisket in the palm of his hand.

Ginger is only able to resist for a few seconds before her sniffer starts scanning the air and she eases closer. First, she cautiously butts JD's fingers with her nose, but then slowly stretches her neck so she can snatch the meat from his palm.

"Good girl," he mumbles as he gets to his feet, not even attempting to pet her.

But as he joins me in the kitchen, I see the dog's eyes following his every step. He certainly got her attention.

"Drink?" I ask, pulling open the fridge and hoping I have one or two beers left. I spot a couple rolling around in my vegetable drawer. That illustrates the current sad state of my kitchen. "I have beer, cranberry juice, or tea."

"It's a beer kinda day."

That sounded loaded, but I wait with the question burning on my lips until I have the bottles open and hand one to him, holding up the other. He taps my bottle with his.

"Cheers."

I take a sip and set it on the counter while I unwrap the dinner of brisket, mashed potatoes, and roasted vegetables. I stifle a moan as I plate the food. It looks and smells delicious.

Pointing JD to the kitchen table, I slide a plate in front of him and hand him some cutlery. Then I take the seat across from him.

"So...what makes this a beer kinda day?"

"After dinner," he says, his eyes pleading.

Must've been a doozy then.

I nod and dig in, enjoying my food and not caring in the least I must look like a pig, the way I'm scarfing it down.

"God, that was good," I mutter, leaning back in my chair as I cover my full belly with both my hands.

"Best barbecue around," he agrees.

His eyes are on me when I lift mine.

"I needed that," he shares, and I have a feeling he's not just talking about the food we shared. "We got called out on a search. Twenty-two-year-old woman went missing up on Swede Mountain. We found her, but she didn't make it."

"Oh no..." I lean forward and reach out a hand to cover one of his.

I get the feeling that's not the whole story, but it clearly affected him, and I'm not going to push it.

"Part of the job," he states dismissively as he retrieves his hand.

But he doesn't fool me. Euthanizing animals is part of my job, taking care of animals who have been badly abused is too, but that doesn't make any of it easier to deal with. It doesn't mean I don't lie awake at night, agonizing over some of the things I deal with in my line of work.

I don't interfere when he gets up and gathers the dishes and the empty beer bottles. Not even when he starts washing the plates and the cutlery, even though I have a perfectly functional dishwasher right next to where he's standing over the sink. He rinses the bottles and leaves them sitting on the counter, and stores the leftover food in my fridge. Then he turns to me.

"I best get going."

"You don't have to go."

A smile briefly tugs at his mouth.

"Yeah, tonight I do. Walk me to the door?"

I do as he asks and follow him to the front of the house. He opens the door, but before he steps outside, he turns around to face me. My breath catches in my throat when his hands come up to frame my face. His thumbs brush my cheeks.

"Gonna kiss you now," he warns.

"Okay," I whisper, as his head lowers.

My eyes stay locked on his as his mouth covers mine, but drift shut as his kiss deepens. I'm lost to everything but those lush lips and his skilled tongue.

Oh my. I'm in trouble.

Six

JD

I grunt with the impact when she throws herself at me.

"Hey, you," my sister says, beaming as she leans back in my arms.

"Hey."

I pull her closer for another hug.

She looks good. Strong and healthy, although I miss her long shiny hair. She's cut it short, wearing it in a messy pixie. It suits her, but I still miss the long braids she used to wear. I guess it's easier in her line of work. I remember when we were still living at home, it would take forever for her hair to dry after a shower.

When I let go of her, her eyes narrow on me.

"What's wrong?"

"Nothing," I brush her off.

"I can see something is," she insists.

Despite sharing a meal and a kiss that lingered until I hit my bed last night, the dream I woke up from, in the early morning hours, was far from pleasant. In fact, it was pretty gruesome, every detail still etched in my mind.

"Leave him alone, Una," my father mumbles from his chair.

I'd hoped to delay showing up at my parents' house as much as I could, but Una was blowing up my phone from the moment she arrived.

"Am I not allowed to ask what's wrong with my brother?" Una immediately reacts to our father's words.

Pa was there yesterday; he saw what I saw. Hell, we had to stand guard over that poor woman's body for hours—making sure no wildlife could get at her—before law enforcement could get their crime team in. I'm sure her image has been swirling around his head as well.

So, I know why he made that comment, but my sister doesn't, so all she hears is criticism and rejection. I understand both, stuck in the middle again, so no matter what I say or how I react, it's gonna piss someone off.

I can see the shutters come down around Pa at my sister's reaction.

Fucking eggshells.

"We were out on a search yesterday that didn't end well," I explain in an attempt to mitigate the damage. "Had to call in law enforcement. Was an ugly scene."

A flash of regret skirts over Una's face before she stubbornly sets her jaw.

"Then why not just tell me that? You don't have to shield me, I'm a firefighter, I see my share of bad stuff."

"Jesus, Una. Maybe because I don't wanna be reminded of the images already seared into my memory. It has zero to do with you."

I close my eyes and pinch the bridge of my nose against the headache already forming.

"Una, did you get your brother something to drink?" Ma asks, walking up from the basement with a couple of jars she went to grab from the cold cellar.

I'm glad she wasn't privy to our little exchange, or she'd have a thing or two to say about that.

"I didn't want anything, Ma," I quickly answer her, trying to avert another possible confrontation.

I can see from the look on my sister's face, her bristles are up at Ma's question, which clearly rubbed her the wrong way.

"Nonsense." My mother—the bulldozer—casually waves me off. "Grab your brother a beer, Una," she insists, setting her jars on the counter.

Instead of objecting—which I know will get Ma going —I shoot my sister a silent plea not to engage. With a low growl, she spins on her heel and darts out to the beer fridge on the covered porch in the back. She returns a moment later with three beers, dropping one beside Pa, handing one to me, and tossing back half of the third one herself.

Ma shoots her a sharp look before turning and fixing her eyes on me. "You sit down at that table and keep me company. You can tell me what's going on with you and Doc Richards."

I can hear Pa's groan, and Una looks at me with a little too much interest.

I swear sometimes living in a small town sucks. Or maybe it was those tough cowboys back at the ranch yapping, they're nothing but giant gossips.

"Christ, Ma..." I mumble.

"Doc Richards? Who is that?" Una pipes up, taking a seat at the table across from me.

"You wouldn't know, since we hardly see you here," Ma snaps, getting a dig in as she transfers the contents of the jars to bowls. "But Doc Richards took over for Doc Evans last year. From what I hear, your brother has taken a shine."

Una's eyes bulge out at me behind our mother's back. "You're getting it on with the vet?"

I open my mouth to respond, but Ma is faster.

"No need to be crude, Una," she chastises her. "She's a nice girl."

"The vet is a woman?" my sister blurts out.

Mom swirls around, shock on her face. "Of course she's a woman, what else would she be?"

The pointed look Una sends me speaks volumes, but I already recognized the thin ice we are on.

"Was just asking, Ma. I didn't realize Doc Richards was a *she*."

"I figured that'd be clear, given that she *is* seeing your brother."

"*Fucking hell,*" Pa mutters from his chair.

My sentiments exactly.

I glance at the oven timer to see how much longer before the enchiladas are done, so I can dine and dash the hell out of here.

"In that case," my sister drawls, the calculating gleam in her eyes not particularly reassuring. I discover how accurate an assessment that is, when she adds, "Why don't you invite her for dinner tomorrow night? I'd love to meet her before I head back."

From the wide smirk on her face, I can tell she is right pleased with herself. I can't believe she is throwing me under the bus to get the focus off her and let her know with a dirty look. Not that she's at all impressed.

"Great idea," Ma predictably agrees. "Ask her. Or I can always call her myself."

"Ama..." Pa warns from his seat. "You're meddling."

"I am not. Is it a crime to be happy at least one of my children is giving me hope, maybe one day, I'll be blessed with grandbabies?"

I love my mother, but there are times I wish I lived at the other side of the fucking country. I can try and deny anything is going on, but that's just going to make Ma more determined.

I catch a glance from Una.

"Please?" she mouths across the table.

I close my eyes and shake my head. I want to expose Janey to our dysfunctional family dynamic as much as I want a root canal, but I know it would, at least temporarily, divert attention from my sister.

"She's probably busy," I mention, in a last attempt to stop this runaway train.

Ma has a ready answer. "You won't know 'til you ask."

I hum in response and leave it at that.

After dinner, which was surprisingly uneventful as family meals go, I take my leave. Una walks me out to my truck.

"Are you going to invite her?"

I stop and turn to her. "I will, but with full disclosure."

Una looks a bit alarmed. "What do you mean by that?"

"She's a nice woman and I'm not going to pull her into a situation she is not prepared for. If she agrees, she's gonna do it knowing what she's in for."

A brief struggle plays out on my sister's face as she processes my intent to share her secret. Her expression settles on resolute.

"Fine. Tell her. It's gonna be a matter of public record soon anyway."

She abruptly turns back toward the house, leaving me to wonder what the hell that was all about.

Knowing my sister, probably nothing good.

∼

Janey

Despite feeling flattered, my knee-jerk reaction was to say no.

The excuse of being too busy seems an easy out these days.

I mean, it's true, I *am* busy, but it's not an excuse to shut out the world and stop living your life. I could end up like my dad, a stroke at fifty-six, and everything he worked so hard for his entire life, gone. That was almost nine years ago. Dad is still around, but the farm is gone, sold to pay for the small bungalow my parents bought in Eureka, and to cover his medical bills.

My parents are well into their sixties, and their life now is not even close to what they'd envisioned and planned for their retirement.

I'm like Dad, a workaholic. Never leave for tomorrow what you can do today. It was a principle I was raised on as it pertained to chores and work ethic. I never realized until Dad had the stroke, it could translate just as easily to enjoying what you can today because tomorrow is not guaranteed.

It's only one of the reasons why I ended up agreeing to have dinner tonight with JD and his family. Another reason, of course, was that turning down a dinner invite to the parents could be construed as disinterest, which is far from the truth. But after the background JD provided, and his transparency about the situation I was walking into, there was no way I could refuse.

Besides, I've met both his parents and like them. James comes across as stoic, but I've seen the wrinkles left by laughing plenty, and the small tugs at the corner of his mouth betraying a sense of humor. His son is obviously cut from the same cloth. I've encountered Ama mostly from a distance, except after that breech delivery when she fed me breakfast. As intimidating as she seemed at first, I could sense the big heart she tries to hide behind a stern exterior.

It doesn't mean I don't have butterflies dancing in my stomach as JD takes my hand and walks me from his truck to the front door of his parents' place.

The gorgeous woman who opens the door is clearly his sister. They share the same dark eyes and generous mouth. She grins wide and pulls me into an unexpected embrace.

"I can't tell you how excited I am to meet you," she whispers next to my ear. "And I apologize in advance for the spectacle you're about to witness."

"Uh, nice to meet you too," is all I can think of to say, a bit flummoxed by the odd apology.

"All right, Una," JD rumbles. "Unhand her already."

"Hello to you too, brother dear," his sister returns as she releases me and focuses on JD, who shakes his head at her, wearing a barely-there smirk.

I'm led into the house, where we find James and Ama working side by side in the kitchen. James greets me with a simple, "Doc," and a nod, but Ama goes right into hostess mode.

"JD, get our guest a drink, yeah? Beer, ice tea, lemonade, water?"

"I wouldn't mind an ice tea, thank you. Can I do anything to help?" I add immediately.

"We're almost done. Hope you don't mind game meat; James made his venison poyha."

I'm not sure what poyha is, but it looks like some kind of meatloaf James is cutting in thick slices. It is being served with some kind of succotash—a blend of pan-roasted corn, lima beans, squash, onion, and red peppers—dirty rice, and some kind of apple slaw.

"Sounds delicious," I mumble, accepting the glass of tea JD hands me.

"I hear you're working the rodeo?"

I turn to James. "Yes. Phil Jericho called and asked if I would. I'm not sure of the details but, apparently, Mackey Livestock is under some scrutiny, and rather than let them bring their own vet, Jericho thought it prudent to get an impartial vet instead."

"Animal cruelty. Heard about that," James comments. "And I'm pretty sure Jericho is more concerned with his reputation than he is with the welfare of the animals. Always covering his ass."

"You don't like him," I conclude, taking a sip of my tea.

Ama snorts. "Understatement of the century. Their rivalry goes way back. Have you heard of Indian relay racing?" she asks me.

"Three-horse relay with one bareback rider? Yes, I've seen it. Quite impressive, and dangerous."

"Yeah. James and Phil were daredevils back then. Always trying to beat each other, until one race—JD was a toddler—James got trampled and ended up with half a dozen broken bones. I told him if he ever got in the ring again, he'd seen the last of me. I'd walk and take our boy with me."

"Only fucking way for that bastard to win that trophy from me," her husband grumbles. "Steered his horse right at me. Once a cheat, always a cheat. Watch yourself around him."

Apparently, the injury extended beyond the physical, and that part hasn't quite healed. A man's ego is a fragile thing. I curb the grin that wants to form.

"So noted."

"Dinner," Ama announces, passing out dishes of food to carry to the table.

I end up with the bowl of dirty rice and set it on one of the trivets on the dining table. Then I'm directed to take the seat next to JD, who is sitting across from his sister. It reminds me a lot of growing up at the farm, sitting down at the table for family dinners. Instead of passing around the bowls of food, the plates are sent around, and whoever is closest to a dish doles out a portion.

There's a strange energy at the table, and I think it's coming from Una. She hasn't really said much since I walked in the door. When I catch her eye across the table, she shoots me a nervous little smile.

"Eat," James orders, when everyone has their plate in front of them.

I immediately dig into the poyha, which I'm very curious about. It looks like meatloaf, but has some whole kernels of corn, and the moment I put that first bite in my mouth, I'm immediately in love with the savory flavor with a hint of slight tangy sweetness I can't quite place.

"This is delicious," I tell James. "It has an almost sweet aftertaste"

"Chopped cranberries," he volunteers. "Pairs well with game."

"It sure does."

"It's Una's favorite," Ama shares. "Her father made it in honor of her."

My eyes dart to JD's sister, who looks like she's sitting on pins and needles.

"I have an announcement," she suddenly blurts out.

In the dead silence that follows, I feel JD's hand squeezing my knee under the table. I have a feeling whatever it was she apologized for at the door, we're about to find out.

"Una..." JD says softly in a cautionary tone.

But she ignores him.

"I'm getting married."

JD's fingers dig into my knee and silverware clatters on a plate, as this news apparently comes as a surprise for the family. A good one, judging by the look on Ama's face, who is clearly smiling behind the hands she presses to her mouth.

"I had no idea you were seeing someone," Ama exclaims. "Who is he? Why didn't you bring him to meet us?"

The long pregnant pause is filled with so much tension, I'm on the edge of my seat. Una darts an anxious glance at her brother and at me, then straightens her shoulders and lifts her chin, before focusing her attention on her mother.

"Her name is Rachel."

From beside me I hear JD's soft, *"Fuck."*

JD

I could murder my sister right now.

I have more than a strong suspicion she didn't just decide to spill the beans.

I'm pissed, she should've given me a heads-up she was going to do it, but I bet she realized I'd never have agreed to invite Janey into what is now sure to be a major family drama. Hell, the whole Rachel and getting married thing is as new to me as it is to my parents.

"I'm sorry?" Ma looks confused as she slowly sinks back down in her chair.

Una darts a glance at our father, who is keeping his eyes firmly fixed on his plate. He's not giving her anything to go by. No sign as to how he's receiving the news.

Ma, on the other hand, couldn't hold back her reaction if she tried, as is evident from the range of emotions playing out on her face. She usually has a pretty decent poker face, but there's no hint of one now.

"Rachel asked me to marry her and I said yes."

"Rachel?" Ma echoes, her eyebrows raised. "Marriage?"

"Yes, I'm gay, Ma, and I'm marrying a woman who is amazing. She owns an apple orchard near San Luis Obispo, which has the most amazing views of Prefumo Canyon, and—"

"Stop." Our mother claps her hands to her ears. "I need a minute."

It's funny, for years I've tried to convince Una to speak up about her sexual orientation, told her she wasn't giving our parents enough credit. She always held back, waiting for the right time to let them know. Well, I'm pretty sure telling them when you're about to get married is not exactly the prime moment.

"Congratulations," Janey says in a soft voice, shooting my sister a tentative smile.

She courageously chooses sisterhood over strategic silence and, although I appreciate her kindness and her courage, I'm not sure Ma will agree. Her eyes snap to Janey before coming to me, narrowing to slits.

"You knew?"

It's more of an accusation than an actual question, which is why I feel it doesn't need a response. She already knows.

"I expected this kind of betrayal from her..." She indicates Una. "But never from you," she directs at me.

"Ama..."

Pa reaches out a hand to put on Ma's arm, but it's too late, she's already on her feet, reaching for her plate, and slamming it down so hard it breaks apart in pieces and sends shards of china flying.

"Ma!" I yell, trying to pull Janey out of the way.

Ma has a temper that doesn't show itself often. Silence is

her tell when she's angry, but when she's hurt, her temper flares.

"Enough!"

My father's bark has Ma spinning on her heel and taking off for the back door. Then he turns his eyes on Una, who looks like she's about to cry. He slowly shakes his head.

"There are better ways, baby girl, and you know it," he scolds her gently. "Could'a been a happy occasion for everyone."

Una looks like she's been slapped. Then she turns to look at me, and I know she's remembering all the times I tried to convince her our parents would be accepting. But the silent apology in her tearful eyes feels a little thin after the stunt she pulled tonight.

I grab Janey's hand and pull her up with me.

"We're leaving."

"I'm sorry, Janey," my sister mumbles.

"Not cool, Una. Not cool," I manage to grind out before leading Janey to the door.

"Son..." my father calls after me and I stop to look over my shoulder. "Best let her cool down for a bit."

I nod and walk outside, Janey beside me.

We're silent the entire drive back to her place. It's not until I turn off the engine and blow out a big breath that I break the silence, my eyes fixed on the reflection of the truck's grill in her front window.

"I would never have put you in that situation, had I known. That was fucked up. I'm sorry."

She chuckles softly beside me and reaches for my left hand, resting on the steering wheel.

"Hey, that's family for ya," she returns easily. "Trust me, my family has had our own share of scenes like that. Usually with me at the center of the drama."

I turn to look at her. "I sincerely doubt that."

It only makes her laugh harder.

"You have no idea," she assures me. "When I was a teenager, my mother used to say I could get on Mother Theresa's last nerve. She had to walk out of a room plenty of times."

"Una is thirty," I point out.

"Yeah, I know. But sometimes you get stuck in a family dynamic that is hard to get out of. People have certain expectations of you, you have expectations of them, and even though we all change over time, it can be easy to fall back into those old patterns."

I have to think about that for a moment. It's forcing me to look at myself with a critical eye, as much as I look at others in my family. I always kept my mouth shut, even growing up. Not that I was an angel by any stretch; I rebelled on my own time, got into trouble plenty, but I was quiet at home. Una provided all the drama we could handle. I still rarely speak up, and choose to wait for shit to blow over.

"You're right."

I turn my hand, palm up, lace my fingers with hers, and lift her hand to kiss her knuckles.

"I don't think I can match your father's poyha, but I can whip us up an omelet?" she suggests, changing the subject.

My intent had been to apologize for the disastrous family dinner and then make myself scarce, sure she would've had enough of the Watike clan for tonight. But maybe not.

"I only had two bites of my damn dinner," I grumble, still pissed at my sister.

"Me too." She grins. "I'm starving."

Without waiting for my answer, she retrieves her hand and gets out of the truck.

I catch up with her by the door.

Her dog doesn't growl at me this time but is still a little tentative when she greets me.

"Does she need to go out?" I ask.

Janey, who is already pulling stuff from her fridge, shoots me a glance over her shoulder.

"Shoot. Yeah, probably. Sorry, girl."

"I can take her."

"Make sure you grab the leash, it's on the hook by the door. I don't want her to try and go after some critter. I don't take her too far yet, usually just out on the side of the house."

I find the leash and clip it on the dog's collar.

"I should probably fence in part of the yard for her. I'll add it to the other million-and-one items on my to-do list for this house."

She mutters the last, but I catch it.

"Show me that list when I get back. I can help," I offer as I walk Ginger out the door.

I've got tools, am pretty good with my hands, and enjoy the work. I helped Dan when he was building his house, and worked on Jackson's bathroom renovation a few months ago. I wouldn't mind another project to keep me busy, with as an added benefit that I'd get to hang around Janey more. I could get started on her list this week; I already have a few extra days off.

Plus, I could do with the distraction.

"Oh, that's Logan."

JD wanted to know whose vehicle he'd seen pulling out from behind the clinic, which is where Logan usually parks his car.

"Who's Logan?" JD asks, still standing by the front window, peering out.

He insisted on doing the dishes after dinner, but I then shooed him out of the kitchen. I'm just putting away the dishes.

"He's my assistant," I explain. "We've got a sick potbelly pig who needs regular injections, so Logan is staying with him in the barn. There's a small bedroom, with a bar-sized fridge and a microwave in the barn for situations like this, but no real place to cook. He's probably just gone to grab something to eat in town."

I should probably check in with him when he gets back, to see how our patient is holding up.

"Do you want tea or coffee?"

JD turns away from the window and heads back to the kitchen. "Coffee would be good."

I load a coffee pod in my Nespresso and slide a mug underneath the spout, before plugging in the kettle for tea for myself. If I drink coffee, I'll be up half the night. I lean against the counter, listening to the machine gurgle while I let my thoughts drift.

It's nice both JD and I are quite comfortable sharing silences. It allows me to be myself and not constantly worry about making awkward small talk.

After our brief conversation in the truck, his family

hasn't come up again, and I'm not about to be the one to broach that sensitive subject. I feel it's safe to assume communication is a bit of a challenge, which is really no different in my family.

There is love, but that doesn't mean we necessarily understand each other. The fact I live less than seventy miles from my parents but have seen them maybe four or five times in the past sixteen months should tell you enough. Sure, I have a very busy clinic, but a lot of that is my own doing as well. I like working hard, but it's a convenient shield at times as well.

Much—if not all—of my identity is rolled into the work I do and being good at it. There isn't a whole lot to me when you strip away the vet. It's what gives me substance, otherwise I'd fade into the background.

"So where is that list of yours?" JD reminds me when I hand him his coffee.

"You don't have to do that. I'll get to it eventually," I tell him, a little embarrassed I haven't even made a start on all the things that need attention.

He raises one dark eyebrow. "Wouldn't ask if I didn't want to help."

"Fair enough."

I'd be an idiot to argue the help he offers. I gave him a chance to back out and he didn't take it. If he doesn't mean what he's saying, he's going to regret saying anything when he sees all the stuff that needs doing.

I grab the pad from my kitchen junk drawer, where I keep it for ready access when I think of something else that needs to be added, and slide it in front of him.

"It's already three pages long," I warn him, adding, "Also, the list isn't particularly organized since I simply add things as they occur to me."

He immediately tears a couple of blank pages from the pad.

"Got a pen?"

I grab him one from the drawer, and he immediately starts dividing the first page with a line lengthwise down the middle. He writes at the top of one column in clear block letters, *kitchen,* and *bathroom* at the top of the second column. On the next sheet of paper he does the same, until each section of the house has its own list. Then he starts copying my listed items in the appropriate column.

When he's done, he tears off one more blank sheet and writes, *general,* at the top, before adding items I hadn't even thought of yet. Electrical, plumbing, HVAC, roof, all with a question mark beside them. I'm feeling a little nauseated.

He chuckles softly. "Better to check those things before you start doing renovations, if you discover problems when you've already done work, you'll have wasted money and time."

I groan, thinking of the meager budget I have allocated for work on the house. It'll be a little better once I get paid for working the Libby Roundup, but nothing that would also cover any major overhauls.

"I just hope this place won't turn out to be a major money pit," I grumble. "Doc Evans is an old friend of my father's, so I trusted him when he said the house was solid and a little TLC was all it would need."

The truth is, I didn't even think to ask for an inspection or anything like that. I never owned my own property before I bought this.

"Don't borrow trouble," JD rumbles as he gets to his feet. "I'm sure Doc Evans wouldn't have sold you a lemon, but let's check to be sure anyway. Where is your electrical panel?"

"Laundry room." I point at the door off the kitchen.

I walk in, flip on the light, and quickly swipe the dirty laundry I dumped on top of the dryer into a basket of clean sheets. I'll just have to wash it all again. Something else I'm falling behind on.

"Over there."

I indicate the little door in the wall Doc Evans pointed out to me when I moved in.

"Good," JD mumbles when he opens it up. "He must've had that redone within the past ten years or so. It's a fairly new panel and looks well organized."

"That's a relief."

My knees wobble a little as he brushes past me in the confined space, the mere hint of a smile on his face, when he bends down so his mouth is right by my ear.

"Nice undies."

My eyes flash to the laundry basket, which shows the cow print panties and bra set Frankie got me last Christmas lying on top. I quickly turn off the light and pull the door shut behind me. JD is already ducking into the cupboard underneath the kitchen sink, pulling the cleaning products I store there out. Then he goes down on his knees and the top of his body disappears into the cupboard, his shirt riding up at the back.

"Noticed any leaks anywhere? Any pipes dripping?"

My mouth goes dry and I have to swallow when my eyes get caught on the strip of exposed skin above the jeans that stretch tightly over his fine ass.

"No," I manage, after clearing my throat.

When I see him back out, I quickly turn around and, grabbing for the first thing to busy my hands with, remove the used coffee pod from the machine and toss it in the garbage.

"I'll bring some tools tomorrow," he volunteers. "Probably easier to check things by daylight anyway."

He's standing a few feet away, leaning his hip casually against the counter and with his arms crossed in front of him. I wish I could snap a picture of him like this, just to remind myself this gorgeous man in my house isn't just a figment of my imagination. He's so far out of my league, it's not even funny.

But when I catch the warm look in his eyes, I know he must see something in me that appeals to him. Who am I to question that? My body tingles under his quiet scrutiny.

"What I wouldn't give to know what goes on in that head of yours," he finally says.

I feel heat crawling up my face. Good thing he doesn't know, since I was imagining lowering myself on my knees in front of him, slowly freeing his cock from his jeans, and sliding it into the heat of my mouth.

"Thinking about electricity and plumbing, that's all."

The grin I shoot him feels forced, and my heart hammers in my chest when he slowly pushes away from the counter and stalks toward me. I may be a bit of an Amazon in size, but JD makes me feel almost dainty when he towers over me, all big and dark and broody.

Sliding his hand along my face and into my hair, he forces my head back a little farther with a slight tug. Then he slowly lowers his mouth to mine.

Like the first time he kissed me, I am swept clear off my feet. My hands come up his chest and grab on to his shirt to steady myself. His kiss is deeper this time, hot and slick, and full of a promise that turns my nipples into peaks and sends tingles to my core.

I feel the groan rumbling from his chest under my

hands, and I'm so addicted to his mouth, I try to follow when he moves his lips to my forehead.

"I should go," he mumbles there.

I close my eyes, take a deep, shuddering breath in, and whisper, "Okay."

Eight

JD

Dan is already waiting for me on the steps of his porch, the baby perched on his knees.

This morning, I was about to load my tools in my truck to head over to Janey's when I remembered I'd loaned Dan a few things I might need. He's close to being done with the horse barn he decided to build behind his house. He already bought Aspen a pony. The kid just turned one a couple of months ago, gonna be a while before she'll ride, but when Dan gets an idea, there's no stopping him.

"Morning, JD," Sloane calls out when I get out of the truck. "Coffee?"

"Don't get up on my account," I try to stop her when I see her struggle to get out of the porch chair.

Sloane looks about to pop, pregnant with kid number two, who is due in about a month, I believe.

She waves me off. "If I don't move regularly, my ass'll get

glued to that chair. Besides, I need an excuse to sniff the coffeepot again."

"In that case, sure, I'll take a coffee."

I wasn't going to stay long, just pick up my tools and go, but I'm not going to deny Sloane that small pleasure. She groans as she stretches, one hand pressing the small of her back as she shuffles inside. Pregnancy looks fucking uncomfortable, but I'm happy for them.

"So what are you working on?" Dan asks, gesturing for me to sit on the steps with him.

"Fixing a few things."

My evasive response isn't enough to brush him off. In fact, it only seems to pique his interest as his eyes narrow on me.

"At your trailer?"

"Nah, I'm giving Doc a hand at her place."

I feel his eyes on me so I keep mine fixed on the view in front of me, which is prime. Dan picked a perfect spot to build his log home, with a view of the Fisher River and Kenelty Mountain beyond from his front porch. I've spent plenty of time here, drinking a beer while watching the sun go down.

My little patch of land backs onto Libby Creek, and although the view isn't bad from my trailer, it pales in comparison to this.

"You're making a move," Dan states.

I turn my head and briefly lock eyes with him. Then I return my gaze to the river.

"Good for you," he adds in a low voice, setting Aspen, who is getting restless on his lap, down on the ground.

She takes a few steps on unsteady feet before plopping on her butt in the grass. She immediately grabs for a clump of harmless dandelions under Dan's watchful eye. Some of the wildflowers here can be quite toxic.

"Here..."

I quickly get to my feet when Sloane tries to bend down to hand me my coffee.

"Thanks. How's that little one?" I ask, pointing at her substantial baby bump.

"A gymnast," she shares, wincing. "And real estate is getting sparse in here. Makes for restless nights."

I hadn't noticed until now how tired she looks. Dark circles curve under her blue, red-rimmed eyes.

"I'm sorry," I mumble, not sure what else to say.

"Don't be." She smiles, patting her belly. "We're excited. One more month to go. And I catch up in the afternoons with naps, although I'll be working for a bit today."

"You're still working?"

Sloane is a deputy with the Lincoln County Sheriff's Department.

"I'm supposed to be on bed rest," she clarifies. "But lying in bed, doing nothing, is driving me insane, so I check in with the office and help out if I can. But after you guys found Maggie Aldridge, it's been all-hands-on-deck."

Immediately an image of the woman's sprawled body flashes in my mind. I shake to dislodge it.

"Any developments on that?"

"Yeah." Her face turns serious. "Junior just called twenty minutes ago. They found another one."

As I'm heading out to Janey's fifteen minutes later, I'm trying to visualize the barista at Bean There, a coffee shop in town I sometimes pop into.

According to Sloane, she was the victim found at the Cabinet View Golf Club this morning. A groundskeeper discovered her body in the trees by the water feature on the third hole. Jennifer Wilson was found partially stripped, likely raped, and even though cause of death looked to be blunt force trauma in this case, the similarities suggest this is the same perp. Apparently, the women even looked alike.

As I come up to the turnoff to the veterinary clinic, I notice a billboard for the golf club up ahead. It's only a couple of miles up the road.

The driveway to Janey's place curves through a strip of trees shielding it from the road, but then it opens up with the Big Cherry Creek on the south side of the property and woods and mountains to the west. It's a nice piece of land, a little closer to town than I am and in a more populated area, but still fairly private.

Janey is just stepping out of her door with Ginger on a leash when I pull up in front of her house. The moment she sees me, a smile spreads on her face. That's a pretty damn good welcome, if you ask me.

"You don't mess about, do you?" she states as I get out of the truck.

I notice her hair is haphazardly piled on top of her head, held in place with what looks like a pair of chopsticks, and she's wearing a pair of striped, men's pajama bottoms. When I get closer, I see sleep creases from her pillow still imprinted on her cheek.

"I'm sorry if I'm early," I apologize, feeling guilty.

Nine thirty seemed like a decent time to show up, but in hindsight, I should probably have checked. For all I know, she was trying to catch up on sleep she missed during the week, or maybe she got called out after I left last night.

"No, don't apologize." She waves me off. "I couldn't get

to sleep. I ended up reading until the wee hours of the morning when I finally dozed off. Ginger woke me up in desperation a few minutes ago, so it all works out. I just need to hop in the shower real quick, but go ahead and make yourself a coffee."

Great. Her mention of a shower immediately calls up an image of Janey, water sluicing down her naked body, and my body's response is instantaneous.

It doesn't help when she turns to head back inside and I catch the enticing jiggle of her ass in those threadbare pants. That good morning kiss I'd planned to lay on her is going to have to wait until I can get my body back under control.

I'm determined to take things slow to show her I'm not in this for a quick lay.

But *damn*, it's getting hard. No pun intended.

~

Janey

"You must be Doc Richards."

I'm not sure what I expected a former bull rider to look like, but it sure wasn't this well-dressed silver fox. This man clearly doesn't care he's standing ankle-deep in mud, with rain teeming down. Wishing I'd grabbed my slicker on the way out, I tug my ball cap low over my eyes and get out of the truck.

"Phil Jericho? Nice to meet you," I lie, shaking his hand.

I'm not exactly happy he called me out here a day early to *go over some things*, which is what he indicated when he called earlier. It had already started coming down good outside and I was happy to putter around the house, sneaking peeks at

JD, who is currently ripping apart my en suite bathroom. He discovered a soft spot in the floor between the toilet and the bathtub, and since the bathroom was near the top of my list of things to do, I told him to go for it.

I glance around the rodeo grounds, noting a couple of trailers and some fencing which is already being put up. I assume those are for pens for the livestock, although the guys working on it are currently huddled under a shelter. We're still standing out in the open and I'm fast becoming drenched.

"What are we doing here?" I ask, a little annoyed.

"Why don't we go into the trailer and I'll tell you."

He starts walking to one of the trailers and I follow behind, my shoulders hunched against the miserable rain. Inside the trailer, Jericho takes off his hat, and hangs it dripping on a coatrack by the door before running a hand through his thick, gray, impeccable hair. Then he walks over to a large desk and takes a seat in the leather chair behind it.

For a temporary office at a rodeo, the furnishings are a little over-the-top fancy, if you ask me.

Still, my ball cap stays firmly on my head, because I know the hair underneath is a disaster. I feel—and most likely look—like a drowned cat, while this man looks like he came straight off the pages of *GQ*.

Life can be so unfair.

"Have a seat." He gestures to a visitor's chair across the desk from him.

I perch on the edge of the small club chair, not wanting to ruin the leather upholstery by dripping all over it. Jericho steeples his hands together, the fingertips pressing against his lips as he observes me silently. It gets uncomfortable real fast, so I try to move things along.

"What did you call me in for, Mr. Jericho?" I prompt him.

"Please, call me Phil," he corrects me immediately. "We'll be working closely together these coming days, so no need to stand on formalities. I thought we could have a quick walk-through of the days to come, and then, if the rain allows, I can show you around the site. A bit of an orientation so you'll know what to expect."

"Sure."

"As you know, tomorrow Mackey will start bringing in livestock. They've got trucks coming Monday through Wednesday. Some of his stock is coming in from Alberta, which is why all the trucks aren't arriving at once. That's the reason we need you here most of the week. I want to make sure each load is checked."

"How many animals are we talking about?" I inquire, suddenly nervous about the potential scope when I hear him talking about three days of trucks arriving. It sure sounds like a lot.

"A fair number. We've got bucking stock, calves, some steers, horses, and whatever Mackey has going on auction. Those are the main ones I want you to worry about. A few other ranchers are trucking in livestock for the auction as well, but those will come with paperwork required for inspection. Then there'll be the rodeo contestants' own horses, but those aren't your concern either, unless they get injured."

I'm glad I asked Logan to come with me, it sounds like we're going to have our hands full.

"And every animal needs to be cleared beforehand?"

"For the rodeo, yes. The herd for auction will have to be signed off on, as well, before the livestock agent gets here

Thursday morning, but a random sampling might do for those."

I don't like the idea of signing a clear bill of health based on the random sampling of a herd, but if we have a chute to run the animals through it can be a fairly quick process. I may need a little more help than just Logan for that though.

"Do you have a plan for the layout of the grounds? So I'll know where to go tomorrow?"

"Over here."

He gets up from behind the desk and moves to a couple of folding tables along the far wall, pictures of aerial views and site drawings spread out on top. Jericho points out where the stockyard will be, and the network of gates to move the cattle to the corral where I'll be working. I'm glad to see they already have a cattle chute planned.

It's amazing, the logistics to fit a large number of animals, and people, on a relatively small patch of land.

"So the auction is on Thursday afternoon and will be held here." He points to a larger fenced-off section, two-thirds of it flanked by spectator bleachers. "Also on Thursday, we'll have vendors setting up here." He indicates a large open field on the other side of the parking lot. "You'll want to get here early that day because it'll be hell trying to get in here later. A lot of the contestants will be showing up then as well."

"Auction is the only event on Thursday though?"

"Yes. Friday morning the gates open to the public at eleven. We've got a fair on the grounds of Airfield Park for the kids. Pony rides, petting zoo, food vendors, that kind of stuff. The rodeo doesn't officially start until two. I'll print you out an itinerary."

We forfeit the tour—it's still coming down hard outside —but I've got a pretty good idea of the layout from those drawings when I get ready to run for my truck half an hour later. While we fruitlessly waited for the rain to abate, Jericho recounted a few amusing stories from his days as a bull rider and, surprisingly, had me laughing more than once, but I was eager to get back home.

"Are you sure I can't convince you to join me for an early bite in town?" Jericho wants to know as he opens the door for me.

He's already asked once and I turned him down but, apparently, the man isn't used to hearing no for an answer. Don't get me wrong, he's a nice enough guy, is handsome and charming, even funny, but I'm more interested in the man who is currently at my house, gutting my bathroom.

"Quite sure. It looks like I'll be spending quite a bit of time here this coming week, and I have a pile of things left to do at home."

He flashes me a grin. "Understood. Maybe we'll find an opportunity in the days to come."

It's not very likely, but to say so now would seem unnecessarily rude.

Instead of responding, I shoot him a friendly smile and dart out the door, yelling, "See you tomorrow," over my shoulder.

Nine

JD

How long are you going to avoid me?

I tuck my phone back in my pocket. Since the disaster on Saturday, my sister has left me three voice messages before resorting to texts, which have been coming in pretty steady.

I'm not ready to listen to what Una has to say.

Ma is still pissed and ignoring me, and Pa is trying to be a peacemaker, but so far has only managed to get Ma angry at him as well.

I don't know what my sister thought was going to happen with a dramatic announcement like that, to be honest. It's almost as if, by creating a circus around the revelation of her sexual preference, she was trying to force a bad reaction from our parents; in order to justify keeping it from them for all those years.

Don't get me wrong, I'm happy for her she found someone she wants to spend her life with, but I have a sneaking suspicion this woman, Rachel, might have been the catalyst for the grand reveal this past weekend.

"Talk to her."

Pa is standing in the door opening, his hands in his pockets, looking a little forlorn.

So much for hiding out in the tack room until the end of my last workday before I take off for the rest of the week. I sigh, put down the rag I've been oiling my saddle with, and wipe my hands on my jeans.

"Not sure that's going to do any good."

"Fucking try. She's not listening to me. She's banging around the kitchen, huffing like a damn bull at anyone who even crosses her eyesight. Everyone is tiptoeing around her, and I think Jonas has had just about enough. You know there's gonna be fireworks if he calls her out."

Shaking my head, I curse under my breath. Yeah, I know. Jonas and my mother adore each other, but both are blunt and headstrong. It could get ugly.

"Fine. I'll talk to her."

I can hear her moving around the kitchen when I step in the front door of the ranch house. Walking down the hall, I pass Jonas's office and glance inside. He's sitting at his desk, his jaw clenched, and his eyes on me.

"Make it fucking stop," he grinds.

I nod. *Shit*. No pressure.

The moment she catches sight of me, she slams the pan she was holding on the stove with a loud bang, puts her hands on her hips, and locks her eyes on me.

"What?"

"Two minutes, Ma. Out on the deck." I move to the sliding doors and reach for the handle. "Two minutes you can yell at me, but then I want two minutes to have my say."

She stays put and tries to stare me down, but I've learned from the best and stare right back.

Finally, she starts moving, looking down at the ground in front of her feet. I slide the door open to let her pass and follow her out on the deck, making sure to close it again. Ma keeps walking until she reaches the edge, bracing herself on the railing as she looks out at the view. I move up right beside her and lean my back against the railing, turning my head toward her.

"All right, let me have it," I invite her, but it's like the starch has gone out of her.

"You lied."

I expected that one, but I'm discovering it hits harder when it's delivered in a soft, pained voice, rather than yelled in my face.

"Both my kids lied to me. Did I raise you like that? But you know what the worst part of it is?"

When she turns her face to me, I see rare tears swimming in her eyes. There's a gut punch.

"What, Ma?" I prompt her gently.

"That you two would feel the need to hide that from us. Have we ever given you reason to believe we wouldn't accept either of you, just the way you are?"

"No. I know you haven't."

"Then why?" She throws her hands in the air as her frustration returns, and with it her temper. "For how long? Since Una went off to college? All those wasted years."

"You need to talk to her. Not yell, but talk. You are more alike than you know, you two. Go from zero to full blast in a second, and when everyone's yelling, no one is listening. It's been like that since she was barely in her teens."

One fat tear finally manages to escape and rolls unchecked down her face. As much as I want to wipe it away for her, I know it would sting her pride. So like her, I pretend it's not there.

"She was always spirited," she muses.

"Still is."

"Unlike you. You were more like your father. Calm, with a quiet strength. Protective, even as a little boy you were your sister's keeper." She turns to face me, and I see anger simmering there. "None of this would've been necessary if you'd told me."

I shake my head.

"No. That wasn't mine to share, it was Una's. Don't try to put this on me. And if you're doling out the blame, don't forget to include yourself. You had as many years as Una to work on your relationship, but you were both too stubborn to do anything about it. If you had, perhaps none of this would've been necessary either."

Her lips form a thin line as she presses them together, and I know whatever else I say will fall on deaf ears, so I don't bother. I leave her standing by the railing and head inside, hoping some of what I've said will filter through.

I find Jonas and Pa keeping old Thomas company on the porch. All three of them with a thick cigar between their lips.

"And?" It's not a surprise Thomas is the one to ask. He rarely holds back. "Did you get the woman under control?"

"Jesus, Dad." Jonas shakes his head. "Don't fucking let her hear you say that, or we're gonna have bigger problems."

My father doesn't say a thing, he just looks at me with a steady gaze.

"Had my say," I volunteer. "And I hope some of it sticks, but it was a lot, so give her a little time."

I get a set of harrumphs as confirmation and start down the stairs to go back to the barn, but Jonas stops me.

"Aren't you supposed to be off starting tomorrow?"

"Yeah."

He jerks his head to the side. "Go. Take off early. It's quiet anyway."

"Thanks. I'll head out after I finish up in the tack room."

Maybe I can head over to Doc's place and finish putting in that new subfloor in the bathroom before she comes home.

∼

Janey

"What the fuck are you on about now?"

I swivel around to find John Mackey stalking toward me, thunder on his face. I swear his boots touch the tips of mine as he stops to hover over me. With his bulbous, blue drinker's nose inches from mine, I can feel the spit hitting my face as he continues yelling at me about my bleeding-heart incompetence. Slapping his dusty hat on his thigh and stomping his foot for emphasis.

I've dealt with men like him, bullies looking for the first sign of weakness to pounce on, so I don't even flinch or blink an eye. Eventually, he runs out of steam when I show no reaction, and that's when I speak. Calmly.

"Was there some kind of issue, John? I couldn't quite hear you clearly."

Some of the hands standing nearby chuckle, and Mackey swings around to glare at them, letting out a frustrated growl. It makes me smile. A bit more composed, he turns back to me.

"There's nothing wrong with that bronc." He waves his hand at the jittery roan I just pulled aside.

The horse has an open rubbing wound, right where a flank or *bucking* strap would be tightened. In addition, his left front fetlock—the ankle joint—is swollen and warm to the touch, suggesting inflammation. I suspect it's damage to or deterioration of the flexor tendon, which is pretty common in bucking horses.

I sent Logan home after we were done inspecting today's arrival of animals, but I kept this horse aside.

I outline my findings to Mackey and explain the horse needs rest to heal, and is a write-off for the rodeo. Despite my calm tone, I can tell he's getting all fired up again, cursing up a storm at my expense. More accusations of incompetence, a general contempt of my gender, and a few juicy, bigoted insults I'm trying not to respond to.

In my peripheral vision I catch the approach of Jericho, who has been around the past two days, keeping an eye on things. He's not my favorite person, but he hasn't really bothered me much and I'm glad he's coming to check out this confrontation. I'd rather have him as a witness if this escalates than Mackey's own crew, even if they did laugh at him.

Apparently, Mackey caught sight of him too, because he immediately tones down.

"Then put him the fuck down. He's no use to me now and I ain't gonna waste good food on a bad horse."

"Are you kidding me? Put him down? All he needs is a few weeks of rest and some proper care and he'll be good as new."

I know it's his right as the owner, but I can't believe he'd ask me to kill the horse over something that can be easily fixed. It goes against everything I stand for.

"I run a business, not a goddamn hospital. My horse, and if you're too fucking soft to do your job, I'll do it my goddamn self."

His eyes are fixed on me as he pulls a gun from a holster on his belt. For a moment I'm frozen, wondering how the hell we got to this point, but then he walks up to the roan and puts the barrel to the horse's forehead.

"I'll take him," I blurt out, impulsively grabbing for his arm. "Save you the bullet and the mess."

Since I've managed to pull his gun away from his target, he tries to dislodge me, sending me stumbling back. That's when Jericho steps in.

"Mackey! You hurt my vet or shoot that horse and we've got issues."

His tone is calm, but his voice holds an authoritarian threat which is impossible to miss. This is not a man to be messed with.

Apparently, John Mackey realizes it too, because after only moments of facing off with Jericho, he grunts, holsters his weapon, and turns on his heel.

"Take the useless carcass then," he fires off his parting shot as he stalks back to the stockyard.

Great. Now I have a bucking horse I have no use for and I sent Logan packing. I could've had him run up to the clinic to grab the small horse trailer from behind the barn.

"Tomorrow we've got the cattle coming in," Jericho reminds me, interrupting my thoughts. "The trucks should get here around ten. Are you bringing the kid?"

"Logan? Yes, he'll be with me."

He nods. "Good. You're gonna need the extra hands. It'll be a long day."

"We're prepared," I return, perhaps a bit defensively.

Jericho flashes a grin. "I'm sure you are. But maybe stay out of Mackey's way tomorrow. You hit any problems, send the kid to come find me." He glances at the horse. "Best get that animal out of here before he changes his mind."

Right.

As I pull my phone from my pocket and dial the clinic, I watch him walk back to his trailer.

"Libby Veterinary Clinic."

"Frankie, it's Doc. By any chance did Logan stop by there?"

"No, I haven't seen him."

Shit, I was hoping maybe I'd catch him there and could get him to run the trailer over here. I don't really want to leave the horse because I don't trust what'll happen to it if I'm not here.

Plan B, and I'm keeping my fingers crossed.

"Okay. By chance have you towed the horse trailer before?"

I know it's a long shot, but I've noticed the hitch on her older GMC Jimmy. I'm hoping maybe she's hauled something before. It's not ideal, but it's not that far and the trailer would be empty coming here. But her answer knocks the bottom out of that plan.

"No," she scoffs. "That would freak me out."

"I have a horse here I need to move ASAP. Got any brilliant ideas?"

"Maybe...I saw JD's old pickup come up the drive earlier. He must be working on your house. I could ask him."

"That's okay, I'll call him."

He answers my call a minute later and I explain my need. Twenty minutes after that, I watch him pull my little horse trailer onto the rodeo grounds. He skillfully backs it up to the gate of the small enclosure I have the horse confined in.

"Hey."

He grins, stalking toward me, his long legs eating up the distance. A large hand hooks me by the neck as he bends his head to lay a kiss on me. It's what he's done the past few days; kiss me when he sees me, kiss me a little harder when he leaves, but nothing other than the promise of more. Lord knows I'm ready for *more.*

"This the horse?" He nudges to the roan.

"Yeah, that's him. He's a bit skittish," I warn him when he approaches.

I'd been able to handle him okay, but I noticed his response had been distinctly different when a man came close.

"I'd expect so," JD returns, taking the lead from my hand.

Then he slowly approaches the animal with an outstretched hand as he mumbles soothing words in a low voice.

The horse is on high alert, his ears are pricked, his nostrils are flared, and I can see a slight tremble in the muscles of his neck. Still, when JD offers him the palm of his hand, the animal tentatively brushes it with his lips. Still alert, but not fearful.

"Can you get the gate for me? Or do you want to do the honors?"

"Either way is fine by me," I assure him.

As JD soothes the horse with his touch and clips on the lead, I quickly release the latch and open the gate to the pen. Then I release the ramp of the trailer which is lined up with the opening.

But the moment JD tries to get the horse to move, he rears on his hind legs.

"Whoa, easy boy."

Instead of forcing the horse, JD moves with him, turning tight circles in the small pen. After passing by the wide-open gate a few times, the horse seems to relax a little. Then on the next pass, JD firmly leads the horse through the open gate, and this time the roan follows him straight into the back of the trailer.

"Nice work," I compliment him when he climbs out of the small escape door at the front of the trailer.

"He could smell the hay I tossed in there before I left the barn. He's already munching on it," he points out as he follows me to the back of the trailer, where we lift the ramp back in place and bolt it shut.

Food is a great motivator, even for a bucking horse, apparently.

Showing my appreciation, I put my hands on his chest, lift up on my tiptoes, and press a kiss to his lips.

"Thank you. I'll follow you home."

I watch him as he heads for his pickup and climbs behind the wheel. Then I turn to walk to my own truck when I notice Phil Jericho standing in the open door of his trailer, watching me. I lift a hand in greeting, but instead of returning the gesture, he turns away and shuts the door behind him. Weird.

Instead of turning to the clinic, I park my truck in its usual spot outside the house, and walk over to where JD is already lowering the ramp of the trailer beside the barn doors.

"Before you get him out, let me check if Frankie got the stall ready for him."

"Does he have a name?" JD wants to know.

I shrug. "I heard them call him Big Red, but I don't know if that was referring to his color, or his actual name."

His coat graduates from the deep red chestnut color of his head and neck, to the almost white blend on his hindquarters. But his tail is red like his mane and he has a white blaze down his face.

"Call him Red, everyone can see he's big," JD suggests.

I give him a nod in agreement before I poke my head into the barn to see Frankie left the stall door open and appears to have spread fresh straw inside. Then I give JD a thumbs-up, indicating he can bring the horse inside.

Ten minutes later, with a little coaxing from JD and some fresh oats from me, we're hanging over the half door, watching Red explore his new stall.

"What are you gonna do with him?"

I glance at JD and shrug my shoulders. "I'm not sure. Get him better first, I guess."

"You can always talk to Lucy at Hart's Rescue. Maybe she can take him in."

The thought crossed my mind when I was waiting for JD to get there with the trailer, but I don't really want to pawn the poor animal off on someone else.

"As a last resort," I concede. "I was thinking maybe I could see if he could be retrained to ride."

JD turns to me with a dubious expression on his face.

"These bucking horses are notoriously difficult to rehabilitate," he cautions me. "If bucking is all they've known their whole life, it may be an impossible feat."

I hold out my hand when Red closes in, curiously sniffing, and I feel a small sense of triumph when he lets me stroke his soft nose.

"But he's fairly young still. I think maybe I'd like to try."

"It's gonna be a lot of work."

Red seems to have satisfied his curiosity with us and returns to the bucket of oats hanging on the wall. I step away from the door and turn to face JD.

"I know, but I feel like I owe it to him to try."

One side of his mouth tilts up. On its own it's barely a smile, but when you add his warm, dark eyes, fine lines fanning out from their corners, it couldn't be any clearer.

"In that case, I'm happy to help," he shares, grabbing my hand and pulling me to the door. "But first let's eat."

I snort. "It'll have to be takeout because my fridge is empty."

He lifts my hand to his mouth for a kiss on my knuckles.

"No need. I made us chili and cornbread."

Ten

"Have you talked to your sister yet?"

If it wasn't for the brief hesitation before he closes the tailgate of his truck, I'd have thought he didn't hear me.

He hasn't said much about Saturday night at all. I haven't pushed him on the subject, but he's been here every free moment since then, and this isn't the first time I've seen him ignore a call when his phone rings.

"No."

He turns to face me and I expect to be told to mind my own business, but he surprises me.

"I've been thinking about what you said last Saturday. About falling back into old patterns. Well, I'm breaking them. I'm done getting stuck in the middle. If Una wants to fix things, she shouldn't be calling me, she should be calling Ma."

He's right, she should. Still, it's clearly not easy for him to ignore her, he's been looking out for her for so long.

"It may take her a while to clue into the fact expectations have changed," I offer tentatively. "But maybe if you communicate it to her. You don't have to talk to her, but there are other ways to convey the message. If the new rules aren't made clear to her, you're just setting her up to fail."

For a moment I wonder if I'm overstepping—I probably am, but sometimes it's easier to see the big picture when you're on the outside of a conflict—but then the corner of his mouth pulls up in a lopsided smile. One that makes the butterflies in my stomach dance.

"You're wise."

"It comes with age," is my response.

At some point over the past few days, I've come to realize I'm more than a couple of years older than JD. I think it may have been last Saturday at his parents' house there'd been some mention of a four-year difference between JD and Una. I know he stated later that night his sister is thirty, but for some reason—maybe the drama playing out was too distracting—I didn't immediately put the two together.

I'm four years his senior, and I'm trying hard not to let that fall on the insecure side of my character. I've been trying to focus on the fact he's known about our age difference since our Mexican picnic at the riverside, and he hadn't even kissed me yet then. He doesn't seem bothered, so why should I be?

Still, I can't resist putting it out there.

He takes a step closer and slips his arms around me, pulling me close so I'm plastered against his front. There is no mistaking the hard length of him pressing against my lower belly.

"Wisdom is a major turn-on," he shares, his dark eyes swirling with surprising heat. "Everything about you is, which is why I'm dealing with a permanent hard-on anytime I'm around you." He rolls his hips, making it impossible to ignore the significance of his words.

A pathetically needy whimper escapes me. It feels like I've been craving a more carnal connection with him than the admittedly excellent kisses for days. It's left me with a deep ache—a gnawing hunger—that is causing me restless nights.

"Yes," I whisper, pressing my lips to the hollow at the base of his throat, where I can feel his heart beating.

"Later," he promises. "When I don't have a dump run to make, and you don't have a horse and a dog to feed, as well as a few truckloads of cattle waiting to be cleared."

"Spoilsport," I groan, making him chuckle.

"Nah, just something to look forward to."

He lays a hard kiss on me before tipping his hat and getting into his truck. I watch him roll down the driveway, passing Frankie in her Jimmy who is just arriving. I give her a wave before heading inside to grab Ginger and drop her off at the clinic where Frankie can feed her.

JD showed up here early this morning, so we could load up the old tub, toilet, and vanity from the master bathroom. I'd been too tired last night to be of any help, and aside from that, the landfill was already closed. This coming weekend we're supposed to head to the Home Depot in Kalispell to buy my new bathroom.

I'm feeling a little guilty over all the time he's spending at my house, but he swears up and down it's what he likes to do, work with his hands. A lot of it is stuff I intended to tackle myself, even though I have no idea how to lay a subfloor or tile or hook up a new faucet. I guess I've been a little blinded by the numerous home improvement shows I've been watching on TV. They make it look so easy, and I figured I could watch some DIY YouTube videos to learn.

Maybe after the rodeo, I'll have some more time and energy to invest in my to-do list.

"Come on, girl. You're going to hang out with Frankie and Red today."

Ginger has become quite agile with her cast. It doesn't seem to be slowing her down much anymore. Last night after dinner, JD was even throwing a ball for her in the backyard. I still don't have a fence, but as JD predicted, Ginger didn't make any effort to take off. Regardless where she came from, she knows she has a good life here.

I leave Ginger in Frankie's good care, and she also promises to look in on Red, who I found moping around his stall. He's used to being around lots of other animals and I bet he's lonely here, which is something else I need to think about.

It's not until I get behind the wheel, I start feeling a little anxiety for the day ahead. Yesterday's confrontation with Mackey was not something I care to repeat. Not that he scares me—I think he's more bluster than substance—but I hope to heed Phil Jericho's advice, and avoid him all the same.

Instead of parking at the trailer and walking over to the stockyard, I drive straight there when I pull into the grounds and see two large trucks have already arrived. It's only eight twenty, so they're earlier than expected.

I'm relieved to see Logan's pickup already there. He'd called in last night to ask what time he should be here, so I wasn't expecting him until nine thirty. He's way early, which I suspect has something to do with his excitement about the rodeo in general. He's been lapping it up these past two days. I don't care about the motivation, I'm just glad he's here, so we can get an early start.

I park my truck next to his and go in search of him. Unfortunately, it's Mackey I bump into first. He's just coming out of the rear of one of the trucks. He seems surprised to see me at first, then his expression quickly morphs into anger, but he doesn't say a word as he ducks back out of sight. I see movement inside through the ventilation holes and can hear urgent voices. A moment later he appears again, this time ignoring me as he comes down the narrow loading ramp and brushes past me. Then he stalks off to the impromptu campground set up behind the livestock pens. It's where Mackey and his employees, as well as some of the contestants, parked their RVs.

Curious, I walk over to the back of the massive trailer. Each of these probably holds anywhere from thirty to fifty head of cattle. When I start up the ramp, I recognize one of Mackey's hands along with Logan standing among the cows. It's not exactly safe, it wouldn't be the first time someone got trampled and seriously injured in a situation like this.

"What are you doing?" I ask sharply, drawing the men's attention.

"One of the cows is sick and went down," Logan answers. "We're trying to make sure she doesn't get crushed by the others."

"The boss went to grab a few more hands to set up the gates so we can unload them," the other guy shares.

Rather than try to maneuver these large trucks into position, given the limited space, it's easier to create a chute to lead the cattle into a pen. Once Mackey returns with a couple of men, it doesn't take them long to put one together, and I help, opening the dividing doors inside the trailer to release the next handful of animals down the ramp.

When I get to the section where the cow went down, Logan and the hand usher the rest of the cattle out, while I crouch down beside the motionless animal. It's obvious she's dead, her eyes are fixed and dull. Her tongue is protruding and slightly swollen, and what looks like vomit is crusted on the side of her muzzle and in her nostrils.

That's odd. Cows rarely ever vomit unless they've chewed on a noxious weed, or ingested bad feed or some kind of poison. I'm going to need to get some samples from this cow.

"Logan!" I call out when I see him hustling the last of the animals down the ramp. "Can you grab the kit from the back of my truck?"

When he brings it to me a few moments later, I quickly collect a variety of samples, including blood and vomit, and slip the vials into my pocket.

"She was still alive when you first saw her?" I ask Logan, who crouches down beside me.

"She was, but barely. She was down and struggling to breathe."

"Did you try to get her to stand?"

"There wasn't any room, that's why we were gonna unload, but I guess it was too late."

"Yeah. I don't think there was any saving her," I assure him.

"What do you think it was?"

I shrug. "Not sure. It looks like some kind of poisoning but until I can figure it out, we're going to be extra cautious and isolate the other cattle that came off this truck."

"You think it could be some infectious disease?" Logan probes.

"Doubtful. I just want to be cautious, and isolating them also makes it easier to monitor the others for any signs they may be getting sick."

"What's going on?" Mackey walks in, followed by a portly older man wearing a ball cap.

"You've got a dead cow," I inform him.

"Dead? *Fuck*. More fucking paperwork."

This comes from the man in the ball cap who, I'm guessing, is the truck driver.

Mackey claps him on the shoulder. "Can't be the first time an animal gets trampled on your truck, George?"

"I'm pretty sure she wasn't trampled," I interrupt. "I don't see any evidence of any kind of contact on her, but what I do see are signs of some kind of poisoning. I was just saying to Logan, we're going to have to monitor the rest of the cattle from this truck so they'll have to stay isolated from the rest until we know what we're dealing with."

Mackey bursts out in a litany of curses, expressing his displeasure with both me and the situation. Ignoring him, I turn to the other man.

"George, is it? Are you the driver?"

He nods.

"If you could move this truck away from the stockyard, I need to open this cow up. I want a look at her stomach contents."

"You wanna cut her open in my truck?"

"Best place for it," I return. "I assume you were gonna hose it down anyway?"

He doesn't seem happy, and neither is Mackey, who seems near apoplectic with rage as he rants on about having me kicked off the grounds, making sure I'd never work again, and threats of that nature. I'm ignoring him pointedly, which is the best thing to do with bullies; don't give them the satisfaction.

"But first I need to have a quick look at the other animals," I continue to explain to George.

I close my kit and get to my feet, grimacing at the pop and crackle of my knees.

"Come with me," I instruct Logan.

He's a good kid and instinctively places himself between me and Mackey, as we walk past him and down the ramp.

There are thirty-seven other cows in the pen. By the time we have the cattle chute set up and run each of them through, taking blood and stool samples, almost two and a half hours have passed. The second truck has been unloaded in a neighboring enclosure, and a third truck is just pulling in.

"Did you see where they took the truck with the dead cow?" I ask Logan as I scan the grounds.

"I thought I saw him head that way." He points toward the road heading out of the park.

Goddammit.

I shouldn't have let that truck out of my sight. Mackey doesn't want anything standing in the way of getting his cattle to auction tomorrow. I wouldn't put it past him to try and haul that cow off somewhere before I get a chance to examine it.

I immediately grab one of Mackey's guys, the one who'd been in the trailer with Logan when I first got here.

"Where did your boss send that truck?"

"Which truck?" he asks, feigning ignorance.

"You know which one I'm talking about," I push.

"Tell her."

I swing around to find Phil Jericho walking up, JD is

right behind him. Jericho is staring down Mackey's hand, while JD sidles up beside me.

The guy shrugs, like he really doesn't care what the outcome will be, and points at the public parking lot.

"There's a clearing on the other side. I'm guessing he's there."

When I look in that direction, I see a plume of smoke rising above the trees.

"That son of a bitch," flies from my mouth as I start running toward my truck.

I hear JD's heavy footfalls right behind me.

Eleven

JD

"Wanna tell me what the fuck is going on?"

I hang on to the handle above the passenger side door, as Janey takes a turn a little too sharp, and the back of her truck fishtails in the loose dirt.

"Mackey," she forces out between clenched teeth. "There was a dead cow on one of the transports. Looks like some kind of poisoning, and I was gonna have a closer look after clearing the rest of the load."

"Let me guess," I volunteer. "He doesn't want the delay."

"He was irate when I told him to separate those cows from the rest of the herd," she adds.

"So he's afraid of what you might find? Like an infectious disease or something?"

"Who the hell knows. It may just be he's pissed I'm here and wants to make my job extra difficult. He's a miserable excuse for a man, and I wouldn't put anything past him."

Another turn that would do a rally racer proud, and then I catch sight of the fire. Janey aims her truck straight for it. She's out of the vehicle before I can stop her, but the fire is too hot for her to get close. The smell of burning animal fills my nostrils when I get out of the truck. Whoever set it on fire not only used some kind of fuel, but covered the carcass with brush and old wooden pallets. It's burning fast and hot.

"That son of a bitch," Janey mutters softly as I step up beside her. "He knows damn well unless I can find another sick cow in the bunch, I can't keep the rest of the load from auction."

"So now what?"

She turns to me with a smug little smile on her lips as she pulls a plastic baggie with vials from the side pocket of her cargo pants. "I still have the samples I took."

She walks over to the back of her truck and grabs what looks like a small lunch bag and places the samples inside. Then she pulls out an instant cold pack, activates it by scrunching it between her hands, and slips that in the lunch bag as well.

"Does that have to go to a lab?" I ask, when we get back in the truck.

"I can do some testing back at the clinic, but I have two more truckloads of cattle to check before I can get to it. It's getting warm, I want the samples to stay fresh."

I would offer to run them to the clinic to refrigerate them, but I don't want to leave her alone with this Mackey guy and that slime bucket, Jericho. Janey doesn't seem in the least intimidated, but I didn't like the way Phil Jericho tried to run me off when I came looking for her, so for that alone I'm going to be sticking around.

Neither man is anywhere in sight when we return to the

stockyard, it's only Janey's assistant, Logan, sitting on the fence of the cattle chute, chatting with a couple of guys who look like they work here.

"Where is your boss?" Janey asks the two guys.

"Left. Him and Jericho both. Some lunch meeting in town," the younger of the two volunteers. "Said he'd be back this afternoon."

"Call him," she orders the guy.

He does what she asks, but it's clear he's not having any luck getting a hold of Mackey.

"Fine. All right," Doc finally says, throwing her hands up in defeat. "Let's get this show on the road, with or without him. Any change in these cows?"

The question is directed at Logan, who shakes his head. "No. They seem fine."

"Good. Let's hope it was an isolated incident. We'll need to clear the animals that came off the second trailer, so we can get the third transport unloaded as soon as possible," she outlines. "It's already getting steamy out here."

She's right. It's almost midday and the sun is high in a cloudless sky. The weather forecast promised sunny and warm conditions heading into the weekend and, so far, that seems to be accurate. Those cows will be overheating quickly in that trailer.

"If I can make a suggestion," I start, looking at the two holding pens that are only separated by a walkway. "Those cows are gonna get hot in the trailer, offload those guys with the unchecked herd and then set the chute up between the two pens. Unless you still want to keep that first group separate."

She shakes her head. "No. I think you're right. It's probably fastest that way."

Logan and the two hands jump into action, tasked with

moving the chute into the pathway between the two pens, while I follow Janey to where the driver of the third transport is sitting in his rig.

"Hey, we're getting ready to unload," she informs him. "Is it possible to back up to the other side of that pen?"

"No can do," the guy responds with a shrug. "I was told by the boss to sit tight right here. So that's what I'm doing."

"You're talking about Mackey?"

"That's right."

I can feel the irritation come off Janey in waves.

"Well, I'm the vet who's responsible for the well-being of these animals, and keeping them in a trailer that must feel like a sauna by now is not in their best interest. Besides, I need to clear them."

The driver looks her up and down and shrugs again. "Be my guest, check them out, but they ain't coming off the truck unless the boss says so."

I swallow a grin when I hear her mumble, *Motherfucker,* as she marches back to where Logan and the others are moving the metal fencing. I hustle to keep up.

"Change of plans," she announces when she reaches them. "Logan, once you have the chute up, start moving the cows through. You know the drill. Don't forget to mark tag numbers and note any observations on the log. Anything out of the ordinary, pull the animal aside until I can have a look."

"Where are you gonna be?" the kid asks her.

"On the trailer." She cocks a thumb over her shoulder. "Driver won't release the load so I'm going in there."

"I can do it," Logan offers.

"That's okay. You keep going here. I'll jump in when I'm done."

Next, she heads back to her truck and opens the tailgate, reaching for her veterinary kit. I get my hand on it first.

"I've got it."

She shoots me a glance but doesn't argue. Instead, she grabs a few other odds and ends from the bins in the back of her truck.

"I never asked what you were doing here. Were you just popping in?" she asks as we start walking back to the transport truck.

I didn't really have a good reason to stop by, other than feeling the need to stick close to her. Both because I wanted to, but also because I don't trust Jericho. I caught him watching us the other day and I didn't like the vibes he was giving off.

Now that I'm here, I have even more reasons to want to stick close to Janey.

"I'm staying."

"Good," she states. "As you can see, I can use an extra pair of hands."

The truck driver introduces himself as Trent when he gets down from his rig to open the gate on the trailer. He doesn't appear to be a bad guy, and reiterates he's only following the boss's orders when he follows us up the gangway.

Working on a ranch, I'm used to the smell of animal manure, but—despite the ventilation holes all around the sides—the stench inside the trailer is overwhelming. The heat doesn't help; a combination of the sun beating down on the trailer and body heat from the forty or so large animals occupying it.

"We'll work from the front to the back," Janey suggests.

"I'll wait here," Trent announces, sticking close to the door and fresh air.

I can't say I blame him, but Doc needs a hand, so I follow her inside, pushing through heavy bodies and climbing over the occasional partitions, until we reach the very front of the trailer.

There's barely any room to put down her kit. I end up keeping it slung over my shoulder so she can grab what she needs. I'm also keeping notes on the clipboard she handed me, jotting down the tag numbers and any other entries she wants me to make.

It's by far not the first time I've seen Janey work, but I'm fascinated all the same. She's apparently as easy and comfortable with these cows as I've seen her with horses, and mumbles nonstop, keeping the animals calm as she pokes and probes.

I lose track of time as we make our way through the trailer, settling into an easy rhythm where I can anticipate what her next move is going to be. Even though I feel a bit more accustomed to the heat and the smells, I'm sweating like a pig and my shirt is plastered to my body. Doc isn't faring much better; a few strands of her hair have come loose from her braids and are stuck to her slick skin.

A sudden thud right behind me has me swing around. Looking over the next divider, I see one of the cows has gone down. Her eyes are wild and her breathing seems labored.

"You've got one in trouble here," I alert Janey.

She immediately hops over the divider and crouches down beside the animal. I am right behind her as I climb over as well and do my best to keep the other cattle away from her.

"What's wrong with her?" I ask, watching Doc examine the cow.

"Heart rate is up; breathing is shallow and labored. The

lungs sound fine, but she's clearly in pain. Help me try and get her on her feet."

I hop into action, but with the two of us pushing and shoving at what I'm guessing to be in the range of a twelve-hundred-pound animal it takes a while to encourage her back on her feet. As soon as she's standing, Janey runs her hands along the cow's flanks.

"Slightly distended," she mutters to herself before putting her stethoscope where her hands were. "Lots of bowel sounds."

Next, she moves to the back of the cow and lifts her tail. "No fresh stool."

Grabbing a glove and a tube of lubricant from the kit, she examines the animal manually, a deep frown between her eyebrows.

"What's wrong?"

"I thought maybe she was impacted, but it feels like something is constricting the anal canal. I think I'm going to need the portable ultrasound from the back of my truck," she shares.

"I can go get it," I offer.

I leave her with her kit and the cow, and start making my way to the back of the trailer, where Trent is hanging out by the gangway, smoking a cigarette.

"Everything okay in there?"

I'm not sure why, but something about the anxious way he's trying to look inside the trailer has my antenna ping. It only adds to my suspicion something fishy is going on here after that cow's carcass was set on fire earlier. So, I decide to keep Trent in the dark for now.

"Yup, you've got some of the animals overheating though. Do you think you could find some water? There's gotta be a hose around somewhere? They need to be cooled down."

"Yeah, sure."

As he heads off in search of water, I jog to Doc's truck and grab the portable ultrasound before heading back to the trailer, without anyone paying me any attention. Good.

Inside, Janey makes quick work of getting the machine up and running. She slides the wand along the cow's flank as she stares at the small screen I'm holding up in front of her.

"That's weird. See that?" She points at an area that looks white on the screen. "That's her vaginal canal. It's supposed to show up dark, but it shows white, which would indicate high density."

She puts the portable unit down and grabs a fresh glove, squirting lubricant on it before positioning herself behind the cow again.

"It's like she's got something stuck in her vaginal tract. What on earth?"

She retrieves her hand, pulling what appears to be a silver sausage of some kind from the cow.

"What is this?"

She holds it up in the palm of her hand and when I take a closer look, alarm bells immediately go off.

"Shhh," I shush her, grabbing the package from her outstretched hand and shoving it in my pocket. "Drugs," I whisper my suspicion.

I don't want to draw any attention to the discovery. Not until we know what this is and who is involved. I've read about this, it was an article on the smuggling of narcotics in cattle, they call it narco-ranching. If that's what this is, it's apparently not only growing in popularity in South America as the article claimed.

"Drugs?" she hisses back at me.

"Yeah. There's probably more in there."

"That could explain what killed the other one, if it somehow burst inside her," Janey contemplates in a hushed tone. "I need to get these out of her."

My instincts are to leave them right where they are, so their discovery can remain undetected.

"We need to call in law enforcement before we do anything," I whisper urgently.

But Janey has other ideas. "Look, this cow may die if I don't get these out of her now, which will definitely alert whoever is responsible for putting them there and focus attention on us. If we can save her, we can walk out of here safely and *then* alert law enforcement."

I reluctantly have to agree with her. The sooner I can get her out of here the better.

Twelve

Janey

"You should've left them."

I swing around and glare at the young deputy standing by Sheriff Ewing's side. Ginger softly growls beside me. I quickly scratch her head to let her know everything is fine.

Frankie has my key and dropped her off at the house after she closed the clinic for the day. The poor girl had been happy to see us, until the sheriff and his deputy showed up a few minutes ago.

"And let the cow die?" I return, trying to keep my voice calm for the dog. "Because that's what would've happened. Those packages were shoved up inside her none too carefully and were causing her to be in serious distress."

The packages I'm referring to are lined up on my kitchen table. Nine duct-taped, plastic-wrapped, sausage-shaped packages.

I've never been so scared in my life, working side by side with JD to clear the rest of the herd as if nothing was wrong, while all the time those packages were hidden in our clothes. JD had me scan as many cows in that trailer as we could get away with without it being noticed, and he recorded everything on his phone. The same high density showed up on the ultrasound of four more cows we were able to examine, and we made note of their tag numbers.

When we finally walked down the ramp of that trailer, I was almost surprised no one was paying much attention to us. Except the driver, who'd finally managed to find a hose and was dragging it to his truck. Despite my shaking hands, I managed to sound fairly stern as I left him with instructions to spray some water on the animals to cool them down.

I don't think even the driver noticed the portable ultrasound JD was carrying, and even if he did see it, I doubt he'd have known what it was. The unit was back in the truck before we joined Logan in the pen and finished up checking those animals.

They were the most harrowing couple of hours of my life. Logan looked at me funny a few times when I'd fumble or drop something when my nerves got the better of me. But JD and I agreed not to talk to anyone but law enforcement. Besides, telling him would only put him in potential danger too. It's safer not to know.

"In this case, I think removing them was wise," Sheriff Ewing tells his deputy. "It may have bought us some time so we can get surveillance in place." Then he turns to me. "You said this herd came from Alberta?"

I nod. "Yes, as far as I know, the transport crossed the border early this morning. The first two trucks were already there when I got to the rodeo grounds a little after eight this morning, and the third one got here around midday."

Ewing instructs Deputy Bastian to collect the packages

in evidence bags, while he probes us for more details, jotting down the information we're able to give him in a small notebook.

"I'm going to head out there, I'll call it a routine check, which I probably would've done tomorrow anyway. I'll also have a look at where you said they were burning the carcass of that cow, see if there's anything left. But first I'm going to call the FBI office in Kalispell. My department is already spread thin because of the rodeo and all the extra traffic it brings to town, but aside from that, this case is bigger than we can handle."

Then he turns to his deputy. "I want you to run the evidence straight to the office. Log it in, secure it, and then meet me at the park. We'll have a look around the grounds."

JD and I walk outside with them. The sheriff is about to get in his cruiser, when he turns around.

"I'm gonna need you both to stick around here. I have a feeling things might move fast once I get a call in to the feds, and I'm sure they'll want to talk to you themselves."

"We'll be here," JD answers for both of us as he drapes an arm around my shoulders.

"For now," I amend.

"I'll give you a heads-up if I know anything more, once I've had a chance to talk to them," Ewing promises before getting behind the wheel.

We don't even know if and when the FBI will get here. It's already late in the day, they may not arrive until tomorrow, which would be a bit of an issue. I'll be expected to show my face at the rodeo arena at some point or my absence might raise suspicions.

Shoot, I didn't even think of the larger implications. I took this job for the nice paycheck attached, but at the very least this investigation will impact the auction scheduled for tomorrow. Although, I'm sure the cloud will hang over the rodeo as well; I'll be lucky to get paid at all once all is said and done.

I'm not sure where exactly those cattle came from, other than somewhere in Alberta, but I know Mackey arranged the transport. There's no way he's not involved somehow. How could he not be? If anything, his hurry to get rid of the dead cow from the first transport was a glaring red flag.

I wonder where he took off to this afternoon.

"I need a shower," I announce when the sheriff's cruiser disappears down the driveway. "I reek."

I start walking toward the house.

"I don't smell anything."

I turn my head and shoot a grin at JD, who is right behind me. "That's because you reek too."

"Maybe I should take a shower as well then," he suggests.

"Take a number." I stop in the hallway to kick off the boots I wore outside. "In case you forgot, I currently only have the one working shower."

JD ditches his boots as well and follows me inside. I head straight for the kitchen counter to grab my phone I left there to charge. I don't want to miss Ewing's call if he gets back to us with more information while I'm in the shower.

"We could always share."

I almost jump when his voice sounds right behind me. I didn't hear him move, he's quiet without his boots.

The moment I turn around to face him, he braces a hand on the counter on either side of me, effectively caging me in. His brown eyes are only inches from mine, reading my face. Thoughts of his slick tawny skin sliding against my much paler tones as our wet bodies come together in my cramped shower put a burning blush on my cheeks.

He chuckles softly. "Good to know," he says, even though I haven't said a word. Then he drops a kiss on my lips. "But we'll save it for a time when we don't have to worry about interruptions."

I'm not sure what annoys me more, that I'm so transparent, or he's the male version of a cocktease. Putting both hands against his nicely sculpted chest, I shove him aside and stalk toward the hallway to the bedrooms, followed by his chuckles.

"You know..." I stop in the doorway and turn my head to taunt him. "I'm starting to think you're all talk and no play. Maybe you can't deliver?"

Even from all the way across the room, I can feel the heat from his narrowed eyes as he slowly slides a hand down to cup his junk. Although, I'm not sure junk is the appropriate term for the enticing bulge in his jeans he drew my eyes to. The sight of his arousal sends a delicious tingle through my body, which is only enhanced by his deep, velvet voice.

"I can deliver, Beautiful. The anticipation only makes it sweeter when I do."

~

JD

Everything comes to you in the right moment. Be patient.

Right.

I'm not sure where I read that, but I'm about done with patient. Trying to ignore the sound of the shower running, mental images of Janey naked in the shower, do little to calm the hunger in my blood.

At this point, I'm more inclined to go with *carpe diem*.

I'm already standing right outside the bathroom door when I hear Janey's phone ring over the sound of running water. Abruptly the shower is turned off and I hear her voice as she answers the call. I quickly retrace my steps to the kitchen, and by the time I hear the bathroom door open, my head is stuck in her fridge. From the outside giving the appearance I'm looking for food, when really, I'm attempting to cool down the blood still running hot through my veins.

Patience.

Not that there's any food in here anyway. A couple of beers, milk, a container of Greek yogurt, a limp stalk of celery, a questionable piece of cheese, and an assortment of condiments, but not much else. It's close to dinnertime and I'm starving. I'm sure Janey must be as well. Neither of us had any lunch today. Depending on what that phone call was about, I'm thinking a quick takeout or even delivery may be the way to go.

"That was the sheriff," Janey announces as she walks in, wearing a pair of leggings and an oversized shirt. Her hair is wrapped in a towel on top of her head, and her face is flushed from the shower. It's not hard to imagine putting that color on her cheeks when I make her come. *Hard.*

"Yeah?" I manage, after clearing my throat.

"The Kalispell office is apparently sending a couple of agents straight here. We've been asked to stick around."

I glance at the digital clock on the stove. It takes about an hour and a half to get here, so even if they leave immediately, I don't see them arriving before eight, eight thirty at the earliest.

"I'll have enough time to run into town and grab us some food. Your fridge is empty."

"I know. It's been so busy; I just haven't had a chance to—"

"Not a criticism," I interrupt her, as I reach for a wet strand of hair that escaped her towel and tuck it behind her ear. "Just an observation. What do you feel like eating?"

She slowly shakes her head. "I'm too hungry to care. Something quick and easy; burger, pizza, whatever you feel like. I'm easy."

"Ever tried a pizza from Cheesy Pies?"

"No. I've never even heard of that restaurant."

"Cheesy Pies is another food truck. It's usually parked beside the VFW club off California Avenue."

She smirks. "You have a thing for food trucks, don't you?"

I shrug. "Maybe."

The truth is, you can get some of the best grub at food trucks. They're small businesses, often run by an individual or a family whose entire livelihood is dependent on that income. Their reputation is everything. They're invested, cook with passion, and it shows in the food they serve.

"Sure, I enjoyed the last food truck you took me to."

"Any preference for pizza?"

"I'm not big on anchovies, but other than that, I'm game for just about anything."

"Their signature pie is topped with potato, onion, bratwurst, and beer cheese," I describe my personal menu favorite.

Her eyes widen at the unusual list of toppings.

"That's unique. Sure, I'm game, and while you're picking up dinner, I'm going to run over to the clinic to check on Red and grab any messages."

I put in a quick call to place my order so it's ready when I get there. Then I turn to Janey and cup her face in my hands. I notice her nose has a faint sprinkling of freckles and her lashes are long and dark against the blue of her eyes.

"You know you're way too tempting, right?"

"I didn't, but now I do," she replies in a soft voice, a faint smile on her lips.

My thumbs brush the downy skin of her cheeks. "I can't wait to find out if your skin is this soft all over."

She grabs my wrists with her hands and holds on. "There you go, teasing me again."

For a moment, I stare into her eyes before dropping a hard kiss on her mouth. Then I release her and head for the door, before I find another way to spend the small window of time we have before the FBI gets here.

I've just turned left on the main road toward town, when my phone rings. It's Una again, but this time I answer, remembering Janey's advice on communication.

"Finally," my sister says by way of greeting.

"Hello to you too," I respond dryly.

"Well, you've been ignoring my calls and my messages for days," she immediately accuses.

"And I may go back to ignoring them if you don't have something constructive to say," I warn her.

That shuts her up, but only for a moment. She quickly gets to the point of her call, looking for an ally.

"Ma is such a bitch, she—"

"Una, if you're calling me to gang up on Ma, you can save it. I don't wanna hear. I'm done being put in the middle. If you have an issue with Ma, call her. If you wanna talk about why the hell you pulled that stunt last Saturday night, not only throwing me under the bus, but using Janey as a pawn in your little scheme, be my guest."

"I didn't use Janey as a pawn," she fires back.

I note she doesn't try to deny throwing me under the bus.

"Give it up," I scold her. "You pushed me to invite her, knowing you were going to create family drama over dinner. I'm not sure what you were hoping to achieve by doing that, maybe a more moderate reaction from Ma? It obviously failed. And now you're hoping I'll listen to you whine about Ma some more?"

"I told you she'd never accept me being gay."

I pinch the bridge of my nose.

"Una, you're my sister and I love you, but that chip on your damn shoulder is so big, it's impairing your sight. This has nothing to do with you being a lesbian and everything to do with you lying to our parents your entire adult life. Not only that, you forced me to lie as well. Ma is pissed because Ma is hurt, and I don't blame her."

I hear her scoff on the other side, but she doesn't say anything, so I push on.

"And I'm hurt too, and pissed off. To put me in that position after covering your ass for all those years feels like a betrayal. So, forgive me if I'm not eager to hold your hand or be your go-between right now. Those days are over. Fix your own problems, talk to our mother, and then—maybe—try calling me again."

With that I end the call, and despite my frustration with my sister, I'm feeling a weight has lifted by the time I pull up to the Cheesy Pies truck. I quickly collect my pizza order, tell them to throw in a couple of iced teas, and beeline it back. I'm uneasy leaving Janey alone for too long.

When I get to her place, I dig through the back seat of my truck to find something cleaner to wear than the clothes I have on now. I dig up a sports bag that must've been in there for a couple of months, since I haven't been to the gym in at least that long. But at least it holds a pair of clean socks, a shirt, and some sweats that smell better than the jeans I have on. I didn't realize how foul I reeked until the beautiful aroma from the pizza was overwhelmed by the smell of cow shit. No way I can eat smelling like this.

Using Janey's bathroom—which is permeated by her scent—is the worst kind of torture. I briefly contemplate polishing one off in the shower, but decide against it. Instead, I turn the faucet to cold for a few minutes before I step out.

Janey is on her couch, her feet tucked under her as she's watching the news on TV. The pizza and iced teas, along with a couple of plates and napkins, are waiting on the coffee table.

"Unless you want to sit at the table?" she asks when I walk in.

"Not particularly."

I drop down beside her.

"You could've started without me," I suggest.

"You weren't that long," she returns, reaching to flip open the pizza box.

My stomach rumbles loudly as she loads three pieces on a plate and hands it to me, before serving herself.

I was wrong; sitting next to Janey as she moans through her first tastes of a cheesy bratwurst pizza has to be the worst kind of torture *by far*.

Thirteen

Janey

"Are you nuts?"

My eyes snap to JD, who, in turn, is glaring at Special Agent Kramer.

To her credit, Agent Kramer doesn't seem in the least intimidated by his outburst.

"Not in the least," she returns calmly. "In fact, it's probably safest for her to simply go about her business as planned. It would definitely draw attention if she suddenly didn't show up tomorrow."

The *she* they're talking about is me. Agent Kramer has asked me to return to the rodeo grounds tomorrow, act as I normally would, but with my senses on full alert. She suggested I was their best possible option for eyes and ears on the inside, without raising suspicion.

"As of tomorrow, when the fair and auction open up to the public, we'll have agents inside as well, but they won't be able to get into the livestock area without risking detection," the agent continues. "There's no time to get one of our own set up on the inside."

She turns to me with a kind smile. "You'll be wearing a wire so we can hear what goes on at any moment, and we'll be close by at all times in case of an emergency."

"I'll do it."

This time JD's angry scowl lands on me.

"Like hell."

Now, that gets my hackles up.

Don't get me wrong, it's flattering he cares enough to be protective, but last time I checked, I was an independent, grown-ass woman. I've long passed the age where I let anyone make decisions for me.

"Not your call to make," I tell him sharply.

"This isn't your business, Janey," he returns. "Drug smuggling is way out of your wheelhouse."

"That may well be, but this is more than that, it's animal abuse, which makes it very much my business."

I see a muscle ticking in his jaw as he tries to stare me down with those dark eyes, swirling with a different kind of heat.

"If it makes you feel any better," Sheriff Ewing, who returned shortly after the FBI agent got here, addresses JD. "I have a couple of guys handling security at the livestock pens who'll be able to keep an eye on her as well."

"Hey, guys, stop talking about me like I'm not even here," I cut in, annoyed. "I'm not some wilting flower. A lot of these almost two-hundred pounds you see are muscle, earned by wrestling large animals—some dangerous—every damn day of my life. I make my own decisions and can do my own talking, thank you very much."

There's an abrupt silence after my outburst, and I make sure to look each of them in the eye, starting with JD, and ending with Agent Kramer, who at least looks mildly amused.

"Fine," JD is the first to speak. "I'll be your assistant for the next few days."

"I'm not sure that's a good idea," Agent Kramer starts, but I interrupt.

"It's actually not a bad idea at all," I suggest, before explaining. "He was helping me almost all day today. I don't think anyone would think anything of it if he showed up with me again tomorrow. You'd have two pairs of eyes and ears on the inside."

It might also give him some peace of mind, and I would feel a little less anxious with someone I trust beside me, but I'm not about to admit to that after my rant about independence.

"We'll have to wire you as well," the agent concedes.

"I'm fine with that, Agent Kramer."

JD's answer still carries a bit of an edge, but he'll get over it.

"The name is Stephanie," she offers. "If we're going to do this, you two have to be careful what you say to each other. Someone could overhear, so stay away from any mention of an investigation or the FBI. Get used to calling me by my first name, it's safer."

She shoves her chair back from the table and gets to her feet.

"We should get going," she directs at the sheriff. "It's already getting late and we've got a lot of ground to cover yet."

Ewing stands up as well. "What time were you planning on heading over to the grounds tomorrow?" he asks me.

"Around eight thirty or so? That way I can catch Frankie when she gets in."

"Frankie?"

"My assistant," I clarify for the agent.

"I thought that was Logan," she returns.

"He works during the summer months. He's a veterinary student. Frankie is my full-time assistant."

"Gotcha," Stephanie confirms as she leads the way to the front door. "In that case, I'll be here at seven with our tech guy to get you miked, and we can be out of here before she arrives. We need to keep this investigation quiet. You two can't share any of this information."

"Of course," I agree.

I follow them out with JD close on my heels. They're about to get into the dark SUV they both arrived in when Stephanie swings around.

"Oh, you mentioned something about taking samples from the dead cow, do you still have those?"

"They're still in my truck, let me grab my keys."

I dart inside and grab my keys off the hall table. The vials of fluids I took are still in the cooler bag in the back of my truck. With everything going on, I'd almost forgotten about them.

I hand them to the agent.

"I was going to get them tested."

"We can bypass a lab," she says, heading to the back of the SUV and popping the tailgate. "I have a portable chemical analysis device in my kit."

The back of her SUV is outfitted with an impressive storage system, holding a large number of drawers in all sizes. I'm a little jealous. The twenty-dollar plastic storage drawers, I thought I was so clever to pick up for the back of my truck, suddenly seem inadequate.

The portable spectrometer she pulls from one of the drawers consists of two devices. Both fit in your hand. One is a scanner the size of a deck of cards, and the display monitor looks more like a fat cell phone.

"Did you label them?"

"I did."

She opens the cooler bag and pulls out one of the vials, holding the scanner against it. Within seconds the results display on the small monitor.

"Positive for cocaine," Stephanie shares.

Even though it's not really a surprise, the confirmation still sends shivers down my spine.

~

JD

"I'm gonna stay here."

"All right."

I should've known Pa wouldn't question me or be surprised. He probably already expected as much, even though he wasn't aware of the circumstances. Now he is.

"In case it wasn't clear, I've been asked not to share what I know," I tell him. "I'm telling you so at least someone knows where I am and why."

Plus, my father isn't a talker on the best of days. He'll take a secret to the grave.

"I figured," he replies. "Look out for her."

"You know I will."

I get a grunt in response before he ends the call.

Sliding my phone in my pocket, I glance through the curtains inside, where I can see Janey putzing around her kitchen. After the sheriff and Agent Kramer left, I told Janey I had to make a quick call and would be right in. We haven't had a chance to discuss arrangements, but there's no way I'm going home tonight. I'm just not sure how to best convey that without pissing her off again.

She swings around when I enter. As much as she's managed to appear pretty cool and collected, I can tell this situation has her freaked out. She's hypervigilant, her senses seem on high alert, and a nervous energy comes off her in waves. I'm thinking maybe reality is finally starting to set in.

I kick off my boots and walk right up to her, taking her in my arms. Her body feels rigid.

"Are you heading out?" Even her voice has a higher than normal pitch.

"Wasn't planning on it."

She leans back slightly to examine my facial expression.

"No?"

I guess I should be more clear.

"I'll need to run a load of laundry though. Don't wanna be wearing the same dirty clothes tomorrow."

No sooner are the words out of my mouth when all the tension seems to drain from her body, and she drops her head against my shoulder.

"You're staying here," she mumbles by way of confirmation.

"Yep."

There's no objection from her, which only proves she's more shaken than she cares to let on. *Good*. I'd rather have her on her toes and cautious tomorrow than cocky and reckless.

But for tonight, I want her to feel safe, relaxed, and get a decent night's rest. It's been a long-ass day.

I drop a kiss on her forehead and release her from my hold.

"Why don't you get ready for bed? I'm just going to

throw my stuff in the washer. Want me to toss something of yours in?"

"I can do it," she offers.

"I've got it."

She's still standing in the kitchen, looking a little forlorn when I get back with the laundry basket from the bathroom.

"Go to bed, Janey," I tell her as I walk by. "You're swaying on your feet."

Her laundry is right off the kitchen and I dump the entire contents of the basket in the washer. I hope she's not too fussy about separating stuff. I find a setting I hope is enough to get rid of the caked-on gunk from my jeans, but not too much so it cooks Janey's delicates. The display says it'll be forty minutes.

Janey's gone when I walk into the kitchen, but Ginger is standing by the door, whining softly. I shove my feet back in my boots and take her out for a quick pee. As soon as we get back inside, she heads back to her bed and curls up.

In the sink, I find a couple of dirty dishes left from dinner I quickly wash up and put away. Then I grab a cold slice from the leftover pizza Janey put in the fridge, settle in on the couch with my feet up on her coffee table, and flip on the TV to an all-day news channel with the volume turned way down.

Waiting for the washer to run through its cycle, I must've dozed off at some point. The machine's soft buzzer wakes me up. It takes me a moment to clue in where I am, and what that sound signifies. I stretch, work out the crick I got in my neck, and go check on the laundry. After switching the load from the washer to the dryer, I walk through the house, turning off the TV and the lights. Then I make sure the doors are locked before I head to the bathroom.

On the counter, Janey left me a brand-new toothbrush.

I wasn't sure where I'd end up for the night; on the couch or in her bed. Given the circumstances, the couch seemed the more appropriate choice, even though that wouldn't have been my preference. Seeing that toothbrush sitting on the counter tells me that despite being dead on her feet, Janey was thinking about me when she hit the sack. I'm going to take it as a sign, so after I brush and do my business, I turn toward the bedroom instead of the living room.

She's on her side facing the door when I walk in. Her eyes are open.

"I thought you'd be asleep."

"I wish," she returns in a soft voice. "My mind won't shut up."

"I can help with that," I offer.

"Would you?"

She won't have to ask twice. Hell, she didn't have to ask at all. I'm already pulling my shirt over my head, tossing it on the floor. My hands stop on the waistband of my sweatpants. My boxer briefs are currently tumbling in the dryer so I went commando. I'd better leave these on for now.

"Don't stop. Take it off," Janey says, pushing herself up on an elbow in bed. "All of it."

My cock jumps free the moment I shove my sweats down my hips. I was already at half-mast just walking into her bedroom, but it didn't take much to get me rock-hard. When I kick off my sweats and straighten up, I find her eyes on me, taking in every inch. It almost feels like a caress and I instinctively wrap a fist around my length, stroking slowly.

"Jesus," she mutters.

Then she sits up, the covers falling down to her waist and her dark hair draping over her naked shoulders. The slopes of her heavy breasts look pale in the moonlight, their tight peaks dark in contrast.

Jesus, indeed.

I already have a knee on the mattress when she flips aside the covers, revealing all of herself as she leans back against the pillows. My mouth waters at the lush curves softening the firm muscles underneath. Beautiful. There is nothing fragile about this woman, and it's the strength and courage in the offer of her glorious body that has me falling for her even deeper.

If I could find adequate words, I'd tell her everything I'm feeling and thinking, but I'd rather show her. Grabbing an ankle in each of my hands, I lift and spread her legs wide open, and let my eyes, hands, and mouth do the talking. Her skin is so soft under the rough calluses on my hands as I touch her reverently, brushing a fingertip through the slick folds when I find her trimmed curls.

Bending down, I inhale her essence as I nip at the inside of her thigh, testing the resilience of her flesh between my teeth. Her responding hiss stokes the fire in my belly.

I want to lap her up, eat her out, and make her come with my mouth over and over. But this isn't about what I want, this is about what she needs, so I make do with a few strokes of my tongue before I continue my way up her body.

Her hands explore unapologetically in return. Her nails raking along my back as I carefully roll a nipple between my teeth.

"Please..." she whimpers, reaching down to dig her fingers into the globes of my ass.

The crown of my cock butts against her slick folds, and I groan softly as I lift my hips. I had the presence of mind to pack a condom in my wallet, but left it sitting on the hall table by the front door.

"Under my pillow," Janey shares, a gleam in her blue eyes as I shove my hand underneath and come up with a foil wrapper.

She'd clearly been more prepared than I was. It takes me a few seconds to roll on the condom and resume my position between her thighs. Then I kiss her, deep and slow.

"Please..." she repeats against my lips, her hold on my ass a bit firmer now.

She feels hot and tight as I sink into her. My eyes almost roll back in my head when I feel her entire body clamp down on me. Her legs wrap around my hips and her hands on my ass push me deeper. I try to be gentle, but she's strong, and when she encourages me to go hard, I give in.

Sweat is running down my face and my heart is beating out of control, as I follow the pace she sets. At some point I slip out, sit up on my knees, and lift her legs in the air, before plunging back in. She feels every inch of me as I piston inside her in this position.

Her body shakes with the force of her orgasm, and when I follow moments later, I don't fare much better.

My heart rate is still coming down, and my knees are still weak when I return to bed after getting rid of the condom. I brought a wet washcloth for Janey, but she's already curled up on her side, fast asleep.

Discarding the washcloth, I slip between the covers and curl my body around hers.

It's the last thing I remember.

Fourteen

"Is she okay to race?"

I tie off the last stitch and smile at the worried young woman.

"She should be fine. Keep it as clean and as dry as you can."

The barrel horse probably got caught on a piece of fencing or something, and tore a four-inch gash along her shoulder. But it wasn't that deep and I was able to clean and close the cut with a tidy row of stitches. The minor injury shouldn't impact the horse's performance.

I pet the pretty pinto's neck. "You're sure she's up to date on her tetanus shot?"

The girl nods. "I'm pretty sure, but I'll check. I brought her vaccination records. They're in my trailer."

I turn to Logan, who's been observing, and give him a nod.

"Would you walk back with her and check the date?

And then you may as well grab some lunch."

My assistant appears to be quite pleased with my request as he flashes a grin in the pretty girl's direction.

"Sure thing."

Clearly his lanky good looks haven't gone unnoticed by her either, as she shyly smiles back.

"You may not see him back for a while," JD warns me.

"I was just thinking the same thing," I consider as I watch them walk off.

I tuck a few strands of my hair back under the ball cap I wore to cover my eyes from the sun. It's a hot one today and we've been standing out in the baking sun without even a hint of shade, so I'm sweating buckets. Adding to my discomfort is the itching of my skin underneath the wires and the tape used to secure the minute microphone between my breasts. I'd almost forgotten I was wearing it while I had my hands full, but I'm annoyingly aware of it now.

When we got here this morning, Phil Jericho showed us to a small corral where he wanted me to set up clinic. I actually thought it was a good idea, being able to keep my gear in one spot rather than lugging it around the grounds. When possible, the animals were brought to me, which suited me just fine. Most of my patients this morning were horses with relatively minor issues, and one goat with a clogged teat.

The goat is part of this afternoon's kids' fair. All kinds of children's activities like kids' barrel racing, best-in-show farm animal contests, a petting zoo, greased pig wrangling, and a goat milking race, among other things. I'm personally not a fan of any of these events, other than perhaps the best-in-show contest—at least those animals are generally treated well—but I'm not here to make moral judgements.

What I didn't realize, until the gates opened to the public earlier, was the corral Jericho assigned us to is actually right beside the petting zoo. Which means we've had a fair number of onlookers and curious kids asking all kinds of questions. To my surprise, JD ended up fielding a lot of those in his calm, steady voice that seemed to have the kids mesmerized. Some mothers too, and I discovered I actually do have a jealous bone in my body.

"You're getting a sunburn. You need a proper cowboy hat," JD suggests when I wipe the sweat off my forehead with a wad of gauze.

"I tried. They don't stay on my head for long in this line of work."

I did put on sunscreen this morning, but that was sweated off a while ago.

"What I need is some shade and a cool drink," I declare, looking longingly at the fair, where some food vendors set up picnic tables under the cover of tents or large umbrellas.

"Let's go. It's quiet now," he points out. "We'll grab some lunch, and find a spot in the shade where we can keep an eye out."

He's right. There's no one waiting, and once the auction starts later this afternoon, I'll be stuck there.

"I'll grab us some food, you find us a table," JD suggests. "Fry bread tacos okay with you?"

"Sounds good. I'm just gonna hit the bathroom first."

Of course there's a line-up at the small building housing his and hers restrooms. There are also a number of Porta-potties, but I avoid those. I'd rather wait so I can have running water to wash up a bit. I feel gross, the dust and dirt are sticking to my damp skin.

When it's my turn, I quickly pee before cleaning up at the small sink. Hand soap is probably not the best choice to wash my face and neck with, but I do feel a lot better when I step outside.

I manage to procure a picnic table under a large awning, and sigh in relief to be out of the sun. But the relief doesn't last long.

"It was you, wasn't it?"

I look up to see Mackey stalking toward me, his face once again an unhealthy red and purple color. My entire body tenses up as he walks right up and into my space.

"What are you talking about?" I ask, getting to my feet so I take away his advantage of hovering over me.

"You took my cow."

He jabs a finger at me and I have to hold back from grabbing on to it and hurting him. He's creating enough of a spectacle without me adding onto it.

"What cow?"

For a moment I'm confused. Is he talking about the dead cow? Because I would've bet he was the one who took it and burned the carcass.

But then he clarifies, "A cow from that last trailer yesterday is missing. We're getting them ready for auction and I'm told we're missing one. My driver says he left you alone on that trailer when you sent him off to find water."

I might've scoffed at him if I wasn't so worried. Obviously, I didn't take the cow, but I'm pretty sure what I did take is what really has him pissed off. There's no way for him to know though. Is there?

"What would I do with a cow? Why would I take a cow? You're not making any sense," I tell him. "Besides, didn't you count heads yesterday when they were unloaded?"

"Everything all right here?"

Phil Jericho walks up behind Mackey, who appears to stiffen at hearing his voice.

I take the opportunity to explain.

"Mackey seems to have lost a cow and is accusing me of taking it."

Jericho drops a manicured hand on the other man's shoulder.

"Now, John, what on earth would Doc Richards want with your cow? The animal probably just slipped in with another herd. Let's go have a look, shall we?"

With a wink for me, and a benevolent smile for a few nosy onlookers, he firmly guides Mackey back to the stockyard.

"What was that all about?" JD asks when he joins me a few minutes later. "I was about to come check it out when Jericho showed up."

I relay Mackey's strange accusation as JD slides a bottle of water and the largest fry bread taco I've ever seen in front of me. His reaction surprises me.

"Hmm. I bet you I know which cow went missing."

~

JD

I'm observant, so it doesn't take me long to spot him.

He looks like just another middle-aged rancher; dusty Stetson, denim shirt, weathered face, toothpick in his mouth to compensate for the cigarettes he probably cut out for his health. But what makes him stand out is his keen focus on the interactions in the auction arena. He isn't looking at his program, or chatting with the other ranchers in the stands, but his eyes track everything that goes on below.

He also places just a few bids, early on in the process—

probably in an attempt to blend in—but only buys one small lot and doesn't seem too interested in following through on the others. That is, until one of Mackey's lots comes up for auction. Now, all of a sudden, he's all business.

"Tan Stetson, fifties, denim shirt. Second to last row of the stands on the south side," I mumble into my shirt. "Number three, eight, one," I read off the placard he's holding up.

I've been to my share of livestock auctions. Horses, not cattle, but the principle is the same. When I mentioned that this morning, when Janey and I were getting miked up, Agent Kramer suggested I take an observing role at this afternoon's auction. Not only keeping an eye on Doc, who is currently in the arena below, standing near the gate where the animals are led in, but also on the stands. She asked me to report any irregularities or individuals who looked out of place.

This guy would fit that bill.

I watch as he waits out another interested bidder and swoops in at the last moment to drop his higher bid. As cautious as he was on his earlier bidding, he is clearly motivated to buy this load and willing to go as high as he needs to.

By the time the second of Mackey's lots is led into the arena, a man sidles up to the railing beside me. I'm pretty sure he's a fed; his attention is fixed on the bidder like mine.

"That him?" he mutters under his breath.

"Uh-huh."

"Okay, take a walk, I've got him from here."

Probably smart. I was looking at him pretty hard.

I don't want to venture too far, so I get a bottle of water from the concession stand and find a shady spot from where

I can keep an eye on the auction arena, the cattle holding pens, and the numerous cattle trailers behind it.

Buyers tend to come prepared to an auction and bring their wallets and transportation. Once they win their bid on a lot, they can pay up, and receive their bill of sale. They need to show that when they drive their transport trailer to the loading chute at the back of the pens to collect their cattle.

I hope the FBI has eyes on that process as well, because sometimes buyers load their animals while the auction is still going on. They probably do—from what I can tell Agent Kramer is thorough—but that doesn't stop me from wanting to have a look myself.

Natural curiosity combined with leftover professional instincts from my years as a game warden have me casually sauntering around to the rear of the arena. There are two guys leaning against the end of the loading chute, smoking and chatting. I can't see anyone else near the pens.

There isn't a ton of security on the grounds, other than a few sheriff's deputies who are mostly concerned with crowd control, and a couple of guys I've seen around the past few days who looked like private hires. Still, with the increasing volume of trailers going in and out of the grounds these past few days, it probably wouldn't have been too difficult to sneak out a cow with no one noticing.

I'm pretty sure the cow-napping was the FBI's doing, if it was, in fact, the animal Janey retrieved those packages from. It's a way to delay the discovery of those missing drugs, giving them more time to identify all the important players and get suspicion off Janey. It wouldn't be the first time a cow ends up in the wrong pen, with the wrong herd.

Except, judging by Mackey's reaction, he's not buying into it, and the fact he went straight for Doc with his accusations is a bit concerning. Good thing the feds were listening in, I hope it'll make them extra vigilant when it comes to her safety.

Nobody stops me when I wander over to the transport trailers parked at the back. There's a group of guys sitting at a picnic table in the shade by the trees, but they're not paying attention. Probably ranch hands hanging out while they wait for a signal from their bosses to meet them with the truck at the loading chute.

I'm not sure what it is I'm looking for as I wander between trailers of all sizes. Maybe the missing cow is in one of them. Also, I'd love to have a look at the trailer belonging to the buyer I pointed out to the agent, but there's no way to know which one would be his. I know it'll be one of the big transport trucks. It would have to be to haul the number of animals he's bidding on.

I focus on the big ones, peeking in ventilation holes and checking any markings. Perhaps something will jump out at me.

No sooner has the thought formed, when I hear a footstep behind me. Whirling around, I see only a hint of movement before something hits me hard in the head, sending me face-first in the dirt. Disoriented, I catch a blurry glimpse of a boot as I try to push myself up on my arms.

Then I'm hit from behind again, knocking me right back down in the dirt.

The last thing I remember is a distant voice calling out, "Hey!" before the lights go out.

Fifteen

My skin crawls every time Mackey looks in my direction.

Still, I will not let him intimidate me and stare right back at him.

This was the last of his herd that was just auctioned off, and from what I could see, four of the six lots his cattle were divided into went to the same bidder. Only someone who knows what is hiding in some of those cows would find that suspicious.

When I suggested to Agent Kramer this morning the drugs would've probably been removed already, she explained why she didn't think that would be the case. It turns out, this type of smuggling isn't new to the FBI. She called it narco-ranching, and it's something they've already had on their radar.

Apparently, Mackey would likely only be a cog in a much larger operation. In this case, he'd simply be responsible for transporting the drugs. He wouldn't have been the one to supply them, nor would he be responsible for distributing or selling them.

From what Stephanie explained, I understand he likely didn't even know who would be taking them off his hands. The structure of these organizations is such that each link in the chain knows as little as possible of the next one. It's designed so if anywhere along the line they get caught, the other links in the chain are safe and the compromised one is easily replaced.

Keeping the drugs hidden in the cattle would add an additional level of protection, both against possible sticky fingers, or outside detection.

Only the head honcho, and perhaps one or two of his most trusted henchmen, would have knowledge of every level of the organization. That's why, rather than stepping in and taking down Mackey and confiscating the animals, the FBI wants to observe and follow the chain. They want to identify all the players, top to bottom, so they can dismantle the entire organization at once.

My eyes drift to the man who bought up the bulk of Mackey's cattle. I wouldn't have guessed he's involved with drugs; the man looks like any other rancher. Of course, it's always possible he's being used as a proxy and has no idea what it is he's actually bidding on.

"No incidents?"

Phil Jericho is waiting for me outside when I leave the auction arena. I was looking for JD, who I lost track of when he disappeared from the stands earlier. I hate to admit it, but I feel safer wandering around the grounds with him by my side.

"Nothing that needed any intervention from me," I tell him.

"That's good. Well, I was thinking about heading into town for a quick bite. Why don't you join me?"

"Thanks, but I'm actually exhausted. Tomorrow will be another busy day so I think I'll pass."

I'll say that for the man, he's persistent, even though he clearly knows I'm with JD.

Speaking of JD, where the heck did he go?

"Are you sure?"

"Positive."

With a tight smile, I start walking toward the stockyard where my truck is parked, and sigh a breath of relief when Jericho doesn't follow me. Pulling my phone from my pocket, I call JD's number, which rings five times before bumping me to voicemail. I leave a brief message, telling him I'll be waiting for him by the truck, but as soon as I end the call, my phone rings. I see it's him calling me back.

"Hey, where are you?"

"Janey?" I stop in my tracks when I recognize Stephanie Kramer's voice.

"It is. What's going on?"

"Listen to me carefully. I need you to get to your truck and drive straight home. One of my agents will be right behind you. Don't stop for anything, just go straight home."

Something is very wrong.

"What's happening? Where is JD?"

"He's here with me. Listen, I need you to go home right now. We'll see you there."

She hangs up before I can ask to speak to him. Something is obviously happening, giving me a sick feeling in the pit of my stomach. I start walking again, a little faster now.

I catch sight of Logan when I pass our improvised clinic. He watched things while I was at the auction.

"How did it go?" He wants to know, walking up to me.

"Fine. Nothing major. You?" I ask, mostly by reflex.

"Same. It's been quiet for the last forty-five minutes or so," he shares.

"Good, good. Go home," I tell him. "I'm heading out too. Long day, and it'll be another one tomorrow. I'll see you at eight?"

"I'll be here."

He shoots me a wide grin, reminding me of one of those happy-go-lucky puppies. Normally that would've triggered a smile, but right now I'm feeling nauseated with worry.

I'm not sure how I manage to get home in one piece. After getting stuck in a bit of a jam getting out of the park—everyone seemed to be leaving at the same time—I wove like a maniac through traffic in my rush to get here. I'm lucky I didn't hit anyone and escaped getting pulled over. I never even thought about the agent who was supposedly following me home until I see the SUV pulling into my driveway right behind me.

He doesn't follow me to the house though, but instead steers toward the clinic, driving around to the back of the barn. There are no vehicles parked in front of my house and the lights are off. I sit here for a moment, wondering what the hell is going on, but when I look back at the barn, I spot someone standing in the shadows outside, waving at me.

I'm a little spooked, so rather than get out and walk over, I take the truck, following suit and pulling around the back of the barn. There are three vehicles already parked here, including the one that followed me home. I assume they're tucked out of sight from the road. None of it does the sick worry in my stomach any good.

Neither does Stephanie Kramer's serious face when she opens the clinic's back door for me.

JD

I'm pissed.

For a multitude of reasons, but right at this moment I'm mostly angry at the fucking feds for scaring the crap out of Janey.

Her face was ghostly white and her expression panicked when she walked in a few minutes ago. She's a little better now, sitting beside me, clasping my hand in a viselike grip while Special Agent Kramer gets her up to speed.

Of course, I'm ticked off at whoever hit me over the head hard enough to knock me out, leaving a nice gash in my scalp at the back of my head. The cut bled like a stuck pig, which makes things look way more dramatic than they should.

One of Kramer's colleagues, who'd apparently been monitoring the transport trailers, interrupted the attack. Unfortunately, the guy who knocked me out took off running before the agent could get a good look at him. Instead of going after the asshole, he decided to check on me.

I was still on the ground between the trailers when I opened my eyes to find Kramer leaning over me. A brief discussion ensued on whether or not EMTs should be called in, which wasn't something I was a fan of. For me to end up in the hospital would create a snowball effect no one would be able to control.

In the end, it wasn't that difficult to convince Kramer not to compromise her investigation like that. I told her I worked with a trained medic, who could have a look at my head, but it had been her idea to ask Bo to meet us at Janey's clinic.

I'd stupidly assumed someone would let Janey in on what was going on but, apparently, she had no idea until she walked in here and saw me with blood all over my shirt.

"So, you don't know who did this?" Janey asks.

"No. The guy was wearing a black hat, dark T-shirt, and jeans, nothing more descriptive. Agent Wilcox only got a glimpse and by the time he went after him, the perp had blended in with the crowd."

"But why would they attack JD?"

"Maybe they didn't like me poking around the trailers," I offer with a shrug.

Bo cuffs the side of my head. "Sit the fuck still," he grumbles, as he tries to stitch me up.

"About that," Stephanie Kramer picks up, shooting me a scathing glare. "What the hell were you thinking?"

"After I identified the buyer, your buddy, Wilcox here, told me to take a hike. I thought I'd make myself useful instead."

"Next time, don't," she orders sharply. "This is a highly sensitive investigation; I don't need civilians blundering all over it."

"For your information, I'm a trained law enforcement officer," I fire back.

"You were a game warden. *Were* being the operative word," she retorts, before firmly putting me in my place. "And clearly out of practice, given your current state."

Bo chuckles behind me. "The woman's got a point."

Fuck.

My head already hurt and now my ego is bruised as well. Maybe it's better to keep my thoughts to myself.

Thankfully, Janey steers us back on subject.

"What about the buyer? Are you letting him get away with the cattle?"

"No. We know who he is and we have another team of agents tracking his transport truck. This is a coordinated effort," Kramer explains. "We have more than just one team involved. With each new link of the drug chain we expose, another team is assigned so, once we have all the players in our sights, we can concurrently step in and take them all out at once."

"So you're sticking around?"

"Three of us are. Agents Wilcox and Furstner," the agent answers her. "In fact, we were hoping we might be able to bunk here."

That seems to throw Janey for a moment.

"I don't know if I have room for everyone."

"Not in your house, but here at the clinic. We'd only be two at a time at most, since one of us will be on surveillance day or night. We'd rotate, and one of us would man the command post at all times. I wouldn't ask," she adds, "if everything within a thirty-mile radius from town wasn't booked full. This rodeo is pretty popular. Your place is close to town but off the beaten path, which makes it a lot easier for us to come and go without attracting attention."

"I guess that's okay," Janey says hesitantly. "But maybe I should call Frankie and tell her we're shutting down the clinic for the next few days."

"There's a couple of empty cabins at High Meadow I'm sure you'd be welcome to use," I offer as an alternative.

"Yeah," Bo pipes up. "It's a bit farther from town, but you'd have beds."

Kramer turns to him. "Actually, we've got cots and sleeping bags, we came prepared. I appreciate the offer, but a lot of people come and go at the ranch, and we'd prefer to keep as low a profile as possible. I'm sure you understand."

I have no doubt she intended to remind us not to share any of this information. It's not an issue for me, I wouldn't want to compromise the investigation and with it, Janey's safety, but from the sound of Bo's deep grunt behind me, it's not that easy for him. I highly doubt there's much, if anything, he keeps from his wife, Lucy. Aside from that, the original High Mountain Trackers members—Bo, Jonas, Sully, Fletch, and my father—were brothers-in-arms and still work side by side daily. I don't think there are many secrets between them.

"One request though," Janey adds. "If whoever is here wouldn't mind letting out my dog around lunchtime, and keeping an eye on my horse while I'm gone?"

"Of course," Kramer responds. "And we'll replace the lock on the back door first thing tomorrow."

"The lock?"

Agent Wilcox had to drill out the basic back door lock in order to get into the clinic, but apparently Janey hadn't even noticed. Her eyes had been fixed on me.

I give her smaller hand in mine a squeeze.

"Done," Bo rumbles, clapping me on the shoulder. "Take a couple of ibuprofen for the headache and you need someone to check on you from time to time. I'd tell you not to wash your hair or wear your hat for a couple of days, but I won't bother since I already know you're gonna do whatever the hell you want anyway."

I let go of Janey and get to my feet, ignoring the brief wave of dizziness as I bump his fist.

"Appreciate it."

"Anytime." Then he turns to Janey with his signature

grin. "Stay safe, Doc, and call me if this idiot steps out of line."

I have no trouble identifying myself as the idiot in question. Bo likes to tease, rattle cages, but I think I've been rattled enough for today, because I don't even react.

"I should let the dog out and call my assistant," Janey announces. "And you should come with me, so I can feed you and give you something for the pain."

I'm not going to argue that, my head is throbbing and, although I'm not hungry, I could probably do with something in my stomach.

"There's one bedroom and a small bathroom with a shower in the barn, through that door," she points out to the agents. "You're welcome to use them."

Then she takes my hand in hers and leads me to the door.

I follow willingly.

JD

I stifle a yawn as I watch Janey and Logan try to control a squealing pig.

The unfortunate young animal was injured in his attempts to evade a crowd of seven-and eight-year-olds trying to catch him in this morning's main event—pig wrangling.

Pig wrangling always draws a good crowd. The event takes place in several rounds, each of which sees a slightly older group of children try to catch a slightly bigger, greased pig. The kid who catches the pig, gets to keep it.

I remember being ten or eleven and winning one of these at the Lake County fair on the Flathead Reservation near Polson, when we were still living near there. At the time, Pa was on active duty and stationed out of a base near Seattle, but with two young kids, Ma opted to stay closer to the reservation where she had the support of her family.

There'd been some lean years, and I recall feeling like a hero when I was able to catch that pig for my family.

Another yawn has me shielding my mouth with a hand.

I didn't sleep that much last night, and not because of any fun activities. Even if I'd been in any condition for those, Janey would've shut me down in a hurry.

Instead, I was lying awake half the night, wracking my brain to try and remember any little detail that might help identify who the hell blindsided me behind the auction arena. Then, when I'd finally exhaust myself and doze off, Janey would wake me to make sure I was still alive.

All in all, a rather restless night, leaving me seriously sleep deprived. The persistent headache isn't helping much, and I've already downed more than my quota of painkillers. It's going to be a long-ass day.

But you won't hear me complaining, at least not out loud. Janey didn't want me to come in the first place, insisted I stay at her place and rest, but that was not an option. To my surprise, Stephanie Kramer agreed with me. She pointed out that whoever was responsible might show a reaction when they see me up and around.

Janey isn't too pleased though, and has been giving me a bit of a cold shoulder ever since.

"James Dean!"

I turn my head at the sound of my mother's voice. She's marching straight for me, a stern expression on her face.

"What the heck are you doing here, Ma?"

"Been waiting for you to get your head outta your ass and call your mother, but we both know that wasn't happening."

"Geeze, Ma. I was giving you some time."

She plants her hands on her hips and tilts her head. "Lemme guess, your father's suggestion?"

I shrug, she obviously already knows it was.

"How'd you know where to find me?"

She shakes her head. "You underestimate me, just like your pa. I know when that man is brooding on something but tries to hide it. Took me all of ten minutes to pry it out of him." Her eyes drift to Janey in the pen. "Sticking close, are ya?"

"Ma...you shouldn't be here."

Last thing I need is my mother poking around the rodeo.

"Oh, relax," she shushes me. "I came with Jillian and Hayley, it's their first time at the rodeo." She points in the direction of the arena where the pig wrangling is taking place. "They're in the stands over there. We happened to see you, and it would've been weird if I hadn't stopped by to say hello to my son."

Jillian is my teammate Wolff's girlfriend, and Hayley is her eleven-year-old foster daughter. Mom makes it sound like she happened to be here with them, but I'm sure the entire setup was more calculated than the accidental encounter she'd like me to believe this is. Still, I hook my arm around her neck and pull her to me, pressing a kiss to the top of her head.

"Hello, Ma."

She briefly leans her head against me and pats my chest with a hand before straightening up. I wonder if she could feel the microphone Agent Wilcox taped to my chest again this morning. It's a good reminder people are listening in to every word I say.

"I know now is not the time to talk, but at some point we should clear the air."

I nod. "We will."

Something makes her pause and scrutinize me. "Are you feeling okay?"

"I'm fine."

Her eyes narrow fractionally.

"Nice try, but we'll add that to our things to address another time." She raises up on her toes and kisses my cheek. "I should head back to the girls, but promise me you'll be careful."

"I will."

I watch her head back to the stands and return my attention to the pen. Looks like whatever was wrong with the pig has been taken care of, as Logan places the animal in the arms of the waiting man and his young son. Janey walks toward me.

"Was that your mom?"

"Yeah, she's here watching the pig races with Jillian and Hayley."

Janey smiles, she knows them. She's the vet for Jillian's search and rescue animals.

"That's great. I hope Hayley has fun."

Life has been pretty rough for the young girl, losing her entire family earlier this year.

Janey glances over at the stands, and when she is turning back to me, I notice her suddenly squinting.

"Is he waving at me?" she asks, looking over my shoulder.

I turn and try to follow her line of sight, zooming in on one of the sheriff's deputies, who is standing on the far side of the stockyard where most of the trailers are parked. He appears to be motioning in our direction.

"Let's go find out," I suggest.

Janey calls out to Logan, "Keep an eye on things, I'll be

right back," and follows me down the path between the pens to the back.

"I'm not good with horses," the young deputy says, when we get within a few feet of him. "So, I tied him to the trailer where I found him, but I noticed he was bleeding."

He points at a pinto tied to a small double-horse trailer, wearing a bridle over her halter. I recognize the barrel horse Janey treated yesterday. The wound on her shoulder looks to be actively bleeding again. She must've torn it open.

"She," Janey corrects him as she approaches the skittish animal. "I just stitched her up yesterday," she explains. "Half of them are ripped, she must've got caught on something."

"Was she not tied up when you found her?" I ask the deputy.

He shakes his head. "No, he was...I mean *she* was loose. I was patrolling the perimeter when she came out of the trees. She looked a bit spooked."

She certainly seems to be with her eyes darting around, her flared nostrils, and her ears twitching back and forth.

"Her rope is torn," Janey points out. "Looks like maybe something scared her and she broke away. She could've easily ripped those stitches on a branch or something, if she darted into the trees."

It's possible, but something about this is nagging me. For one thing, the fact she's wearing a bridle tells me someone was riding her. Bareback, obviously, which would suggest someone who's very familiar with the horse. Also, when Janey carefully probes the reopened cut, I notice some of the blood coating her shoulder appears to be dry.

"This didn't just happen," I suggest. "It looks like she's been bleeding for a while, since most of it has dried already."

Janey brushes her fingertips over the stain on the horse's hide.

"You're right. Some of this is at least several hours old."

Several hours.

I wonder where her owner is?

Janey

"Have you heard anything?"

Logan crouches down beside me and hands me the wrap I asked for, a hopeful expression on his face.

"No, I haven't."

His face falls immediately. Poor kid.

He'd been all starry-eyed yesterday when he returned after walking the pretty girl back to her trailer to check on her horse's vaccination records. Apparently, he'd asked her out and they'd agreed to meet up tonight after her barrel race.

Except, Lacey Del Franco is nowhere to be found.

JD took off with the deputy to look for her, while I took the horse back to our improvised clinic so I could fix her up. Logan had wanted to go looking as well, but Sheriff Ewing —who'd apparently been called in and stopped by to ask a few questions—suggested he'd probably be of more use sticking with me.

The pointed look the sheriff shot me after his comment turned the granola bar I'd just scarfed down into a lump of concrete in my stomach. I don't think Logan read the same implications into it I did, which is a good thing. The only reason my mind immediately went to the two murdered women is because JD told me about finding the first body, and the subject of the second girl came up when the sheriff and Agent Kramer showed up at my house two nights ago. I don't think any of it is public knowledge yet.

To keep Logan distracted, I sent him to pick up some more supplies at the clinic. Only the first official rodeo day and already we're running low on stretch bandages. This is the fourth horse that was brought in lame, and these are only the kids' barrel races.

Great fun for the kids, but unfortunately, because some of their horses aren't necessarily trained for the kind of strain barrel racing puts on their legs—with the abrupt stops and sharp turns—they're easily injured.

"I'm sure she'll show up," I add, trying to sound encouraging, even though I'm pretty concerned myself.

Then I hand him back the roll of bandages.

"You know what? Why don't you finish this one? I need a bathroom break and a bottle of water. Can I grab you something?"

"Water is fine," he mumbles distractedly.

"Remember to use padding, start high, wrap from front to back and outside to inside, and then back up. Even pressure."

If you don't wrap right, you can cause more problems.

"I know."

I can almost hear the eye roll in his response and suppress a smile.

The restrooms are packed—lots of moms with kids about to pee their pants—and I'm getting a little worried myself by the time a stall opens up. This is the first bathroom break I've taken all day and it's been hot, so I've been drinking a lot of water to stay hydrated.

Judging by the rush on the restrooms, I'm guessing the kids' barrel racing is finished. That means the adults will be in the arena next. The schedule I was given shows today and tomorrow are preliminary rounds, with finals on Sunday. The actual rodeo has barely started and I've already had enough. Mind you, that may have little to do with working the event and is more about the stressful circumstances.

Those tensions have only been ramped up now that girl, Lacey, seems to have gone missing. At this point I don't really believe she's gone into town or out for lunch with a friend or something. Her horse is still in the pen next to where we're running the clinic, unclaimed. I saw how the girl was with that horse yesterday, and I don't believe for a minute she'd leave her unattended for any length of time.

It's been hours since we found the freaked-out animal.

I find the food stand with the shortest line, figuring they'd at least all have water, and get in line. This vendor sells basic hamburgers and hot dogs and by the time I get to the front of the line, my mouth is watering and I end up ordering a couple of hot dogs for Logan and myself. I know he only asked for water, but the day isn't over yet and both of us have to eat.

"Late lunch?" I hear behind me.

Phil Jericho definitely looks the part of a rich rodeo benefactor: a crisp white Stetson on his head, a bolo tie with an intricate silver and turquoise clasp at his neck, and what looks like a giant championship buckle on his belt. The ensemble is completed by a pair of expensive snakeskin boots, which would be illegal to wear in some states, but not so in Montana.

All a bit over-the-top for me, but he sure seems to be drawing attention.

"Late lunch, or early dinner, take your pick. It's been a crazy day."

I would assume, being the organizer, he must've been made aware one of the barrel racers is missing, but I can't be sure, so I stop myself from asking him if he heard anything. At this point, I really wish someone could give me an update. I feel out of the loop.

"You've been busy?" he asks, butting in line to place his order for a hamburger.

"It's been steady," I share. "Minor stuff."

I step off to the side to wait for my order, and Jericho joins me.

"No boyfriend today?"

The tone of his question is a bit sarcastic, but at the same time feels opportunistic. The smirk on his face makes the whole thing feel sleazy. Even though I get the sense he's probably this way with any woman who hits his perimeter. Trust me, I'm well aware I'm far too plain for the likes of him to be genuinely interested. He's probably one of those guys who thinks all women should fall at his feet, and this is more about his own ego than it has anything to do with me.

"He's around somewhere, probably taking in the sights," I share, hoping the lie isn't plastered on my face.

Jericho squints his eyes and tilts his head.

"Then he's a fool. Not a sight better than this one around."

Okay, *eww*.

Now I know for sure he's full of it. I had a glance in the restroom mirror and know for a fact I look like shit, and I probably don't smell much better.

Thankfully, the arrival of my order saves me from having to come up with a response to that.

"There's a table over there." He points to a picnic table that is just freeing up. "I'll join you and we can chat."

I plaster what I hope is a friendly smile on my face and remind myself this is the man who'll be signing my check after all of this is done. At least I hope he will.

"I appreciate the offer, but I'm afraid I have to get back; my assistant is waiting for his lunch."

"Of course," he immediately returns. "I just wanted to make sure you didn't have any more unpleasant run-ins with John Mackey. The man can be a bit of a loose cannon, I'm afraid."

Thankfully nothing more than a few dirty looks yesterday afternoon at the auction, but that's about all and not worth mentioning. No more accusations of stolen cows.

"It's been quiet on that front."

He nods and seems relieved. "Good."

"That reminds me, has there been any sign of that cow?" I ask.

I know full well the FBI was responsible for taking it, but it would probably be the question I'd ask if I wasn't aware. Besides, I'm curious to see how he'll answer.

"The missing animal? Not as far as I know, but then I haven't seen much of Mackey since yesterday."

"Oh, I thought I saw you talking to him. Well, I hope he finds it. See you later."

I immediately turn to head back to the improvised clinic, remembering clearly how I saw Jericho in what appeared to be a heated discussion with Mackey on the far side of the holding pens this morning.

I wonder why the man is lying.

Seventeen

Janey

"Careful, Doc."

One of Mackey's wranglers came and got me to come check out a bull.

The animal—going by the name of Crusher—is as menacing as his moniker promises. Already agitated from his performance, and the injury he sustained in his groin when trying to climb the fence exiting the arena, he's none too pleased being contained in the chute. His nostrils flare red as he snorts and huffs, trying to fight his way out of the constraints.

I'm hanging almost upside down over the side of the chute, trying to use a squirt bottle of distilled water to clean the tear in the bull's tender skin. Luckily it was a fairly straight tear and not gaping wide open. I should be able to use a wound sealant, preferable to stitches, since those would require some kind of sedation in order to safely get between the animal's rear legs.

"Can you hand me the can of KeriCure from my kit?"

I'm in a good position to see what I'm doing now and would prefer not to move too much and risk riling up the cranky bull even further. As it is, I'll have to stick my arm between his legs to get close enough to the wound. As soon as the sealant spray hits that bull in the tenders, he's gonna buck hard, and I'm going to have to get my arm out of the way fast.

"This is a one-shot deal," I tell the guy when he hands me the can. "That bull is gonna jump and I don't want him injuring himself even more. So, as soon as I hit him with the spray, you release the front gate so he can take off to his pen, instead of getting himself tangled up in the chute."

"Ready?" I call out when I've lowered myself into an even more precarious position.

"Yup."

I blow out a breath to try and calm my nerves; I may be used to handling cattle, but a pissed-off bull isn't a daily occurrence.

Then I slowly reach my arm underneath the animal, trying hard not to brush against his legs. The moment I hit the nozzle on the spray, he kicks out as predicted.

"Now!" I yell, trying to retrieve my arm and only partially succeeding.

One of the hooves hits me, knocking the can out of my hand as Crusher bolts out of the chute. I scramble down from the fence and immediately check myself for injuries. It hurts like a sonofabitch, and likely will be swollen and bruised by bedtime, but it doesn't look like anything's broken.

"That was a damn fool stunt."

I swivel around to find JD approaching. He immediately

reaches for my hand, which is already starting to puff up, and studies it carefully.

"It's fine. Trust me, I've been stomped on and kicked at more than I care to admit, and this is nothing."

His dark eyes snap up and meet mine. After a quiet stare down, he wisely chooses to abandon that particular subject. I'll do what I have to do to get the job done, whether he likes it or not. His work can be dangerous, but I'm pretty sure he wouldn't appreciate me questioning his methods.

Still, he can't quite keep his protective instincts in check.

"You were supposed to stay with Logan at the corral."

I take in a deep, steadying breath before I answer, even though my natural inclination would be to bite his head off.

"I was called away to tend to an injured animal, which is my *job*," I remind him.

Unfortunately, JD doesn't seem to read the warning signs and digs in his heels.

"Still, you shouldn't have gone off by yourself. You're not safe."

"I wasn't exactly by myself," I fire back, grinding my teeth.

Part of me recognizes the stress of the past few days is probably taking its toll on both of us, and today's added concerns around the missing woman has us all on edge, but that doesn't give him a license to treat me like I'm an idiot.

"You would've been safer with Logan," he stubbornly persists, digging himself a deeper hole, because now I'm good and pissed off.

"And Logan would've what? Protected me?" I scoff. "Do you even realize how sexist it is to suggest a twenty-something-year-old *boy* would be better equipped to look after me than I could? Do you even hear yourself?"

Belatedly, I realize my raised voice is drawing an audience; a few passersby slow down and gawk. When I turn my back, I catch sight of the wrangler, leaning against the chute, his arms crossed and a smirk on his face as he openly listens in to what he probably thinks is a lover's quarrel. Which, I guess, technically it is.

Ugh.

Annoyed, I retrieve my can of KeriCure and toss it into my medical bag, which I then throw over my shoulder. With a nod at the wrangler, but ignoring JD, I start walking back to the other side of the stockyard. Wordlessly, he falls into step beside me, which annoys me even more.

I need a moment to myself, but he's not giving me the space. So instead of heading straight back to the clinic, I make a sharp right and aim for the restrooms. I'd like to see him try and follow me into the ladies' room.

With the rodeo well underway, the restrooms are not as busy as they were earlier. I feel a pang of satisfaction at JD's unhappy grunt when I duck inside. I'm of a mind to leave him waiting out there for a while.

I find an empty stall and slip inside. It only takes me a minute to pee, but I stay seated when I'm done, resting my elbows on my knees and my head in my hands. I'm tired and stressed and now I'm feeling emotionally wrung out as well. Tears burn my eyes, but I don't think I can afford to let even one roll, or all of me might dissolve into a puddle. Instead, I practice deep breathing—in through the nose, out through the mouth—to try and regain my equilibrium.

Another hour or so for today's rodeo events to close down. After that the fair will stay open, but I won't need to stick around. I can do another hour, although the groceries I was planning to pick up on my way home will have to wait, I don't think I have it in me today. All I want is to go home, soak in a nice hot bath, and then go straight to bed after. I'll worry about food tomorrow.

Armed with a plan, and feeling a little better, I get out of the stall and step up to the sink. The bathroom doesn't have the best lighting, but I don't think it would've made a lot of difference to the reflection staring back at me. I look horrendous, my braids half undone, smudges of dirt and God knows what else on my pasty cheek and forehead, sunken, red-rimmed eyes looking shades darker than they're supposed to be, and sharp lines bisecting my eyebrows and bracketing my mouth.

I'm a mess.

I use hand soap to wash myself, scrubbing my hands, face, and neck, and using paper towels to pat myself dry. It actually does make me feel a little better.

But the moment I step outside, JD is there and takes one look at me before grabbing me by the arm and pulling me around the back of the building, which is butting up against the tree line. There he turns me to face him, pressing my back against the wall, as he lowers his head so his eyes can stare straight into mine.

"I almost came in after you," he growls in a low voice.

JD

Fuck.

My heart is still hammering in my chest, and I don't think I'll ever get rid of that sick feeling in the pit of my stomach. Getting back to Janey had been the only thing on my mind after the discovery Deputy Dale Bastian and I made.

We'd been paired up for the search, and I'd been getting pretty annoyed at the young deputy after listening to him chatter on about everything under the sun for hours, while we slugged around the thick brush. In hindsight it was probably nerves that had him run at the mouth.

He'd recognized Janey as his sister's boss—apparently Janey's assistant, Frankie, is Francesca Bastian—which led to a detailed family history. Then he brought up Logan, who was apparently in his graduating class and used to be on the high school football team, and the two of them had a crush on the same cheerleader. Unfortunately, that led the conversation to relationship woes. Apparently, he'd won the girl, and they'd been together until this spring, when she broke it off with him.

I hadn't exactly been much of a participant in the conversation—it was more a monologue than anything else—but it was at that point I started actively tuning him out. At first, he didn't even notice I'd stopped walking and was still talking when I pushed aside the low branch hanging over the ditch, not too far from the main road.

But not for long.

She was lying on her back, one arm up, covering her eyes, and the other stretched out, her hand clutched around a clump of quackgrass. Her jeans and underwear were tangled around her ankles and she was left exposed. My mind was already trying to detach as my training kicked in and I began to catalog everything I could see.

There was definitely blood at this scene, it looked like this girl may have fought hard. The hand clutching the grass looked to have blood under the fingernails, and from what I could see of her face, she'd been badly battered. Her death looked to be the result of a number of stab wounds, visible on her bare chest. The arm covering her eyes had some cuts as well, leading me to believe she was trying to ward off her attacker.

Deputy Bastian lost his cookies on the edge of the ditch, and I have to admit, I almost joined him.

Finding two dead women in a span of two weeks was not fun. Neither was having to stand guard over a crime scene for the second time, waiting for Sheriff Ewing to show up, when all I could think about was getting back to Janey. Only to find, when I finally was able to leave, Janey wasn't where she was supposed to be.

I was sick to my stomach when I couldn't immediately find her, and imagined her lifeless body ending up in a ditch somewhere. So I may have overreacted a bit when I finally located her.

Staring into her pale face, I see a mix of anger, fear, and exhaustion swirling in her eyes. She looks at the end of her tether, and I may be partially responsible for that. Repentant, I cup her face in my hand, stroking my thumb over the dark circles under her eyes.

"I'm sorry," I whisper, leaning my forehead against hers. "That was fear talking."

As her eyes examine mine, they go from hard and cold to shiny and soft.

"You found her..."

I swallow, choosing to nod because I don't trust my voice right now.

Her arms slip around my waist, pulling me to her. We stand like that, holding on to each other in the shadow of the restrooms for a while, when she suddenly straightens up.

"Oh no...Logan. He's been waiting for news all day, they made plans for their first date tonight, after the rodeo."

Shit. Poor kid.

I mean, he just met the girl yesterday, but he clearly liked her. It'll still be hard news to get.

"That's gonna be tough for him," I commiserate.

Janey nods, her expression serious. "Yeah. I should probably go let him know and send him home, before the news reaches him some other way."

But Sheriff Ewing beat us back to the clinic. As we walk up, I can see him standing close to Logan, resting a hand on his shoulder.

"Doc, I was looking for you," he says when he catches sight of Janey. He glances from her to me. "I'm guessing you already heard?"

"Yeah," she confirms, immediately sidling up to Logan, putting a supporting hand on his back.

The kid looks dazed—a bit out of it—like he can't quite believe what happened. But when Janey makes a suggestion, he turns to look at her.

"Hey, why don't you head on home? We're about wrapped up here anyway."

"You sure?"

"Yeah. Go. I'll check in with you in the morning, see how you're feeling. I can always call Frankie to give me a hand here tomorrow, if you need some time."

Logan shakes his head, his jaw set stubbornly. "I'll be here in the morning."

"Are you gonna be okay to drive?" I ask cautiously.

"I'm fine."

The curt answer is firm, his tone making it clear it's not up for discussion, but Janey tries anyway.

"We can easily drop you off at home," she offers.

"I'm good."

He abruptly takes his leave, probably to avoid further offers of concern. I get it, I was that young too, cocky, and feeling all kinds of invincible in my college years. Even though there's only ten or so years separating Logan and I, it feels like a lifetime to me.

We watch as he gets in his truck and drives off.

"I'm sorry to have been the bearer of bad news," the sheriff apologizes, "I didn't realize the kid knew her."

"They only met yesterday," Janey volunteers.

"He mentioned that, but it looked like she made an impact on him. Anyway," he shifts topics. "I came here to have a look at the horse."

He glances at the pinto, who looks to be dozing off in the pen next door, her tail occasionally whipping from side to side to keep the flies off.

"Of course, go ahead," Janey invites him. "Some of her sutures ripped but I redid them. What's going to happen to her?"

"Not sure. I was wondering if perhaps you had room for her until we sort that out?"

"I do, but I'll have to pick up the trailer at the clinic."

She sounds as tired as she looks. I can drop her off at her house, where she'll be safe and can put her feet up, and I'll come back here to pick up the horse.

"I'll do it," I offer. "Let me get you home first."

For a second it looks like she wants to object but then thinks better of it.

"Did you need us for anything else?" she directs at Ewing, who shakes his head.

"Not at the moment, I have my hands full, but I'm

gonna want to talk to you both at some point. Especially you, JD," he addresses me.

"Me?"

The hair on my neck stands on end and I instantly feel defensive.

"I never even spoke to the girl."

Eighteen

JD

"I can pick us up something to eat."

Janey pads into the house on her socks and sinks down on the couch. She reaches underneath the front of her shirt and her hand resurfaces, clutching the wires of the microphone. Tossing them on the seat beside her, she drops her head back and closes her eyes before answering.

"It's okay. I'll whip up something."

I'm not sure what, because there isn't a whole lot in the house. Besides, I doubt she's in any shape to whip up anything. She looks like she'll be zonked out two seconds after I leave.

"No. I'll worry about food; you worry about you."

I bend over the back of the couch and press a kiss to her slack mouth.

"I won't be long."

When I pull her truck in behind the barn, I notice only one vehicle is there, and I quickly poke my head into the clinic. The waiting room has undergone a transformation, two large folding tables set up in an L-shape, housing computers and assorted electronic equipment. Agent Wilcox lifts his head from a monitor when I enter, and Ginger crawls out from under the table, her tail wagging in greeting as she approaches me.

"I just wanted to warn you, I'm taking the trailer to pick up a horse. I'll take the dog with me. Doc Richards is at the house," I let him know, dropping the wire I pulled off my chest on the way over on one of the tables.

Wilcox doesn't say anything, just flicks me a salute before he drops his attention back to the monitor. I hesitate for a moment, curious to find out what, if any, progress has been made, but I have a feeling he'll be redirecting any questions to Stephanie Kramer anyway. I may as well wait until I can ask her.

After letting Ginger have a pee, I briefly contemplate dropping her off with Janey. The likelihood is she's already dozed off, and I don't want to disturb her. Let her nap for a bit.

"You up for a car ride, girl?" I mutter at the dog, who still moves with some difficulty on her cast.

She looks quite happy though, with her tongue lolling and her tail wagging. I pick her up and put her in the passenger seat, cranking the window so she can shove her nose out, which she immediately does. Then I quickly hook up the trailer.

"What are you doing?" I ask Jackson when he answers my call.

"What do you need?" he returns.

"Some clean clothes and food from my trailer, and two portions of whatever Ma has cooked up for dinner."

"Let me guess, you want it delivered to you at Doc's place."

"Ideally."

I hear him mutter something under his breath but can't quite catch the words, although I have no trouble understanding the gist of it.

"So that's a yes?" I prompt him.

"We had a visit from the FBI this afternoon," he says instead of answering my question.

"At High Meadow? Stephanie Kramer?"

"Yes, and yes. Jonas was mighty ticked off he was just finding out what apparently half of his team already knew, and called us all into the office. Drug smuggling. How the fuck did you land in the middle of that?"

I do a mental tally of who was in the know since I only told my father. He obviously shared with Ma, which makes two, and Bo is three, since he was at Janey's last night playing nurse. I guess maybe Dan heard something through Sloane, which would make four, and I guess I'm number five.

Maybe *half the team* is more accurate than I thought.

"Not voluntarily," I clarify before asking a question of my own. "What did Kramer want?"

"Manpower. We're actually loading up the horses as we speak. Sully already has the Matrice in the air, looking."

The Matrice is the team's state-of-the-art drone, which can be helpful on searches. Although, it's less effective in densely forested areas.

"Looking? For who?"

We found the only missing person I know, and she's currently at the morgue awaiting an autopsy in the morning.

"One of the drug peddlers has gone missing," Jackson clarifies. "Guy by the name of John Mackey. He was spotted on the side of Highway 37 about four miles east of the park, near Tub Gulch. The feds think he may be hiding out in the woods on the north side of the highway."

Mackey missing? That's the first I hear of it. If Ewing knew, he never mentioned anything this afternoon. Although I'm sure the guy had other pressing things on his mind at the time. Agent Wilcox didn't mention anything either, but I wouldn't expect him to volunteer anything.

I'm curious to know how the FBI came to the conclusion he must be hiding in the woods, or he was even on the run to begin with. Wouldn't it make more sense for him to drive or hitch a ride instead of walking, to get as far away as he could?

Maybe Kramer will be at the clinic by the time I get back so I can pick her brain.

"So you guys are heading out soon?"

"Within the hour. But I was going to drive myself anyway, so I can pick up your shit and drop it off at Doc's place. It won't take me that long, it's all on the way."

"Appreciate it. Grab me a couple of changes of clothes —there should be bags under the kitchen sink—and take my cooler from the front closet and throw in what's edible from my fridge."

"Little soon to be moving in, isn't it?" he goads me with a chuckle.

"You're fucking hilarious," I snarl, not in the mood for jokes. "I'll meet you at Janey's in twenty."

"10-4."

*

Janey

Shit.

I must've dozed off.

I put a hand at the nape of my neck and try to stretch the kinks out. I had my head back in an awkward position. Turning my eyes to the clock on the kitchen wall, I check the time. I only slept for about twenty minutes, which means JD will probably be back soon. I can still smell myself and it's not pleasant, I should grab a quick shower before he gets here.

But as I get to my feet, my eyes catch on the empty dog bed. *Ginger.* I forgot all about her, she has to be hungry by now. Feeling guilty for forgetting about her, I head for the front door, shove my feet back in my dirty boots, grab my keys, and head outside.

Sundown isn't until about ten in the summer months, but the sky is looking dark. It must be that rain they were promising overnight. Thunderstorms, more likely, given the high temperatures of the past few days. The weather can be unpredictable, especially in the mountains.

I love summer thunderstorms, it's a break from the stifling heat and there's nothing better than sitting on the porch, witnessing the force of nature at work. Everything feels and smells so fresh afterward.

Unfortunately, not all animals share my appreciation, which is why I'm rushing to get Ginger before the storm hits. I'm not sure how she feels about thunder, but I'd rather err on the side of caution. I'll poke in to the barn to check Red is secure. Come to think of it, I should make sure there's a stall ready for the pinto. JD could be back with her any minute.

Ignoring my aching muscles, I duck my head against the wind, which is suddenly picking up, and head for the barn. Halfway there, I can feel the first drops of rain falling.

Wonderful.

I jog the rest of the way, and rather than heading around the back to go in through the clinic, I opt for the big barn door, which is closer. I quickly shove my key into the lock, keeping the latch closed, and slip inside, making sure to pull the door shut behind me.

It's pretty dark in here; the two small windows in the front and two at the back hardly let in enough light with those storm skies outside. I hear Red moving about restlessly in his stall—the rustle of straw gives him away—but I head for the light switches first, which are located near the door to the clinic first.

The barn stays dark when I flick the first switch. Odd. The second one is for the light in the small hallway to the bedroom and bathroom at the back, but that doesn't come on either. Just then lightning flashes in the windows, briefly lighting up the barn, and it's almost immediately followed by a harsh crack of thunder overhead.

That moved in fast, and I wonder if the power is off due to the storm. It wouldn't be the first time I've lost power, which is why we keep flashlights and a camping lantern in the clinic just in case.

I open the connecting door and poke in my head.

"It's just me. I think the power is out."

I fully expect a response, or at the very least hear Ginger's approach as she comes to greet me, but it stays silent. Maybe whatever agent stayed here took her out for a pee in the back. Although, right at that moment I can hear the rain start coming down in earnest, so I don't think they'll be out for very long.

I head straight for the treatment room across from me,

where I keep the lantern. It gives off a wider spread of light and, in a pinch, I can still see what I'm doing if I happen to be treating an animal when the power is off. There's a nail in the wall next to Red's stall for ropes or a halter, I can hang it up there and have my hands free. I just hope it has full batteries.

I blow out a relieved breath when the lantern casts a decent glow. Enough to light my way as I walk toward the back door to poke my head outside and see if someone is out there with my dog. The rain is teeming, and I have to squint to see anything. One of the FBI SUVs is still parked in the back but there is no sign of life out here.

Confused, I retrace my steps back to the barn, where I make an immediate right to check the bedroom. Maybe someone is having a nap and took Ginger with them. But the bedroom is empty, as is the small bathroom next door.

This is weird.

Maybe I should try and get a hold of Stephanie Kramer, see if she knows what's going on. I wish I'd thought to bring my cell phone, which I tossed on the small table by the front door when I walked into the house. I picked up my keys, but left the phone. The clinic has a landline, but my phones won't work with the power out.

Another one of those loud booming cracks thunders, this time in sync with the bright flash of lightning. It's right over top of us. I can hear Red's restless snorts as he shuffles around his stall. Clearly, he's not enjoying the storm, and at this point, neither am I. I'm a little worried about Ginger, wondering if maybe she somehow got out and took off—although I'm not so sure she'd get far with that cast—and the agent went after her in the storm.

All I can do is speculate at this point, and that gets me nowhere. So I focus my attention on Red as I approach his stall. I hang the lantern on the nail and peer over the stall door.

The horse is huddled in the far corner, his alert eyes are turned toward me. There's a slight tremble visible in the skin on his flank.

"Easy, boy," I mumble soothingly. "You'll be okay."

If JD or Logan were here, I'd risk slipping into the stall to try and calm him. Horses can be unpredictable when scared, and I don't know this guy that well. More importantly, he doesn't know me well, and may not welcome my attention.

Abruptly he snorts, jerking his head up at the same time I hear movement behind me.

"Tell me where it is..."

It takes me a moment to recognize John Mackey when I swing around at the sound of his voice. He looks like someone worked him over with a baseball bat. His bruised and battered face is what catches my eye first, but a close second is the gun in his shaking hand. My own hands come up automatically, a useless defense against a bullet.

"I promise, I don't have your cow."

He looks jittery, almost panicked as his eyes seem to dart around at shadows. At my words his eyes slam back to me.

"Bullshit." He gestures with his gun hand toward the clinic. "Why else would the feds be here?" Then he aims it back at me. "You found the drugs."

I could feign ignorance, but I'm not a very good liar, and I can't really come up with a valid excuse why the FBI would be here, so I opt to say nothing. Anything out of my mouth would probably only agitate him more.

I try to hang on to the hope maybe the agent is around somewhere, waiting for the right moment to take control of the situation, but I have a bad feeling.

Suddenly he swings his arm around and backhands me with the gun, knocking me to the ground. My hand instantly comes up to the side of my face where a sharp pain blooms and brings tears to my eyes. But I barely have a chance to assess the damage, when he bends over me and shoves the gun against my temple.

"I need those packages," he hisses, his spit hitting my face. "Whatever it fucking takes. I'll start by shooting that fucking horse, piece by piece. See how long your bleeding heart can hold out. And when there's nothing left, I'll move on with you."

Bile rises from my stomach, burning a raw path through my chest on its way up. I wouldn't be able to withstand any harm he puts on Red, I'd rather he focus on me, and the only way to accomplish that is to tell him the truth.

"I don't have them, I swear." My voice sounds funny and my face hurts with every word. "I handed them over to the FBI. Please, they'll be here any minute."

"You think I'm scared of the feds?" he scoffs harshly. "They're the least of my worries. I'm already a fucking dead man if I can't come up with the missing cargo."

He grinds the barrel of the gun into my scalp, pressing my head hard against the concrete barn floor.

"And I won't need you anymore."

I hold my breath, waiting for the inevitable, when a bright flash outside lights up the windows. Lightning?

But a moment later, instead of the rumble of thunder, I hear the crunch of tires driving up to the barn.

Nineteen

JD

Fucking rain.

Working outdoors most of the time, I'm used to all kinds of weather, but I like rain least.

It started when I was backing up the trailer to the pinto's holding pen at the rodeo grounds. The place was quiet, the only people I encountered were security at the gate, and one of Mackey's hands walking through the stockyard. Whoever else is staying on the grounds must've retreated to the trailers in the back.

At first it was just a few drops as I was getting out of the truck, but that soon turned into a fucking monsoon.

Lowering the tailgate of the trailer, I rushed to get the horse out of the pen. Water was sluicing down the ramp and the first bolt of lightning struck, as I was trying to lead the horse into the back. She spooked and one of her hooves slipped on the slick surface. When she reared back, she almost ripped the lead from my hand.

After that, she hadn't been too keen on repeating the experience, and it took me forever to get her into the trailer. I ended up soaked; not a dry fucking stitch left on my body. Everything is stuck to my skin, and I can't wait to get out of these clothes and into the shower.

It's still raining when I get to Janey's place, but at least it's no longer coming down in sheets. The sky doesn't appear quite as black anymore as the thunderstorm slowly moves out of the region. Driving past, I notice there are no lights on in the house and I wonder if Janey is sleeping. If so, she must be dead to the world to be able to sleep through a storm like this. I should check on her, but first I'm going to unload this horse.

"Almost done, girl." I reach out and scratch Ginger's head. She's been patiently waiting in my truck. "I'll feed you as soon as we get inside."

She has no trouble understanding those words, her tail tapping out a happy rhythm on the old leather seat.

I'm surprised Jackson hasn't shown up yet either, but when I pull around the front of the barn, his truck is parked outside.

What the hell is he doing over here?

I stop when the back of the trailer is lined up with the barn door. I'm about to get out when my phone rings in my pocket.

"Move your fucking truck," Jackson hisses when I answer his call.

"What the hell are you talking about?"

"There's trouble," he whispers. "Keep coming this way, toward me. Park it here, right in front."

My eyes scan the building toward the clinic, where I finally catch a glimpse of Jackson. He's no more than a dark shadow pressed to the right side of the clinic's front entrance. I have no trouble recognizing the shape of the rifle in his hand though, and it feels like a punch in the stomach.

I shove my phone back in my pocket and immediately put the truck in drive, moving slowly forward until the trailer is directly in front of the clinic. I'm not sure what the fuck is going on, or what Jackson is up to, but I'm not about to question the urgency in his voice.

Turning off the engine, I slip out of the truck, reaching for my gun the moment my boots hit the ground.

"What the fuck is going on?" I whisper as I sidle up beside Jackson, my back pressed against the wall.

"Drove up, knocked and rang the bell at the house. No answer. Then I saw a faint light coming from the barn so I figured someone was up here," he explains. "I drove up and got out of the truck when I heard Doc start yelling inside. Something about a gun. Next thing I know a fucking bullet rips through the barn door. Retreated to the truck, grabbed my rifle, and took shelter here. That's when I saw you coming up the driveway."

"Janey is in there?"

"Sounds like it. And clearly, she's not alone."

The urge to barge through those doors, guns blazing, is great, but I resist. It's a sure way to get Janey hurt, if she isn't already. We need to know what we're dealing with first.

"Any sign of the FBI agents?"

At least one of them should be here manning their command center.

"Haven't actually seen anyone."

As I move to the clinic's front window to peer inside, I can hear Ginger's high-pitched whines from the truck behind me. She must sense something is going on.

The clinic is dark, none of the faint light in the barn is filtering through inside, which would mean the connecting door is closed. That may be a good thing. If we can sneak in through the clinic, we may be able to catch whoever is in there by surprise.

I try the front door, but it's locked. However, I walked right in the back door when I came by for the trailer earlier. Hopefully it's still unlocked, otherwise, I may have to put some of my ill-gotten lock-picking skills to use. A leftover of quietly rebellious teenage years.

"Do you have Stephanie Kramer's number?" I ask Jackson.

He shakes his head sharply, so I hand him my phone.

"I need you to stay here, keep an eye on the front, and call her. She's in my contacts. If you can't get through to her, call Ewing."

"And what are you gonna do?"

I cock my thumb over my shoulder. "I'm gonna get us inside."

Just a few minutes have passed since I drove up, but every minute Janey is in there with the gunman—possibly getting hurt or worse—is one too many. So, without wasting any more time, I duck around the corner of the building and hoof it to the back.

Only to trip over a leg.

I manage to keep my balance, but immediately crouch down to check on the body attached. It's Agent Wilcox and he's bleeding from his head. I'm not sure whether it's from a bullet wound or blunt force trauma. I press my fingertips to the side of his neck where I find a pulse, but his breathing is very shallow.

"Hang in there, buddy," I whisper, tapping his shoulder in case he's aware of me. "Help is on the way."

I feel bad leaving him, but there isn't anything I can do for him. Neutralizing the threat has to be my priority, otherwise medical help won't even be able to get to him. Besides, I have to get to Janey before it's too late.

Of course, the rain picks this moment to start coming down hard again and I'm dripping when I get to the back door. When I find it unlocked, I let out a big breath of relief. I very slowly open it, listening for any squeaks. As soon as I fit through the opening, I slip inside. I take off my boots to minimize noise, and use one of them to keep the door propped open.

I wait for a moment for my eyes to adjust to the darker interior before I start moving toward the front of the clinic. As I tiptoe past the connecting door, my ears are pricked for any sounds coming from inside the barn, but I have a hard time hearing anything over the heavy rain hitting the roof.

Jackson is already waiting when I carefully turn the lock on the front door and step outside.

"Found the agent around the side. He's injured and unconscious," I fill him in.

"*Shit*. Kramer is on her way," Jackson shares. "But she was gonna put a call in to the sheriff because she's about twenty-five minutes out."

Hopefully he has someone closer. Plus, whenever the sheriff's office gets called out to a situation that involves gunfire, EMTs are generally on their heels. But, we're about ten minutes from town, and I'm not about to wait around.

I have to get Janey out of there.

Janey

Mackey is losing whatever was left of his marbles.

He's been mumbling to himself, pacing back and forth in the empty stall ever since he pulled me in here.

I had no choice, I had to warn JD when I heard him walking up to the barn door, or he would've walked straight into the barrel of Mackey's gun. I did not expect Mackey to shoot right through the damn door, but I jumped on the momentary distraction to try and wrestle the gun away from him.

Unfortunately, I ended up getting pistol-whipped again, this time hard enough to knock me out. Not for long, probably no more than a minute or two, but it was enough to rattle my brain. It took me a moment to realize he was dragging me into the stall next to Red's.

I decided I was probably better off feigning to still be out. As long as I'm unconscious—or at least he thinks I am—I can't tell him where the drugs are. I've been pretending, staying very quiet while he's mostly talking to himself, occasionally kicking me in the stomach or the legs in frustration.

I'm determined to be tough and grind my teeth to keep from crying out, hoping I'm buying time. Enough time for help to show up, provided that bullet didn't hit JD, preventing him from calling for backup.

"...I'm a fucking dead man. I'm a dead man. This was supposed to be my retirement," he rambles on under his breath. *"Except he's not gonna pay me, he's gonna fucking kill me piece by piece. If the FBI doesn't shoot me first. I wasn't thinking, but when that bitch started yelling, I reacted. Now I'm in big fucking trouble—dumbass—shooting at the feds. I'm a dead man. And if not for this fucking cunt poking her nose where it doesn't belong, I'd be home free. If only he had her under control the way he was supposed to."*

I bite my tongue to keep from yelling out, as his boot

connects with my kidney, but a grunt escapes me anyway. Immediately the barrel of his gun is shoved in my ear.

"Good...you're awake. I need them to hear you scream."

Clenching my jaw, I'm determined not to make a sound. He may think it's the feds outside and maybe has some deluded idea he can use me as a bargaining chip for the drugs, but I know better. I have no doubt the moment I scream, JD will come barreling in here, and when Mackey realizes it's not the FBI out there, he will shoot JD.

I don't think the man is functioning on all cylinders if he thinks the agents are just going to hand over those packages. He's desperate, and a desperate man is a dangerous one.

The next moment he removes the gun from my ear. I jerk at the deafening bang too close to my head, but it's not until a second later I feel the hot burn of the bullet entering my leg.

Then I scream.

~

JD

I'm waiting by the connecting door, ready to barge in as soon as Jackson gets in position.

The plan is for me to draw the shooter's attention, hopefully giving Jackson a clear target from the barn door. He was a sniper before his discharge from the Army, and is the most accurate shot.

I've been picturing the layout of the barn, anticipating where they might be and how I might find cover in case Jackson doesn't have a good visual.

But as soon as I hear the man start talking inside, I realize time is running out.

The moment I hear the shot, I reach for the door. It's followed by Janey's scream, and I'm already busting through.

I'm moving on blind faith my teammate is in the right place, because there is nothing holding me back.

Ignoring the small hallway to my right I'd thought of potentially using as cover, I'm banking on the element of surprise as I head straight for the direction of the sound.

I'm vaguely aware of Red, kicking the boards of his stall in distress, and to my left I see Jackson coming in through the barn door in my peripheral view, his rifle at the ready.

He's taking aim at the last stall on the right side, where the right shoulder and arm of a man are just visible. I just catch the glint off the gun when it goes off, the bullet shooting splinters off a post right next to me.

The sharp crack of Jackson's rifle is loud in the enclosed space, and the man is already down before I make it to the stall.

Inside I find Mackey on the ground, clutching his shoulder, and behind him I see Janey, her blue eyes blinking wide as blood runs down her face.

Enraged, I kick the gun Mackey dropped on the ground out of reach, before hauling back and aiming my boot for his injured shoulder, making him howl in pain. Then I step over him and crouch next to Janey.

That's when I notice the blood streaming from her leg.

Twenty

JD

"Where is she?"

I'm not surprised my mother is the first to show up.

I'm sure word has gone out to the team the guy they were looking for showed up at the clinic, but it would take them some time to pack up and head back to the ranch.

Jackson stayed behind at the clinic to deal with law enforcement, and look after Ginger and the horses, but I expect the feds to show up here at some point.

Agent Wilcox—whose first name is Shane, apparently— was transported by Life Flight to Logan Health in Kalispell. He was barely hanging on, from what I picked up. I'm not sure what happened to Mackey, because I hopped in the ambulance with Janey, who was brought to Cabinet Peaks Medical Center in Libby.

"X-ray. They told me I had to wait here."

I wasn't happy being relegated to a waiting room, but Janey insisted she'd be okay, so I went.

"Talk to me," Ma insists, taking the seat beside me.

"Gunshot wound to her lower leg on the right side. Looks like it may have missed the bone, but they're looking to make sure. That fucking bastard pistol-whipped her and split her face open right along her cheekbone, and she probably has a concussion."

I grind out the words through clenched teeth, burning with rage. For all I know, that lowlife could be right here in the same hospital getting treatment. If he is, it's probably better I don't know. I don't think I can be held accountable for my actions.

"Jesus..." Ma hisses. "Poor girl. Good thing she's tough. She'll recover."

I nod. She's right, Janey is tough and she'll recover from her injuries, at least the physical ones. But that kind of violent trauma can mess with a person's head, and leave far longer-lasting damage than what was done to the body.

"Physically," I modify her statement.

"And mentally," Ma insists. "She's tough. She's got you, and all of us. She'll be fine."

I let that sink in for a bit as my gaze drifts to the window. It's dark now, which means it's after ten. Another long, fucked-up day. Hard to believe it's still only Friday, the past few days have felt like weeks. So much going on, it's hard to keep up.

My empty stomach rumbles loudly in the quiet room, a reminder of another missed meal.

"You haven't eaten," my mother concludes. "I packed up dinner and gave it to Jackson."

"Never had the chance. It's probably still in his truck and he's back at Janey's place taking care of things."

"Well, then why don't I go see if I can find you something?" she offers, but I shake my head.

"It's okay, Ma."

The sandwich shop in the hospital is closed, and the only other thing available at this time would be some greasy fast food I don't think I'd be able to stomach right now. It's doubtful Ma will let it go that easily, feeding people is her way of looking after those she cares about.

She proves me right when she persists with, "You need to eat," only to be interrupted by a nurse who chooses that moment to walk in.

"Janey is back in her room. You can keep her company while we wait for the surgeon."

"Surgeon?" my mother echoes, alarmed.

It's news to me as well.

The nurse turns to her and explains, "We generally call the surgeon in to assess gunshot wounds coming in, it doesn't necessarily mean she has to have surgery. It all depends what the X-rays show as well, and the radiologist is looking at those."

"Oh, okay," Ma responds.

"Normally, we limit it to one person in the room, but I'll make an exception if you want to poke your head in as well. You'll need to leave when the doctor gets there though," the nurse adds.

I'm not sure how Janey's going to feel about Ma showing up at her bedside, but since she gets to her feet before I can, I don't think there's any stopping her.

Half of her face is still wrapped in the gauze the EMTs used to keep the dressing on the cut on her cheek in place. The other half looks a little gaunt. A blanket is draped over her with her injured leg exposed, but they repacked that wound before she was wheeled to radiology and I'm happy to see only a little blood has soaked through the bandages since.

I walk straight to the bed and drop a kiss on her lips.

"Hey. How are you doing?"

"Under the circumstances, okay, I guess."

She tries for a smile when I see her eyes catch on something behind me. *Someone*, rather.

"Ama...hey."

"The nurse said I could poke my head in," Ma explains quickly. "I came as soon as I heard."

"That's really sweet of you. You didn't have to."

Sweet is not something my mother is often accused of. She's more of a tough-love type of person, but I can tell from the faint smile on her lips, she doesn't seem to mind. Of course, she brushes it off with a wave of her hand.

"Did you get something for pain?" Ma gets right down to business.

"Yeah, I'm not sure what, they injected it in the IV, but I think it's starting to work."

Her voice is a little slurred and I suspect a combination of the events of the day, the pain medication, and the inevitable adrenaline letdown are starting to take their toll on her.

Ma doesn't miss it either.

"Listen, I suspect they'll keep you at the very least for tonight. Is there anything you need or want? I'm about to run over to your place to grab the food I gave Jackson for you two anyway. I know you're probably not hungry yet, although you might want something decent later, but I know JD needs his food or he turns cranky."

"Ma..."

I roll my eyes at my mother's manipulations. She's effectively made it impossible for Janey to pass on the offer without making her seem selfish, and I'd risk looking like an ungrateful ass if I told her not to.

"Hush," she scolds me, putting a hand on my arm. "Let me feel useful."

Ahhh.

The words she chooses are "let me" but what I'm hearing is about what she needs.

I slide my arm around her shoulders and give her a side-hug, dropping my cheek to the top of her head.

"All right, Ma," I concede.

"My phone," Janey suggests, observing the dynamic between my mother and me. "I left it on the hall table inside the front door, which may still be open, I'm not sure. And possibly some clothes. My pants were cut off me. *Shit...* my keys were in my jeans. I don't know where they went."

"I've got them."

I reach in my pocket and fish out the key ring one of the EMTs handed me. Ma snatches them out of my hand.

"Anything else?" Ma asks.

She barely gives Janey a chance to respond before she plows on.

"Excellent. I'll be back," she announces. "And if there's anything else you think of, tell my son to message me."

Then she bends over the bed and brushes a stray hair from Janey's forehead before kissing it. I'm not accustomed to the rare show of affection.

"You get some rest," she instructs Janey.

All I get is a pat on my shoulder before she strides out of the room.

~

Janey

. . .

"How is Shane?"

Stephanie Kramer looks exhausted. She didn't even argue with JD when he offered her his chair, and simply sank down in it, her shoulders slumped.

"In surgery, last I heard," she shares. "But at least that means he's still alive."

Very true.

I really hope the agent pulls through. I feel a bit responsible for what happened to him. After all, Mackey was looking for me, or rather, the drugs he thought I had. It's weighing on me, especially since I got off relatively easy in comparison.

My X-rays showed no damage to the bone, so I escaped surgery altogether. It also revealed the bullet, which was lodged beneath the skin at the back of my knee. The surgeon was able to retrieve it with local freezing and a small incision, right here in the room. He flushed out the wound, stitched and dressed it, and then moved on to the cut on my cheek. He ended up using surgical glue on that cut, promising it would leave less of a scar than even the tiniest of stitches would. I wasn't really all that worried about scarring until he brought it up, so the glue seemed like a good option. I guess I have some vanity in me after all.

The surgeon had just left when Special Agent Kramer showed up.

"I hope he makes a full recovery."

Stephanie looks up and shoots me a wobbly smile. "As do I."

Then she appears to pull herself together, sitting up straighter and squaring her shoulders.

"I know it's late," she starts, "but tonight's developments blow this case wide open, and we are in a hurry to piece it together. As soon as word gets out, the rest of the players along this drug pipeline will be scrambling to cover their tracks. That'll make it so much harder—if not impossible—to wrap up this case. I need to know exactly what happened, and what was said."

"I'm guessing Mackey is not talking?" JD asks.

"Nothing useful so far," the agent admits, focusing on JD. "But since you bring up Mackey, you wouldn't happen to know how his face came to look like someone used it as a punching bag, do you?"

JD quietly stares her down for a moment before holding out his hands, showing her both sides. There are no marks, nor is any swelling visible as you might expect, given the beating Mackey received.

Stephanie nods. "I had to ask. The only thing he was willing to talk about was how you assaulted him."

"Mackey already looked like that when he approached me in the barn," I defend JD.

I shoot a glance at him, noting the tension in the careful way he holds himself. I vaguely recall him kicking at Mackey, but that was mild compared to what I might've been tempted to inflict on the man, had I not been hurt myself. Not so much for Mackey's actions tonight, but for the despicable way he treats animals. It's no wonder poor Red had been trembling in his stall; I'm willing to bet that had more to do with his fear of his former owner than of thunderstorms.

"Why don't you tell me how that came about?" Special Agent Kramer smoothly redirects her focus.

I try to relay events to the best of my recollection. Every so often she asks for clarification or poses a question that triggers my memory. She's particularly interested in everything Mackey said, and I try my best to remember the exact words he used.

JD ends up adding his perspective once I get to the part where I thought I heard him driving up to the barn. I wasn't aware it was actually Jackson who showed up first. Something I'm very grateful for, since he was able to alert JD before Mackey took a potshot at him as well, and maybe not missing that time.

He finally takes over, recounting everything happening outside the barn I hadn't been privy to, and what happened in those final moments after Mackey shot me.

"Is this not a good time?" Ama says as she pokes her head around the door.

I'd almost forgotten she promised to be back.

"It's fine," Stephanie is the one to respond, as she gets to her feet. "I have everything I need for now and should get going. You two should get some rest with your matching concussions."

She pauses at the door, waiting for Ama to pass her inside, before adding, "I'll be in touch."

"Matching concussions?" Ama asks, looking pointedly at her son as she sets down a large cooler and a bag on the floor by the window.

"I got knocked over the head earlier this week," he clarifies.

"That was only yesterday," I correct him, glancing at the clock over the door that shows a few minutes before midnight.

"No one told me about that," Ama grumbles.

"I'm fine, Ma. Just a couple of stitches."

His mother huffs audibly. "Just like your father. You Watike men all think you're invincible."

JD glances at me, his dark eyes amused. He doesn't respond, which would seem wise in my humble opinion.

Ama asks me what the outcome of the surgeon's visit

was so I fill her in, as she opens the cooler and pulls out two containers. She hands me one of them and the smell of rich spices wafting up has my mouth water.

"Tortilla pie. Quick and not too heavy. Eat."

She shoves a fork in my hand before giving JD the other container.

"Iced tea and bottled water in the cooler, and I've packed some clean clothes for both of you."

"You didn't have to go to all the trouble, Ama."

She turns to look at me sternly. "It's what I do. Now I'll be able to sleep." Then she drops my keys on the bedside table. "Jackson asked me to let you know he'll stay at your house and look after your animals."

"I appreciate that, and thank you."

As expected, she waves me off. "Eat and rest. I'll check up on you in the morning."

When she tries to pass JD on her way to the door, he wraps her in a hug.

"Love you, Ma."

She lifts her head to look at her son and places a hand on his cheek.

"You'd better," she returns in a suspiciously unsteady voice before darting out the door.

Maybe it's the drugs they gave me, but the brief mother-and-son moment has me a little choked up.

JD

"Wait a minute...you just passed my turnoff."

I haven't told her yet, I have no intention of taking her back to her place. Not only is it still swarming with law enforcement, but it may not be safe for her. Sure, Mackey is in custody, but it's clear he wasn't operating in a vacuum. Janey may still be at risk.

"We're going to my place."

"Why?"

I can feel her eyes on me and glance over.

"I talked to Jackson this morning. He mentioned your place is overrun by agents at the moment, you won't get any rest."

"But what about the animals?"

I reach for her hand and bring it to my lips.

"Jackson's looking after them. He offered to drop Ginger off once we get you settled in, if you want."

"I want."

She drops her head back and closes her eyes. I think she's in more pain than she's willing to let on, otherwise I'm pretty sure she would've put up more of a fight.

I'd gone to grab a coffee and something to eat at the sandwich shop when it opened at seven this morning, and by the time I got back to the room, nursing staff already had her out of bed and moving. It must've hurt like a son of a bitch walking on that leg, but Janey pushed through with steel determination. She even convinced the nurse to wrap her leg in plastic so she could clean up in the shower. The exercise wiped her out, but she said she couldn't stand the rodeo stench clinging to her.

I'm pretty ripe myself. I never even changed into the clothes Ma dropped off last night. I'll grab a shower at home as soon as I get Janey tucked into bed.

The moment I walk into my place, I know my mother was here. A bowl of fresh fruit is sitting on the small kitchen table, and there's a hint of cleaner in the air. Even though she usually respects my space, I'm not surprised, Ma has a way of finding things out. She probably talked to Jackson.

"Wow, nice view," Janey observes when I guide her to my couch.

"Yeah. It's why I bought this piece of land."

She flashes me a tired smile.

"You're tired."

She nods. "A little."

I drop a kiss on top of her head. "I'll be right back."

Before I tuck her into bed, I'll need to change the sheets, but when I walk into the small bedroom, I see Ma beat me to it. The bed is turned down and the sheets are clean.

Janey's eyes are closed when I return. "I don't know why I'm this exhausted," she mumbles without opening them.

"Come on, let's get you to bed. You'll feel better after a nap, it's been a busy morning."

I lead her to the bedroom and have her sit on the edge of the bed so I can take off the slip-on shoes and stretchy pants Ma packed for her. Then I tuck her in, leaving her pain meds and a glass of water on the nightstand, and head for the bathroom.

My shower is small, but the pressure is good, and it feels amazing to let the water beat down on my stiff muscles. It wasn't particularly comfortable trying to catch a few winks on a visitor's chair in the hospital, but I'm feeling a fuckload better when I walk out of the bathroom twenty minutes later.

I check in on Janey, who is out like a light, and head for the kitchen. There I discover my mother hasn't just cleaned up; she's even restocked my fridge. A good thing, since what I had in my fridge yesterday is probably spoiling in the back of Jackson's truck.

Grabbing a beer, I snag my phone off the kitchen table and head out the sliding doors to the deck I built onto the trailer home a few years ago. I drop down on the Adirondack chair and dial my mother's number.

"Thanks, Ma."

"She okay?"

She ignores my thanks and responds with a question of her own. Ma doesn't do well with gratitude or compliments, but I want to bet she's secretly pleased.

"She's okay. Sleeping right now."

"Good. Best thing for her. I'll bring some dinner over later."

"No need. You left plenty of supplies in the fridge, I can throw something together. It'll give me something to do."

At least in part, but mostly, I want to be the one looking after her. With a woman like Janey, I imagine I won't get the opportunity that often, so I'm grabbing this one. I'm not sure how good I'll be with words to let her know I care about her, but I can let my actions speak for me.

"Never could sit still for very long," Ma observes dryly, before adding, "and, by the way, your sister called this morning. She says you're not answering your phone."

I'd ignored two calls from Una since talking to her on Wednesday and told her to first make things right with Ma. It's Saturday today, I'm actually surprised she didn't hold out longer. My sister can be very stubborn.

"Is that the only reason she called?" I probe.

"No," Ma admits. "We talked. We'll probably need to talk more, but it's a start."

Yeah, you don't erase years of strained interaction with one conversation. I'm not exactly a master in the art of communication myself, but I'm making an effort to at least be real and speak the words I feel.

"I'm glad for that. I'll give her a call tomorrow."

"You do that."

I smile when the line abruptly goes dead.

Taking a sip of my beer, I stretch my legs out and slide down in the chair. I take in the fresh air, and force myself to enjoy the moment. I have a beautiful woman safe in my bed, the warm sun on my face, a cold beer in my hand, and one of the best views in the valley.

A small window of serenity in the chaos of the past few days.

∼

It takes me a moment to realize I'm in JD's bed.

Then I'm reminded why when pain washes over me, along with a wave of nausea. I immediately reach for the water and the bottle of pain meds I didn't think I would need.

I've always heard them say the first day after an injury or surgery is the worst. By that rule, tomorrow should be better. Thank God. I'm not a very good patient and I have too much to do.

"You're awake," JD says, walking into the room just as I'm popping one of the pills he left on the nightstand.

He sits down on the edge of the mattress. "Guess I don't have to ask how you're feeling."

"Best not," I advise him, swallowing down the medication with a swig of water. "How long did I sleep for?"

"Almost two hours. I was just coming in to see if you're ready for something to eat."

The hospital tray they brought me this morning had little edible on it, so JD had grabbed me a breakfast wrap from the sandwich shop. That was the last food I had. I should probably eat something.

"Let me get up first."

"Or I can bring it to you in bed," he offers sweetly.

I shake my head. "I need the bathroom, and I think I want to move about a little."

He bends down and brushes a kiss on my lips. It strikes me how natural the attention already feels, even though this is all very new. Although, given the intensity of the past few days, we should count those in dog years.

"Take your time. I put your toiletry stuff Ma brought

over on the bathroom counter, and your pants are over there." He points at the top of the dresser. "Yell if you need a hand."

I take a good look at my reflection while I wash my hands after peeing. My face looks like a bad caricature, swollen in all the wrong places and, with the bandage covering the stitches on my cheekbone, a bit like Frankenstein's bride. Especially with my hair a knotted mess around my head. It needs to be washed. I only got it wet this morning at the hospital and didn't even run a brush through it.

Rummaging through the bag on the counter, I dig up not only my hairbrush—bless Ama's heart—but my toothbrush as well. My teeth feel like they're growing mold, and I'm sure my breath smells like something died in there. I can't believe I let JD kiss me.

I feel instantly better with my mouth clean, and I do my best with my hair, but what little energy I had is fast depleting. I'll try again after I've put something in my stomach.

It's not until I walk into the small kitchen I'm hit with the smell of rich spices.

"What are you cooking?" I ask JD, who is standing at the stove.

"Beef and broccoli stir-fry with cashews. That okay?"

"Sounds delicious. I'm surprised at how hungry I am," I admit.

He turns around and one corner of his mouth pulls up.

"You look a little better."

I snort. "Hardly. I'm a mess, I can't even get my brush through my hair."

"Ah." He runs a hand over my hair. "The hair will have to wait until we get some food in you. But first let's get you off that leg."

He takes my hand and leads me through the sliding doors and onto the deck. I hear the thump of Ginger's tail on the wooden boards before I see her. She's on her bed between a pair of wooden chairs, and gets up to greet me the moment she sees me.

"Hey, girl. Are you glad to see me?" I smile at JD. "I guess Jackson dropped her off? I never heard anything."

"Maybe forty-five minutes ago. We were trying to be quiet."

One of the wooden chairs has a blanket draped over the back and an upside-down bucket with a pillow on top beside it. The bucket serves as a footstool, as I discover when JD helps me into the chair and carefully lifts up my injured leg, resting it on the pillow.

"There's a little chill in the air," he explains as he drapes the blanket over my legs.

Ginger comes to sit down beside me and nudges her wet nose under my hand, looking for a few more scratches.

It strikes me what a surprisingly thoughtful man he is. I've seen it in the way he handles animals—caring, and with respect—but I've only recently discovered he's the same way with the people he cares about. I smile at the thought I'm included in that group.

Dinner is simple but so tasty, exactly what I needed. After we're done, JD disappears to the kitchen with the empty bowls but returns holding my brush.

"Lean your head back."

I do as he asks, keeping my eyes on the pretty view as he carefully works on the tangles and knots. I feel pampered. A full belly, the fresh air, and the feel of those strong, long fingers combing through my hair have me so relaxed, I'm almost dozing off again. But the faint sound of a phone ringing cuts through my moment of pure Zen.

"I think that's yours," JD says, letting go of my hair as he ducks inside.

He returns a moment later and hands me my phone.

"Hey, Logan," I answer, after checking the name on the screen. "I was going to call you later to see how today went."

At least that had been the plan.

I called him from the hospital this morning, after I spoke with Jericho. The councilman had apparently already talked to Sheriff Ewing, so he was aware I was in the hospital and had put a call in to another area vet to fill in. I'd offered to get in touch with Logan to get him up to speed and to ask him to assist the other vet, since he was already familiar with the layout and the procedures at the rodeo.

"Okay, so far. I'll probably be out of here in an hour, maybe a little longer if something comes in at the last minute, but I was just calling to see if you wanted me to stop by and check in on the animals after I'm done? I'm happy to crash in the barn so I can feed them in the morning. My parents aren't home anyway."

I don't think the FBI wants Logan anywhere near my place. Frankly, neither do I, it's much safer for him to go straight home. I don't want him inadvertently landing on the drug traffickers' radar.

"No need," I quickly tell him. "Someone is staying at my house. He'll look after the place and the horses, and I've got Ginger with me."

"With you? At the hospital?"

"No. I was released earlier. I'm staying at—"

JD suddenly taps my knee and shakes his head, putting a finger to his lips.

"...a friend's place," I finish.

"That's good. Well, I'd better go, but let me know what's happening for Monday."

"I will, as soon as I figure it out."

I end the call and turn to JD.

"Why didn't you want me telling him I was here?"

"He can't reveal what he doesn't know," JD explains with a serious expression on his face. "It's for his safety as well as yours."

Twenty-Two

JANEY

I can't believe how quiet it is here.

I've been sitting out here with Ginger snoozing by my side for the past hour, and all I hear is the burbling water in the creek, the birds chattering in the trees, and an occasional animal call I can't really place.

It's peaceful.

I'm peaceful, which is a bit of a surprise, considering I'm usually a bit of an Energizer Bunny and not good at staying still. I couldn't even stay inside on the couch for long after JD left. Yet, I've been content sitting in this deceptively comfortable chair on the deck, simply existing, since I came out here.

Today I'm feeling a lot better than I did yesterday, which I'm sure plays a role, but I think it's more than that. I think that being on my own since I left home in my early twenties, I've become used to everything falling on my shoulders.

There is always something that needs to be done, and "idle hands are the devil's workshop," as my father used to quote.

I'm coming to terms with the fact hardworking is a badge I like to carry. A label I don't mind wearing. It feels comfortable to think that's how others see me, how I've begun to identify myself. It's where I've always seen my value in the eyes of others; my worth. I'm strong, I'm capable, and I don't need anyone else.

But this morning, sitting here completely unproductive and feeling quite at peace with that, I realize that is changing. A hard worker is only part of who I am, there is so much more to me.

I'd love to claim I came to that realization by myself, but I doubt I would've had this epiphany if JD hadn't drifted into my life. He makes me feel fully seen in a way I haven't experienced before. There don't seem to be any conditions or expectations to his desire to be with me.

He simply wants to be around me, look out for me, and I'm learning to recognize it for the gift it is. I may not *need* anyone else, but damn, it sure feels good to have him in my life.

When Phil Jericho called this morning, wanting to know where he could drop off my check and a few items I'd apparently left behind at the rodeo grounds, I didn't argue when JD offered to collect my things. I don't particularly want to deal with Jericho. I was surprised he actually called, I would've thought he'd be busy with the aftermath of the rodeo and the events of the past few days. Everyone's probably moving out today, on to the next event, wherever that is.

I'm not even sure what's happening in terms of the FBI investigation, I haven't heard from Stephanie Kramer since Friday night. We've been living in a bit of a bubble, first at the hospital and, since yesterday, here at JD's place. A little reprieve from what has become an ugly world out there.

So, I'm sitting here, enjoying a peaceful morning, while JD is out there—slaying my dragons—and I'm surprisingly okay with that.

Suddenly Ginger raises her head, her ears tracking for sound. A soft growl sounds deep in her throat.

"What is it, girl?"

Slowly the dog gets to her feet, her head held low as she appears to focus on something on the other side of the creek. I sit up in my seat and squint my eyes against the sun, trying to make out what she could be looking at. It's hard to see anything with the sunlight reflecting off the water almost blinding me.

An uneasy feeling has the hair on my neck stand on end, and I push myself to my feet, all of a sudden feeling too vulnerable sitting down. It's almost like I have eyes on me.

My hand drops down to Ginger's neck, my fingers curling around her collar, seeking a false sense of security. Part of me wants to rush inside and lock the doors behind me, but I'm afraid to turn my back on whatever—or whoever—is out there.

Without taking my eyes off the opposite bank of the creek, I take a few steps to the side before I start shuffling backward, dragging Ginger along with me. The dog fights my hold and suddenly starts barking furiously, as a black bear ambles out of the underbrush and saunters up to the edge of the creek. His head is up and his beady eyes are fixed on us.

Still, I sigh a breath of relief at the sight. When it comes to threats, I much prefer the four-legged kind.

That doesn't mean I don't jump when my phone starts ringing, a loud interruption of a silent standoff. On the other side of the creek, the animal appears startled as well, and as I grab my cell off the small table, he turns and runs back into the woods.

"Hello," I answer, a little out of breath, as I keep my eyes on the trees where the bear disappeared.

"Go inside right now."

I recognize Stephanie's voice, but I'm confused.

"What do you mean?"

How does she know I'm outside? Is she here?

"Right fucking now, Janey," she snaps, just as someone steps into the clearing across the water.

But it's not Stephanie.

A sharp crack reverberates as splinters fly up from the chair next to me, and I dive for the door.

~

JD

What a fucking waste of time.

First of all, it was a bitch to get to the rodeo grounds, since it looked like everyone was coming and going at the same time, causing gridlock on the narrow roads through the park in both directions.

Yesterday was the last day of the rodeo, but the fair is still ongoing today, so the grounds are busy.

When I finally made my way to the trailers to find Jericho, his fancy SUV was parked in front, but the asshole wasn't there. The first place I looked was the stockyard. The place was chaos with animals being loaded up in trailers, pens getting broken down and packed away, lots of people milling about but none of them Jericho. I finally bumped into one of Mackey's hands who thought he saw him heading toward the auction arena, but there was no one there.

Then I got caught up trying to help wrangle a bull who'd managed to clear the gate on the side of the trailer ramp, and was charging toward the crowds of people at the fair. It took half an hour, a dozen men, several lengths of fencing, and a whole lot of cursing to get the animal into the damn trailer. But no one was hurt.

I thought for sure Jericho would show up after that excitement, but he is still AWOL when I get back to the trailer, dirty and sweating fucking buckets.

Damn bull, and damn Jericho.

I wasn't able to find him in the stockyard and there is no way I'll be able to locate him in the high-density crowd at the fair.

Getting in my truck, I briefly contemplate calling Janey to get Jericho's number off her to see where he's at, but I've already left her long enough and I'd rather just get back home. I'll call the asshole from there.

As I turn my key in the ignition, my phone starts to ring. It's Special Agent Kramer.

"Where the hell are you?"

The urgency in her voice has the blood run cold through my veins.

"Just leaving the rodeo grounds. Why? What's going on?"

"Tell me Janey is with you—"

It feels like the air is being sucked from my lungs as I shake my head, belatedly realizing no one can see.

"No," I croak. "She's at my place."

I hear some muffled cursing before she appears to relay

my answer to someone. When she comes back on the line her message is curt.

"Get your ass over here."

Then the line goes dead.

My heart is hammering up in my throat as I break every speed limit and traffic law, trying to get home.

Get your ass over here, Stephanie said, which would mean she's at my house. I don't think she's there for a social visit.

Fuck, how could I have been so stupid? I thought we'd been careful and figured she'd be fine in my trailer for half an hour while I went to pick up her stuff. Of course, that half hour turned into an hour and a half.

I try calling Janey's number several times as I race home, but keep getting punted to voicemail. By the time I reach the turnoff to my place, I'm so frantic, I cut right in front of an eighteen-wheeler heading to town. I manage to skirt past him by a hair's breadth, but the blare of his horn follows me all the way up the dirt road to my trailer.

Two dark SUVs are parked in front as I slide my truck in beside them, jamming the gear into park as I jump out.

"She's fine," Stephanie Kramer volunteers when she opens my front door before I can.

My eyes shoot past her into my trailer where I catch sight of the back of Janey's head. She's sitting on the couch. I push past the agent and in four long strides I'm in front of her, sinking down on my knees. For the second time in as many days, I'm looking into her wide, startled blue eyes, before I scan her body for additional injuries.

"I'm okay," she mutters, as if trying to reassure herself as much as she's reassuring me.

No blood this time, for which I'm eternally grateful, but clearly whatever happened shook her up. I stroke the back of my fingers over her unmarred cheek and she grabs on to my wrist. She seems to need to for the contact, so I lift myself up on the couch beside her and gently wrap her up in my arms.

I hear Ginger whining from somewhere at the same time I see my shattered sliding door. Then I notice a group of several people with FBI printed on the back of their shirts standing at the edge of my deck. They're surrounding an individual in handcuffs.

"Is that..."

"Phil Jericho," Stephanie confirms, stepping into my view. "We've suspected his involvement and have been watching him, hoping he'd trip up and make a mistake."

"Involvement?" Janey repeats incredulously, as if she still can't quite believe what is happening.

The agent nods. "We suspect this wasn't the first time the rodeo was used as a cover for drug trafficking. It made no sense a former rodeo champ and current city councilman like Jericho would continue his association with a livestock supplier who is suspected of animal cruelty. Livestock suppliers are plentiful in these regions, he could easily have gone with someone else. Unless—"

"He had a vested interest in having Mackey Livestock here," I finish for her.

"Exactly. And when Janey told me, in the hospital, she caught Mackey mumbling to himself someone was supposed to have kept her under control, those pieces clicked into place. The only person who could've made that claim—however misguided—was Jericho."

"He wouldn't take no for an answer," Janey volunteers. "He was pretty persistent in trying to get me to go out with him, even after it must've been clear I had no interest in him."

"He probably figured he'd be irresistible," Stephanie suggests. "I'm guessing that was his motivation for contacting you to be the rodeo's veterinarian. He's not bad-looking if you like the suave type, and he's got money and influence. Powerful aphrodisiacs for a lot of women."

"Not this one," Janey fires back.

I give her shoulders a squeeze. "Lucky for me."

"And bad for Jericho," the agent concludes. "We've had him under twenty-four-hour surveillance since Friday night, waiting for him to make a move. Unfortunately, we didn't know where he was heading when he took off in one of the park's maintenance trucks, or we'd have warned you sooner. In fact, I didn't realize where he was heading at first. He took the road to the airport and we thought for sure he was going to make a run for it, except he passed it and kept going. It wasn't until he turned off on a dirt road, pulled the truck into the trees, and continued on foot toward the creek, I realized we couldn't be that far from your place."

I'd told her how to get to my place when she called me yesterday to check in on Janey, who'd been napping at the time.

"Why go after Janey though?" I question. "Surely he'd know by now she no longer has the drugs."

"I don't think he was after the drugs. I'm pretty sure he was trying to kill her."

"That just doesn't make sense," I comment, tugging Janey closer to my side.

"I saw them, you know?" she pipes up beside me. "On Friday morning? I saw Jericho and Mackey; they were arguing about something. It was weird because I remember Jericho mentioning later, he hadn't seen Mackey since Thursday, but I'd just seen them hours earlier near the holding pens by the auction arena. I meant to tell you about that."

"There's your motive," Stephanie deduces.

Twenty-Three

JD

By the time I feel her stirring in my arms, gentle sunlight is already starting to filter through the curtains.

I haven't slept much. It's almost like I'm afraid if I let down my guard, some other threat is going to materialize.

Yesterday was chaos.

My peaceful patch of land invaded, the woman I was supposed to be protecting attacked, and federal agents in my house and around my property. Quiet returned around the time the sun set, but my body remained restless and my mind wouldn't stop churning out images of Janey, bloodied and broken, her vibrant blue eyes dull and unseeing.

My first instinct had been to pack Janey in my truck and hit the road. Take her somewhere where no one would think to look for us. Of course, not exactly a reasonable option.

Agent Kramer's assurances both Jericho and Mackey would remain safely in FBI custody helped. As did my father's calming presence. I'd called him to bring over boards so we could temporarily cover the broken sliding doors, and working side by side with him to make the trailer secure was a productive way to channel my lingering anxiety.

But the moment he left and it was just Janey and me, my muscles tensed up and my senses went on high alert. I had a hell of a time projecting calm confidence for Janey's sake. After all, she's the one who endured the trauma. *Again*.

So when we turned in for the night, I wrapped myself around her and watched over her while she slept.

I'm not stupid, I recognize it for what it is, I'm just not sure why I should experience a stress response to someone else's trauma. I've fucking spent all night practicing deep breathing, trying to calm the erratic beating of my heart.

"Did you get any sleep at all?"

Janey's soft voice and the gentle touch of her hand on my chest are soothing.

"Some."

"Liar," she returns, pushing herself up a little to look at me. "Your body is like a loaded spring. I can feel the tension in the muscles under your skin.

"I shouldn't have left you."

The long night has obviously given guilt a chance to settle at the forefront of my mind. But Janey doesn't hesitate to set me straight.

"Stop," she commands. "I'm responsible for myself. I'm responsible for my choices, and I'm the one who chose to sit outside on the deck after you left, making myself an easy target. Don't take on shit that doesn't belong to you."

"Still, I was supposed to—"

"Nothing," she cuts me off. "You weren't *supposed* to do anything. Not that I don't appreciate you looking out for me and taking care of me when I'm down, but don't treat me like I'm a job—an assignment—because that feels like an insult to me."

"An insult?" I echo, a bit taken aback. "I care about you."

"And I care about you, but if this is anything other than a two-way street, where we are equal partners and look out for each other when the need arises, count me out."

I'm not going to lie, that stings. Mainly because I can't imagine turning my back on her for any reason, I'm already too far gone.

Needing a moment to get my head together and avoid saying something I might come to regret; I swing my legs out of bed and head for the bathroom. Hopping in the shower, I brace myself against the wall and let the water pound down on my neck and back, trying to relieve some of the tension in my muscles.

I told Pa last night I wouldn't be in today, but maybe a solid day of physical labor will be good for me. I need to get out of my head before I risk fucking up what is probably the best thing that's ever happened to me. I don't just care about Janey, I'm pretty sure I'm in love with her and have been for a while. After being so patient in waiting for the right time to approach her, it would be a tragedy if I messed things up now.

I lift my head at the swoosh of the shower curtain sliding aside, revealing Janey, naked as the day she was born. The bruising and the cut on her face have become an almost familiar sight, but the injury to her leg stands out in stark contrast to her pale skin.

"You're not supposed to get your stitches wet," I caution her as she steps into the shower behind me.

"It's been forty-eight hours," she reminds me of what the nurse mentioned when Janey was discharged.

Without hesitation, she wraps her arms around me from behind, her hand sliding down to grasp around my rapidly growing cock.

"Janey," I caution her, grabbing onto her wrist. "You're injured."

"Hush," she mumbles with her lips pressed against my shoulder blade. "Put your hand back up on the wall, honey. I've got you."

She feels amazing, her full breasts plastered against my back, her lush hips rocking into mine, and her hands administering the most beautiful torture. With one strong hand stroking my length, she uses the other to cup and play with my balls while firmly rubbing my taint with the pad of a finger.

I rest my forehead against the tile, my mouth falling open as she plays me like a fine-tuned instrument. My soft pants are drowned out by the constant rush of the shower, until the tip of her finger slides precariously close to that tight sphincter muscle before pressing inside.

I erupt like fucking Vesuvius, coming in long strands that hit the wall and are washed down the drain with the water. She milks me dry, until my legs are shaking with the strain of staying upright. Then she wraps me firmly in her arms, keeping me standing until I can catch my breath.

My body is like gelatin, without real substance; every muscle completely relaxed.

"We take care of each other," she softly reminds me before stepping out of the shower.

She doesn't give me a chance to reciprocate.

I guess she's made her point.

～

I'm surprised how normal everything looks when I walk over to the clinic.

I'd asked JD to drop me off at my place this morning when he was heading out to High Meadow. I think my point in the shower this morning was well-taken, since he didn't launch an objection when I told him I needed to get back to the clinic.

Yesterday, Stephanie had mentioned her team would be packing up and moving out last night. They were transporting their prisoners back to Kalispell, but she indicated she'd be in touch.

"Feel good to be home, girl?" I mutter at Ginger, who walks beside me.

We make quite a pair, hobbling to the barn.

I feel much better today, the pain in my leg is more of an ache now, even without the meds I ditched yesterday, and my face just feels a little tight, even though it still looks pretty horrible. Evidence of that is the shocked look on Frankie's face when I walk into the clinic.

"Oh my God! Dale told me you'd gotten hurt, but I thought it was your leg. Your poor face."

Dale would be Deputy Bastian. I don't recall seeing him here on Friday night or yesterday at JD's place, but either way, I'm not surprised she heard. Libby is a small community, and there isn't much that stays secret for long.

"Looks worse than it is," I reassure her. "Once the bruising and swelling is down, you'll barely be able to tell."

At least I hope so. I'm not particularly vain, but I'd rather not have a gnarly zipper on my face.

"I'm surprised you're here at all," Frankie admits. "I was

about to start calling a few appointments I shifted from last week to this week. Are you sure you're able to work?"

"Absolutely. I'll take it easy if I need to, but I can't afford to let things go. Besides, Logan should be in to help with clinic hours this afternoon. I can let him do some of the work; if I need a break.

"What do I have going on this morning?" I ask, glancing at the appointment schedule she has up on her computer screen.

"Sandra Bowen is coming in with Gremlin for his teeth scaling, you have a follow-up appointment to see Daisy, and we rescheduled that surgery on Chet Weinstein's donkey to ten this morning."

Right, Gremlin, the snarling Chihuahua with serious periodontal issues, the sweet potbelly pig with pneumonia, and the miniature donkey with a large but benign tumor on his neck requiring removal since he keeps rubbing it open.

I'll have my hands full this morning, but first I want to pop into the barn. Jackson assured me the horses were fine when I walked into the house this morning, but I want to check on them myself.

Red sticks his head over the stall door, curious to see who just walked in. I'm surprised he allows me to rub his nose without withdrawing. I'm guessing he's becoming accustomed to his surroundings and starting to feel safe. I hope JD is still up for helping me rehabilitate this horse, because if this little nose rub is any indication, I think I'm going to love seeing Red's personality in full bloom.

But first I'm going to need to get the fencing around that field in the back fixed. It's not healthy for him to be cooped up in the barn all day. Half of the damn fence boards are either broken or hanging off the posts, and some of those are busted too. I'd get a start on it myself, but I'm not exactly in prime condition at the moment. Maybe Logan is interested in making some extra money, otherwise I'm going to have to call around to see who is available to help. I'm pretty sure JD would offer, but he already took days off last week for me, and in the evenings I'm selfish enough to want him spending time with me instead of out in the field.

When I move down the barn to the farthest stall, I'm hit with a flashback. The sound of the shot that hit me Friday night still echoes in my ears and, for a moment, the fear I felt is as real now as it was then. I force myself forward and into the present, taking those last few steps to look in on the barrel horse. She's a bit more cautious, staying out of reach in the stall, but when I open the door to check on her stitches, curiosity wins, and she nudges the pockets on my jeans.

"Looking for treats, girl? I'll remember that for next time."

I realize I don't even know her name, although I'm sure it would be in our notes somewhere. Between Logan and myself, we kept track of every animal we treated.

Her wound looks clean and those stitches can probably come out in the next day or so. I pat her neck and rub her nose before stepping out of the stall again. This time she follows, sticking her head over the door, so I give her some more attention.

I'm still not sure what's supposed to happen with her. I'd like to think the girl had family who would want to collect her horse eventually, but I don't really know. I haven't heard anything from Sheriff Ewing yet, but he probably still has his hands full with the investigation. I may give him a call after this morning's appointments.

Perhaps if she's still here after I get that fence fixed, we can try to introduce her to Red and she can keep him company in the field. Who knows? Maybe no one will claim her and she can stay.

I give her a last scratch under her chin and dismiss my fantasies. I don't really have time for those, I have a clinic to run.

~

By the time I report to the owner of Arthur, the large mass was successfully removed and he can pick up his pet donkey at the end of the day, after the animal sleeps off the anesthetic, I'm dead on my feet.

"I'll be in my office," I tell Frankie. "Oh, and can you check our pharmaceutical supplies and put in an order? We may be getting low on some stuff. I noticed there are only two vials of ketamine left."

I ache and it feels good to drop down in my seat, propping my leg up on an open desk drawer. I'm tempted to tilt my chair back and close my eyes for a few winks, but I have too much to do.

It's amazing how fast things pile up when you're out of the office, even for only a few days. There's a stack of mail I need to look at, bills that need paying, an inbox of emails requiring my attention, and a bunch of follow-up and return phone calls I need to make.

The first thing I do is put in a call to the sheriff's office. Sheriff Ewing is out of the office, so I leave a message for him to get back to me, when Frankie walks in.

"Thought you might need this," she says, setting a steaming mug of coffee in front of me.

"You are a saint," I mumble, reaching for it as I inhale the scent.

She snorts. "Hardly, although I was going to offer to

pick up something for lunch. Do you want a sandwich or something?"

"I wouldn't mind a club sandwich. Thanks, Frankie."

"Sure thing. I'll head out now."

As she's heading out the door, I start working my way through the stack of pink messages she left on my desk. Next, I tackle emails, and I'm still working on those when I hear the front door of the clinic open.

"Logan?" I call out.

"Yep," is the answer, as Logan pops his head in my door. "I didn't think you'd be back so soon," he says, shooting me his boyish grin. "Pretty badass."

I bark out a laugh and roll my eyes at him.

"Where is Frankie?" he asks.

"Gone to pick up some lunch. Hey, how did it go Saturday?"

He shrugs. "Fine."

"How was Dr. Feltner to work with?"

He was the other veterinarian Jericho called in to cover for me on Saturday.

"Okay, I guess. A bit of an ass, if you ask me, he barely said a word and wouldn't let me do anything other than hold the animals. I definitely like working with you better."

I grin at him.

"Flattery will get you everywhere," I joke, before turning to a different subject. "I have a question for you; how handy are you with a hammer and nails?"

His answer is in the way he scrunches up his face, looking pained.

"That good, huh?"

"I'm the only one in my class to fail shop in high school," he shares, lifting his hands and wiggling his fingers.

"It's a miracle I still have all my digits left. Why are you asking?"

"I need to find someone to fix the fence on that pasture in the back so we can put the horses out during the day."

Logan looks surprised. "Horses? More than one?"

That's right, I forgot he'd already gone home Friday afternoon when Sheriff Ewing asked me to look after the pinto. He wouldn't have known she was here.

"Shoot. I guess you missed that part. The sheriff asked me to temporarily board Lacey Del Franco's horse."

A shadow passes over his face at the mention of her name. I feel bad even bringing her up, but there's no way to avoid it with the animal boarded here.

"I noticed the horse was gone when I got to the grounds on Saturday, but I didn't know you had her," he admits.

"Yeah, she's our guest for now. At least until I find out from the sheriff what is going to happen with her."

As if summoned, my phone rings and Sheriff's Office appears on my display.

"Speak of the devil."

Logan slips out of my office as I answer the call.

Twenty-Four

JD

"In a hurry?"

I turn to find Thomas leaning against the railing of the porch as I head to my truck.

As much as I enjoyed the physical labor today, it did little to alleviate the gnawing worry about Janey. Which is why I'm rushing to get to her place.

Still, I tell Thomas, "Not really."

"Good, then you can join me for a drink. I wanna hear all about the excitement at the rodeo."

Guilt has me take the first step up to the porch.

Thomas reminds me of my grandpa, who also spent his last years sitting on his porch, watching the world go by. He'd ask me to sit down with him too, but I always had better things to do. I was too young to appreciate what I was missing out on, and I don't want to make that mistake twice.

Still, I quickly pull my phone from my pocket and shoot off a text to Janey.

How was your day? Are you home?

An answer comes back immediately.

Okay. Productive. Tiring. And yes. I'm just putting my feet up for a bit. How about you?

Done for the day. Having a quick drink with the old man before coming over. That okay?

Of course. Your father?

Ha. Don't be calling him an old man to his face.
No, Thomas. He missed out on all the gossip.

Ah. Gotcha. Spaghetti and meatballs okay? The meatballs are frozen, I don't have the energy for much more.

Leave cooking to me. You relax.

Well, if you insist. (Smiley face)

"Doc?" Thomas asks when I take the seat next to his rocker.

"Yeah. Just checking in."

"Good. Don't get too comfortable," he warns, handing me his empty tumbler. "I need a refill and you're gonna have to get your own."

I take his empty glass into the house, where I find my mother in the kitchen.

"The old coot con you into fetching him seconds?" Ma grumbles.

It's a daily struggle for Ma, who tries to keep Thomas to his one drink a day, and he uses every trick in the book to get his hands on more. I figure he derives more pleasure from besting my mother than the actual drink itself, but for an old rancher who can't do much more than sit on a porch and watch the world go by, it may be one of the few joys he has left.

"Come on, Ma, let up on the guy a little," I plead his case as I top up his glass from the bottle on top of the fridge. "What's the worst that could happen?"

She turns on me, her eyes glistening suspiciously.

"He could die," she says with emotion.

I set the glass down and walk up to her, pulling her into a hug.

"Would that be so bad?" I suggest gently. "What is he, ninety-three? At least he'd die a happy man."

"I'm not ready..."

Her response is barely audible.

"Ma..."

She steps out of my arms and turns her back, lifting her apron to wipe her face before bracing her arms on the counter by the sink, her eyes staring out the window.

"I may not be of his blood, but that old man is the only father I've ever known. I need more time."

My mother didn't have a great childhood. Her mother was an alcoholic, who pawned her daughter off to relatives most of her young life, and she never even knew who her father was. The hard outer shell Ma shows the world is her way of protecting herself and a direct result of her childhood experiences.

Sometimes it's hard to remember Ma shields a fragile heart.

I grab Thomas's glass and lean over my mother's shoulder to kiss her cheek. Then I bump her aside and turn on the faucet, tipping half of the bourbon down the drain and topping it up with water.

"I doubt he'll be able to tell the difference. He'll be too busy enjoying the illusion he got one over on you."

"Sneaky," she says, a faint smile on her lips as she nods her head. "I like it."

By the time I grab a beer from the fridge for myself and head back outside to join Thomas, Ma is by the sink, watering down the remains of the bourbon left in the bottle.

Twenty minutes later, I leave the old man happily dozing in his rocker and head over to Janey's.

∽

"Sterling gets to stay."

I lean back in my seat, while Janey fills me in on her conversation with Junior Ewing this afternoon.

Despite my offer to cook, she already had dinner going by the time I got here. I'd stopped off at the trailer to pick up a change of clothes, since I plan to spend the night here.

I'm not sure who she's talking about, but the news clearly makes her happy. I grin back at her smiling face.

"Sterling?"

Janey nods. "Yes. That's the name of the pinto; Lacey Del Franco's barrel horse."

She stacks our empty plates and starts getting up, when I stop her.

"You cooked; I clean."

She doesn't fight me when I take the dishes from her and carry them to the sink.

"So how did that come about?" I prompt her.

"Sheriff Ewing was in contact with the girl's father, he's her closest remaining relative. The guy works on an oil rig in the Gulf of Mexico and wants nothing to do with the horse," she explains. "Apparently, the father wasn't too supportive of his daughter's life choices. He told Ewing to send the damn horse to a glue factory."

I snort. "Aside from the fact those days are far behind us, he clearly doesn't know how much a decent barrel horse can bring." I turn on the faucet and run hot water in the sink. "Even a trained amateur horse can fetch an easy five grand to start," I add. "One as pretty as that pinto—if she shows promise—could go for quite a bit more than that."

Janey grins. "Obviously you know that, and I know that, and probably Ewing too." Her expression turns serious. "But clearly that man doesn't, and I don't feel even a little bit guilty about it. I find it hard to imagine any father being so callous and vindictive after finding out his only daughter died a violent death. I don't care how big the fight was when she chose her own path."

Point taken.

Still, I feel sad for the girl, and I hope a bitter father and an abandoned barrel horse isn't all she leaves behind in this world.

"You plan on keeping her?" I ask, throwing a glance over my shoulder.

"I thought she might make a good companion for Red."

I put the last plate in the dish rack and drain the water from the sink. Then I grab the towel hanging on the stove door and dry my hands.

I can tell she's excited about it and I don't really want to play devil's advocate and kill her joy, but I'm not so sure she's thought this through.

"You sure you have time for any horse? Let alone two? You're already pretty much burning the candle at both ends. Those horses are going to need—"

She stops me with a raised hand, a warning for caution in her eyes, and a clear reminder not to overstep.

"A little credit, please?"

~

Janey

A leopard doesn't change its spots, at least not in one day.

I'm sure his concerns come from a place of caring,

which is why I'm not jumping down his throat. His wince makes it clear he received the friendly message.

"First of all, I called Big Sky Lumber this afternoon and they're dropping off a load of boards to fix the fence around the field in the back. They put me in touch with a local handyman, who has time this week to come in and do the repairs."

"I could've done that for ya," JD offers with a hint of petulance.

"I know you could've and I figured you'd offer, but you also offered to help me with the house, and I'd much prefer you in here with me."

The scowl is quickly replaced with a wolfish grin.

"Is that a fact?" he drawls, pushing away from the counter as he stalks toward me.

"Hmm."

I tilt back when he braces one hand on the back of the chair, and plants the other on the kitchen table as he leans over me. His lips are soft on mine, but his tongue is demanding. I lift a hand and run my fingers through his short, thick hair, holding him close as he turns my limbs to jelly with only the touch of his mouth.

"What kind of *help* did you have in mind tonight?" he mumbles, his breath brushing the flush on my cheeks.

"Depends on what you feel up to," I whisper back, my body tingling in all the right places.

"Mmm, dangerous proposition, leaving that up to me, Angel. I'm afraid I'm up to more than you can handle in your current condition."

A smile stretches across my face as I challenge him, "Try me."

His nostrils flare as he curses under his breath. In the next moment, he grabs me under my arms and hauls me out of my seat. Next, he swiftly strips me out of my sweats and plants me with my bare ass on the edge of the kitchen table, before he sinks down in the chair I just vacated and gently lifts my legs over his shoulders.

"Lie back," he orders.

Oh, his mouth is talented, and I prop myself up on my elbows, just so I can watch his dark head between my thick, pale thighs as he goes down on me. When he adds his long slim fingers to the manipulations of his forceful tongue, it doesn't take long before my entire body quivers and I'm no longer able to hold myself up.

I can feel myself hurdling toward the edge of release, but just before I fly apart, his mouth and fingers suddenly disappear.

"No...don't stop," I plead, raising my head off the table.

I catch him shucking his jeans down his narrow hips, his fierce-looking cock springing free as he fishes a condom from his pocket and rolls it on.

"Gonna hurt you if I fuck you," he grinds out between clenched teeth. "I need you to set the pace."

With that he pulls me up, sits back down in the chair, and slowly impales me as he lowers me on his lap. No sooner is he rooted deep inside me, when he whips off my shirt, his hands curving around my naked back as his lips latch on to one of my breasts. I feel the deep tug of his mouth all the way down to my core, prompting me to move.

I barely notice the light tugging of the stitches in my leg as I ride him. Time doesn't exist, only the moaned mingling of our breaths, the blissful friction between our bodies, and two hearts racing in concert. It's only after I soar off the edge, and moments later JD spills inside me, awareness slowly returns.

"Are you cold?" he asks, his voice gentle and deep.

I shiver again, not so much from a chill as it is an after-shock of pleasure.

"No. I'm perfect right where I am."

Where I am is still nestled on his lap, surrounded by his warmth with his cock softening inside me. He kisses the hollow where my neck meets my shoulder and gently nips my skin between his teeth.

"I have to get rid of this condom, Angel."

I sit up and smile at him.

"Angel? Me?"

He shoots back a lopsided grin.

"Yeah. But one of those fierce ones, with a shield and sword."

I like it. I like that he sees me like that.

Twenty-Five

The smells of coffee and something deliciously sugary greet me when I walk into the kitchen.

Like me, JD is an early riser and was already in the shower when I woke up. Now he's standing at my stove, a big frying pan on the burner in front of him.

"Is that fry bread?" I ask, spotting the large disks of fried dough arranged on a few layers of paper towel on my counter. My mouth instantly waters.

"Ma used to make this on special occasions," JD says, flashing a smile over his shoulder. "Hardly nutritious. Basically carbs, fat, and sugar, which is why we only got this on birthdays or holidays."

I poke at one of the pieces and come away with a finger covered in sugar and cinnamon I quickly pop in my mouth.

"What's the special occasion today?"

I brace myself against the kitchen counter, facing him. He leans over and drops a sweet kiss on my lips.

"I can think of a few things," he shares, his eyes warm on my face before he returns his focus to the pan. "Simply waking up to you is cause enough for celebration, but I'm also just glad the dust is settling and we can focus on what's happening with us."

He says he doesn't have a way with words, but I sure like the things he's saying. I brush his cheek with a kiss.

"Why don't I get us set up with some coffee," I offer, as he lifts the final piece of dough from the pan and turns off the burner.

While I fix us a couple of mugs, JD grabs two plates and loads up the fried pastry. Then we sit down at the kitchen table.

"This looks delicious."

I pick up a piece and sink my teeth into the sweet, crispy dough. Unfortunately, that is the moment I glance to the front window and see a black SUV pulling up in front of the house. A sheriff's cruiser is right behind it.

"We've got company," I mumble around the bite in my mouth.

I'm already on my feet when JD swings around and catches wind of what's going on. I have the front door open when Special Agent Kramer and Sheriff Ewing walk up.

"Sorry for the early hour," Stephanie apologizes.

"We were up." I step to the side to let them in, noticing the serious expression they're both wearing. "Did something happen?"

JD, who followed me to the front door, wraps his arm around my waist and tugs me to his side.

"Sheriff Ewing has requested my assistance on the murder cases of Maggie Aldridge, Jennifer Wilson, and Lacey Del Franco," the FBI agent clarifies. "There have been some new developments, which is why we're here."

"I'm not sure how much help I can be," I offer. "I only met Lacey briefly and I didn't know the other two women."

"There's another woman missing," Sheriff Ewing informs us.

"Another one?"

He nods at me, before looking at JD. "Britt Jensen."

I feel JD's body go rigid beside me.

"She's a waitress and disappeared in the middle of her shift at Foxy's Bar last night," Stephanie fills in.

Foxy's Bar?

Britt.

I immediately have a vision of the pretty brunette server hopping up in JD's arms. Hard to believe that was just a little over a month ago. It feels a lot longer, so much has happened. So much has changed.

"Britt?" he echoes, clearly stunned.

"Her purse was still behind the bar and her car parked in the parking lot," the agent continues. "She was seen slipping out the back around eleven, presumably for a smoke, but never returned. It was busy last night, but no one saw a thing."

"You know her?" Ewing addresses JD.

"I do," he admits, and I instinctively slip an arm around his waist, holding on tight.

"We were told you're seeing each other."

"*Were,*" JD clips. "And seeing each other implies a relationship, which it never was. We'd hooked up a few times, that's all. And that was a while ago."

"Are you sure?" the agent questions, taking over for Sheriff Ewing. "The bartender saw you two kissing just last month."

"She was kissing me," he argues. "There's a difference."

My head is spinning, trying to keep up with what is

happening. Are they seriously suspecting JD? That's ridiculous.

"Look," I interrupt, positioning myself in front of JD. "I don't know what you are getting at, but he was with me. All night. You are barking up the wrong tree. He had nothing to do with her disappearance."

The look I get from Stephanie is one of pity, and I don't like it one bit.

"Are you positive he couldn't have slipped out at some point during the night?"

"One-hundred-percent," I snap back. Then I look from the agent to Ewing. "I can't believe you would even entertain something so ridiculous."

"We went by the trailer this morning," the sheriff volunteers, looking at JD over my shoulder. "To ask you a few questions. See if maybe you'd seen or heard anything."

"I stopped by my place after work to pick up a few things before I came here, but that was before six last night."

Stephanie Kramer pulls a plastic baggie from her pocket with an empty vial inside. One I recognize immediately.

"Then perhaps you can explain how this ended up next to your front steps?"

"What is that?" JD asks.

"Ketamine," I whisper, as my mind spins.

JD

"Maggie Aldridge, Jennifer Wilson, and Lacey Del Franco all had ketamine in their system. Lacey Del Franco also had the broken needle of a syringe embedded in her neck," Ewing explains.

A cold fist squeezes my chest. I hear the words, but I'm having trouble processing them.

"You happened to be the one to find two out of the three known victims, and are intimately familiar with a possible fourth. We found the empty vial of ketamine at your trailer. You've been spending a lot of time with Doc Richards, and would've had relatively easy access to the drug. All of it is pointing to you. Unless you have some explanation?" Stephanie Kramer lays it out in a gentler tone.

It's like my mouth is glued shut. It feels like a noose tightening around my neck, even though I had absolutely nothing to do with this.

"Are his fingerprints on the vial?" Janey asks sharply.

"No fingerprints," Ewing admits before adding, "but he could've worn gloves."

"Careful enough to wear gloves, only to toss the vial in his front yard? This is such bullshit!" Janey reacts forcefully. "And the worst part is, you both know it. I can see it in your faces. You can't possibly believe what you're suggesting."

Stephanie puts up her hands. "We're not suggesting anything. We're investigating leads, and at this point what we have is leading us here."

"He's being set up," Janey protests. "Surely you can see that."

Feeling crowded in the small hallway, I slip out from behind Janey, turn my back on the group, and walk into the living room. The pressure on my chest releases a bit and I'm able to take in a deep breath.

"Do you have any enemies?" I hear Stephanie ask behind me.

I turn to face her.

"I would've said no prior to last week, but I know Phil Jericho didn't like me around Janey. He wasn't exactly a fan," I suggest. "The only problem with Jericho is that I doubt he knew of my existence prior to the rodeo and, by that time, the first two victims were already dead. Plus, he's in custody, so he couldn't have been responsible for Britt's disappearance."

"Maybe he has someone helping him?" Janey proposes, sidling up to me.

She's reaching, even as she anchors herself to my side. I'm not sure whether it's for her benefit or mine, but I'm grateful for the unconditional support.

"Considering Jericho for these murders is a bit of a stretch," Stephanie Kramer states. "First of all, he's too smart. I can't see him risk drawing that kind of negative attention to the rodeo. He's got too much invested in his drug trafficking operation to jeopardize it by drawing in law enforcement. And that's aside from the fact the first two victims were found prior and weren't related to the event in any way."

No matter how hard I think about it, I can't imagine anyone hating me enough to try and frame me for murder.

"What if it isn't something personal at all?" I suggest. "And I was simply a convenient scapegoat?"

It's clear my suggestion is met with some doubt, but I push on.

"What if the reason someone hit me over the head when I was poking around the trailers the day of the auction had nothing to do with the drugs? The timing could work with Lacey Del Franco's disappearance, unless you have witnesses who saw her that Thursday night."

I catch a glance exchanged between Ewing and the agent, before he faces me.

"Last time anyone saw her was before the auction," he admits. "Okay, let's assume you almost stumbled onto something and our perp panicked, hit you over the head, and took off. The issue I have with that is, the attack on you was witnessed by an agent, and law enforcement was on high alert instantly. If anything illegal was going on in that parking lot, we would've found it."

"Unless...it wasn't so much about *what* JD might see, but *who*," Stephanie contributes. "Someone who would've stood out, who was out of place."

"Who wasn't where they were supposed to be," Ewing fills in.

It would have to have been someone I know. I immediately try to think of who that might be, but those options are endless. I live in this town—I do my groceries here, work here, get my hair cut—I interact with people on a daily basis who would recognize me. It could've been anyone.

A phone rings, and Stephanie reaches for her pocket.

"Excuse me a minute," she indicates, walking toward the front door and stepping outside.

"Hey," Ewing gets my attention, "We're doing our job. Not an easy job and even harder when you have to look at people you know and like. Three women are dead, maybe four, and we can't afford to dismiss any leads, just because we think you're a good guy. Gotta follow the evidence."

I nod. I get what he's saying, even though it doesn't make being on this side of the equation any more comfortable.

I don't get a chance to respond when Stephanie comes barging in, her eyes on the sheriff.

"That was Agent Furstner, I've gotta get back to Kalispell. Jericho has asked to talk to me, claims he has information on the murders. He wants to make a deal."

"Of course he does," Ewing replies. "Do you believe him?"

The agent shrugs. "I don't know, he may be yanking my chain, but I won't know for sure until I talk to him. You've got things handled here?"

Ewing nods. "Call me with any updates."

"Same goes," she answers him before turning to me.

She opens her mouth to say something but appears to change her mind, shaking her head. Then she raises her hand before turning on her heel and heading out the door.

When she's gone, I turn to Ewing.

"Is anybody looking for Britt?"

My tone may be a bit sharp, but the past half hour has been a fucking roller coaster and he's lucky I'm hanging onto my temper. If not for Janey grounding me, I'd have lost it a while ago.

"Of course," he returns defensively. "I have deputies crawling all over the bar and surrounding area."

"Did you call Jonas?"

"I plan to, after I'm done here."

He removes his hat and runs a hand through his hair. He looks like he's aged ten years in the past few weeks.

As sheriff of Lincoln County, I know the man is stretched thin as it is. Especially since the Libby Police Department—which was a tiny department to begin with—has become virtually nonexistent in recent years. It's all on Ewing's shoulders, and the sheriff's department isn't really equipped to handle crimes like drug trafficking or the murders of those women. Even more so now, with his only detective—Dan's wife, Sloane— on bed rest and about to pop a baby.

"I'll get the guys together," I offer, knowing the best

chance Britt has is for the High Mountain Trackers team to get out there as soon as possible.

That is, if she's still alive.

He rubs his face and squeezes the bridge of his nose, apparently struggling to make a decision.

"Divide and conquer," I add when he takes too long to respond.

"Fine," he finally agrees. "Get the team ready, meet up with Deputy Bastian at the bar, and I'll join you when I'm done here."

I turn to Janey—who has been pretty quiet since her passionate defense of me—and cup her face.

"I'll be in touch," I promise, dropping a kiss on her lips. "Be careful."

She nods. "Go. Find her."

Twenty-Six

Janey

"Who has access?"

After Special Agent Kramer and JD left, Sheriff Ewing asked to see the clinic.

I figured it would be about the ketamine.

We walk over, finding the clinic still locked up. Frankie isn't here yet but I expect she'll get here shortly.

"To the clinic? Frankie Bastian, my assistant, and you met my intern, Logan."

"Yes, I know Frankie, her brother is one of my deputies, and Logan is the son of council member David Osborne."

"That's correct."

I open the clinic door and invite him inside.

"Nobody else has a key?"

"No. Not as far as I know. But I never changed the locks after I took over the clinic from Doc Evans. I guess it's possible he may have given a key to someone at some point I'm not aware of."

"You're keeping drugs, you should change your locks."

"All medication is in a locked, steel cabinet and I'm the only one with a key to that. I bought it new when I moved in," I react a bit defensively. "I also keep careful track of what I've used."

I show him into our surgical room where I keep the drugs, and unlock the cabinet.

"Who does inventory?"

"My tracking system does it for me. I don't carry a lot of stock, and as I said, I mark everything I use off the inventory list. When we get down to a certain level, I ask Frankie to order more, and we tend to order a set amount. Ketamine, for instance," I start to explain. "Yesterday morning I noticed we were getting low when I needed it for surgery on a miniature donkey. We were down to two vials, so I alerted Frankie, who was going to put in an order."

"And you've never had one go missing? Not even a half-empty one?"

I shake my head. "No, never."

"Is that the log?" Ewing asks, pointing at the notebook hanging on the front of the cabinet door.

I grab it off and hand it to him.

"You can see every use is marked by date and time. The amount is then deducted, and we list what is left in inventory. Because I only stock small numbers, it's easy to track."

He flips to the section marked ketamine, and starts scanning the entries.

"Who stocks the cabinet when a new shipment arrives?"

"I do that myself. If I'm out on a call, Frankie will sign for the package and hang on to it until she can hand it over to me. Unopened," I add.

I watch him lift the remaining vials of ketamine off the shelf and examine them.

"These are still sealed."

"Yes, like I said, I used some yesterday for a surgery. That vial was empty."

"What did you do with the empty vial?"

"Garbage."

I jerk my thumb at the trash can in the corner next to the cabinet. He immediately pokes his head in.

"Did someone clear out the trash?"

"One of us usually does at the end of the day."

"Who did it yesterday?"

I shrug. "I'm not sure. I spent a lot of the afternoon in my office, so I didn't see."

"Where does the trash go?"

I'm not sure what his fascination with my trash is, but I walk him through the clinic and out the back door. There's a green, steel box with a bear-proof lid installed against the back wall of the clinic.

"I have a garbage collection service come by once every two weeks to collect what's in there."

"When was your last pick up?" Ewing asks as he opens the box and peeks inside.

"Usually on a Thursday. I'm pretty sure they were here last week, but Frankie could probably tell you that when she gets in."

"Only three small bags in there now, so that would make sense."

The sheriff reaches into the bin and pulls out one of the bags.

"What are you looking for?" I ask, when he pulls a pair of gloves from his back pocket, snaps them on, and tears open the plastic.

"The empty vial. Agent Kramer took the one we

collected at JD's trailer, but I memorized the lot number. It matches the number on the vials in your cabinet."

"You think someone took it from my garbage and left it there?"

He shrugs. "If someone was intent on framing JD…"

He reaches into the bag and comes up with the empty vial I dropped in there.

"Damn," he mutters under his breath, at the same time Frankie's car pulls around the back of the barn.

"Morning," she greets us a bit hesitantly, as she exits the car and walks over to us.

"Morning, Frankie," I return.

The sheriff just nods at her.

"Did something happen?" she asks him, looking concerned.

"I have a few questions for you," he replies, before dropping the bag back in the bin and taking off his gloves.

He motions for us to go ahead and follows us inside. There he asks Frankie mostly the same questions he asked me. I know it's his job and he's being thorough, but I still breathe a sigh of relief when she confirms everything I told him.

That is, until she brings up my veterinary kit.

"Yes, I put the order through yesterday. We always order when we get down to two," she explains, before adding. "Although I guess technically it's four, since Dr. Richards always carries two in her medical bag for emergencies."

My mouth falls open, I'd totally blanked on those.

"I'm so sorry. I forgot about those. I rarely use ketamine outside of the clinic."

Ewing looks at me sharply. "Where do you keep the bag?"

"Locked in the back of my truck."

"Who has access to your truck?" He wants to know next.

"I do. I may leave it unlocked when I'm on a call somewhere, but then I carry my bag with me."

"You had it with you at the rodeo?"

I nod. "Yes."

"Had your eyes on it at all times?"

"Well..."

I can't exactly make that claim. Things were crazy busy at times, and I guess someone could've grabbed something out of there without me noticing.

"Where's the bag now?"

I'm already heading outside where my truck is parked, Ewing right on my heels. My heart is lodged in my throat as I unlock the cover on the back and pull out my kit. Setting it on the tailgate, I flip it open and rummage through. When I come up with only one single vial of ketamine, my heart sinks down to my stomach.

Oh my God.

I feel all the blood drain from my face.

The thought I might have in any way—however remotely—been connected to the deaths of those poor women makes me sick to my stomach.

"You're sure you did not use the other vial," Ewing prompts.

"Positive," I whisper.

"And you didn't see anyone near your bag."

At the rodeo, it could've been anyone. One of Mackey's hands, any of the participants, heck, even someone in the public deciding to have a closer look. There were plenty of those, which was the whole purpose of Jericho putting me at the front of the stockyards.

I shrug my shoulders. "Not that I recall. Either Logan or

JD were with me most of the time. They would've seen and said something."

"I'll have to talk to them both. When is Logan supposed to be here?"

"I told him this week he could come in around noon, because he put in a lot of hours covering for me both here and at the rodeo last week."

"I'll track both of them down this morning. In the meantime, do me a favor and keep your damn bag with you at all times."

With that, he stalks back to his cruiser still parked in front of my house.

I grab my kit, close the gate on my truck, and head back into the clinic.

~

JD

"You're kidding."

"Not even a little bit," I tell Jonas.

He hopped in my truck after we loaded up the horses to head over to Foxy's Bar, and asked for an update. I've just filled him in on the early morning law enforcement visit, and the evidence they discovered suggesting I was involved.

The fact Jonas doesn't even stop to entertain the possibility I might have had something to do with these crimes makes me feel a little better. Despite realizing neither Ewing or Stephanie Kramer really believes in my involvement, their line of questioning had left me shaken up. Adding to my unease is the fact someone went through a lot of trouble to implicate me, possibly going so far as to snatch an innocent woman because of her connection to me.

That's the part that makes me sick to my stomach. Because even if we are able to find her alive, I will always carry some responsibility for what happened to her.

"Let me give fucking Junior a piece of my mind," Jonas grumbles, retrieving his phone from a pocket.

I stop him. "Don't. Don't distract him from catching the bastard who is doing this. That's where his focus should be."

He grumbles some more under his breath, but ends up tucking his phone away.

The rest of the relatively short drive to Foxy's is silent, but when I pull into the parking lot, Jonas pipes up.

"I want you to man the command post."

I pull into a spot next to one of the sheriff's cruisers and glance over at him.

"Like hell I will."

He turns to face me. "You already found two of the victims, you don't need to find another one. Especially not a friend."

I want to launch an objection, but the steel look he shoots me has me hesitate and think. I can't forget Agent Kramer listed the fact I found two of the three victims as highly suspect. Probably better if I didn't add a third. I already can't get the images of those two women out of my head, and I didn't know them. Finding Britt in a similar condition would seriously mess me up, and I feel in my gut she's already dead.

I hope to God I'm wrong.

"We're going in with the original team. Fletch, Sully, Bo, and myself. Dan's sticking around the ranch because of Sloane, Wolff is coming in with Jillian but he's helping search with the dogs," Jonas continues. "And I want you and Jackson to fly the Matrice and direct us from above. You're familiar with this area, so you know what you're looking at and are best equipped to navigate for us, even if we were to split up."

I nod. I don't necessarily like it, but what he says makes sense.

I get out of the truck and head around the back to grab the equipment we loaded up, just as Sully pulls up with the large horse trailer.

The bar is closed for business, but some of the staff are in the building with a few deputies, so we set up outside on the covered patio in the back. I much prefer being out here—for one thing, it's easier flying the Matrice drone—and I like the fresh air. It's pretty dark in the bar. Under the overhang we still don't need to set up a tent or even unload the generator, because we can tap into the bar's electrical to run the computers.

While Jonas goes to talk with Deputy Bastian—who was left in charge—Jackson and I set up the equipment. It only takes about fifteen minutes and by the time we're up and ready, the others have the horses ready and are mounting up to head out.

Four tough, aging cowboys, still looking pretty imposing as a group. Everything us younger guys know about search and rescue, about tracking, we learned from these guys. I catch Pa looking at me, sending me the slightest of nods. His way of assuring me they've got this, but I already knew that.

I watch as they ride off before turning my attention to the monitors. The Matrice is already up in the air, scoping out the lay of the land.

"They're still poking around your trailer," Jackson points out.

On the screen I can see two cruisers parked in front of my place and a couple of uniforms standing off to the side. I recognize one of them as Junior Ewing. He must've gone straight there from Janey's house.

Thinking of Janey, I grab my phone and type out a quick message.

> Everything okay there?

I don't have to wait too long for a response.

> Sort of. Vial of ketamine missing from my kit.
> Probably taken at rodeo. Sick over it.

Shit. I was afraid that might be a possibility when she so quickly identified the vial found at my place as ketamine. Looks like an overinflated sense of responsibility is something we both suffer from.

> Don't take that on.

Sage advice I should probably take myself.

. . .

Right. Lumber delivery is here, gotta go. You be careful.

I forgot about the fencing. Well, hopefully it's something that'll help to keep her mind off things.

You too, Angel.

"Angel?"

I turn to Jackson, who is peeking at my phone, grinning wide.

"Fuck off and mind your own business."

He shrugs and turns back to his screen. "It's cute, but Doc doesn't strike me as particularly angelic," he comments.

"Avenging angel," I clarify, grinning at the image of Janey stepping in front of me as she went off on Ewing and Kramer this morning.

"That makes more sense," Jackson concedes.

∼

"Anything?"

I turn my head to find the sheriff behind us.

He stopped by earlier this morning, indicating he was off to run down some leads but would be back to check on progress. Unfortunately, we have little to report. We've had to replenish batteries for the Matrice once already, and are currently providing aerial support for the dog team.

Wolff radioed in about ten minutes ago, one of Jillian's dogs seemed suddenly hot on a trail. Unfortunately, the dog in question is Emo. That news settled heavy on my shoulders.

"Jillian's cadaver dog picked up on a scent. Not sure what it is yet, but we're following with the drone."

I point at the screen where we can see flashes of yellow popping in and out of the tree cover. The safety vests Jillian and her dogs wear when they're on the job.

"Do we know anything more?" I turn the question on him. "Heard from Stephanie?"

Jackson suddenly pays attention at the mention of the agent's name, confirming what I suspected.

"Not a peep. I suspect Jericho is yanking her chain and this is a pitiful attempt at controlling his fate. Other than that, I just wasted almost two and a half hours tracking down Doc Richards's intern without success."

"Logan?"

He confirms with a nod. "Councilman Osborne wasn't too pleased I showed up at his house looking to speak to his son, so that was half an hour of him insisting I tell him exactly what this was about, and me reminding him his son is a legal adult, while trying not to plant my fist in the man's face. The rest of the time I drove around to all the locations his mother finally listed as places I might be able to find the kid. I finally gave up. I'll catch him back at the clinic this afternoon."

I wouldn't have had the patience to deal with difficult parents, which is why the High Mountain Trackers is a much better fit for me than any kind of law enforcement.

Something niggles at me though. Maybe it's the fact

Logan's father serves on the same council as Phil Jericho. They're colleagues at the very least. Probably just a coincidence, Libby is a relatively small town and it isn't hard to find connections between people. Or maybe it's that despite the appearance of being a nice guy, Logan is just another typical, spoiled rich kid like the ones I grew up with, wearing designer jeans and snakeskin boots while the rest of us walk around in worn out hand-me-downs.

Snakeskin boots. The memory is suddenly clear as day.

Just as I'm about to share it with Ewing, his phone rings.

"What've you got?"

I watch his face change as he listens to whoever is on the other side, and I get an unsettled feeling in the pit of my stomach.

When his eyes turn to me, I already know the news is bad.

Twenty-Seven

JANEY

"Some of these posts need replacing too."

I'm out here showing the handyman, who was able to come in for a few hours today, where the fence needs fixing.

"I know," I tell him. "There's a bunch in that pile of lumber behind the barn they dropped off earlier."

"Good."

He nods, giving the rotting post a final shake and marking it with a spray can, before moving on to the next one.

It's a bit silly for me to follow him around the entire perimeter. I may as well head back to the clinic, I need to give my leg a break because it's starting to ache. I've been on my feet too much already today.

I'm about to tell him as much when I hear my name called.

"Doc?"

Frankie comes jogging up to me, her pink Chucks no match for the muddy, overgrown field she finds me in.

"What's up?"

"We have an emergency," Frankie announces, breathing heavily when she reaches me.

"What kind of emergency?"

"A crash involving a truck hauling a small trailer with two horses out on Flower Lake Road near the Nordic ski trails. Both horses injured."

"Shit. No sign of Logan yet?"

"No."

I turn to Will Figueira. "You can find your way around from here?"

"Yeah, yeah," he replies, waving me off.

"Need anything, talk to my assistant."

I start heading back to the clinic with Frankie trying to keep up with me.

"Look, if you prefer, I can try and get a hold of Dr. Feltner. See if he can go?"

I shake my head.

"It'll take too long."

Flower Lake Road runs up the mountain right behind us. It wouldn't make sense to call in Sam Feltner, his office is on the north side of town and it would take him too long to get there.

I rattle off a list of things I might need as we make our way back to the clinic. Inside I quickly change into coveralls, while Frankie stocks my kit with the extra supplies. Within five minutes I'm in my truck, heading out.

Flower Lake Road is little more than a dirt road, snaking up the mountain. There isn't much along here, a few trailheads, the lake, and the ski trails that are mostly used for ATVs in the summertime. There may be a few hunting cabins up farther, but little else. I follow Snowshoe Road past the golf course where I have to take a right turn up the mountain.

I drive for a few minutes without encountering another vehicle, which kind of surprises me. I would've expected maybe emergency vehicles heading to the site of the accident. Personally, I wouldn't want to haul a trailer up this road, but I guess to each their own. I assume these people were looking for a good spot to take the horses for a ride. It's definitely pretty up here.

Driving past the small dirt parking lot of a trailhead, I notice it's empty. There's no sign of any accident, and nothing visible on the road when I pass by the Nordic Ski Club. I'm starting to wonder if maybe we got the directions wrong.

Then I round the next curve and see an ATV on its side in the middle of the road. A pickup and horse trailer are off to the side, butting up against the tree line. I notice the back of the trailer is down.

I pull up behind the trailer and start getting out of the truck, wondering what is going on. Maybe the horses were spooked and took off? I scan the woods around me but don't see any movement. Puzzled, I walk up to the back of the trailer and peer inside.

The next moment a hand clamps over my mouth and, before I can react, I feel a sharp stab in my neck. I try to struggle briefly, before my body grows heavy and my muscles become nonresponsive. I feel myself getting dragged into the back of the trailer, and there is nothing I can do.

Next, everything goes black.

∽

My arms feel like they're being pulled from their sockets.

I cry out as I'm bounced around.

I'm trying to wrap my head around what is happening and where I am, but I can't will my eyes to open. All I know is that my arms are suspended above me and my body is heavy.

My olfactory senses provide the first clues when I notice a few familiar smells; fresh straw, horse manure, and a hint of gasoline.

I'm in the back of the horse trailer, and it's moving.

It's coming back to me now, the emergency call, the Nordic club, the accident. But that wasn't a real accident, was it? That was a setup. Someone had been lying in wait for me, and injected me with something.

Ketamine?

It would fit. It knocks you out quickly and, depending on how much you're given, the effects can wear off in as little as ten to fifteen minutes. It feels like I haven't been out that long. It's possible they underestimated my size and miscalculated the dosage. An unexpected benefit to being a couple of pounds overweight.

I try my eyes again, and this time I manage to open them slightly, blinking a few times to clear my vision. The first thing I see are my hands zip-tied to the horizontal bar across the front of the trailer. It's a safety bar that braces against a horse's chest to prevent injury to the head or neck in case of a sudden brake.

Then I struggle to lift my head, which is tilted back, and see the ATV inside the trailer. I'm guessing the same ATV I saw lying on its side in the road. I notice a set of keys dangling from the ignition just underneath the handlebars.

If only I could get the rest of my body to work, there may be a way I can get out of this. If only I could get my hands out of these damn zip ties. I could get on the ATV, and the moment that gate comes down, I can floor it out of here.

As I wiggle my fingers and move my feet as best I can, I'm trying to think of anything that might clue me in to who grabbed me. I never saw his face, and didn't recognize the truck or trailer either.

Slowly some control returns to my extremities and I manage to get up on my feet, bracing myself against the safety bar. But before I have a chance to test the strength of my binds, the truck slows down and comes to a halt. I pull and twist, trying to get loose, but all I manage to do is break the skin on my wrist.

Too late, I consider maybe I should've pretended to still be out cold when the gate starts coming down. I squint my eyes against the bright sun backlighting the shadowed form peering into the trailer, but I end up identifying him by his voice.

"You're awake."

~

JD

"Where is she?"

Frankie startles when I come barreling into the clinic, immediately ducking past her and poking my head into the treatment room and her office. Both are empty.

"Out on a call? Why?"

Because she's not answering, that's why.

I've been trying Janey's cell the entire drive here but keep getting bumped to her voicemail.

I hopped in the passenger seat of Ewing's cruiser, leaving Jackson to deal with the search. My blood had run cold when he relayed his call with Stephanie Kramer. She hadn't told him much, other than to say Jericho had brought up Logan Osborne, but was using holding the concrete evidence he claims to have hostage in return for his own immunity.

She'd stepped out of the meeting because she was concerned about Janey. As it turns out, from my countless unanswered calls to her phone, a very valid concern I share, and clearly Junior Ewing does as well, since he drove us to the clinic in record time.

"Tell me about the call," I snap at Frankie, leaning over her desk.

Her eyes are wide as she leans back to get as far away from me as she can. Probably wise, because my rage is bubbling right under the surface.

"JD, back off," Junior Ewing barks at me. "You're angry at the wrong person." Then he turns to Frankie, and says in a much gentler tone, "It's urgent we find Doc Richards."

She nods and starts talking. "We got a call for two horses injured in a crash somewhere up on Flower Lake Road, near the Nordic trails."

"Where did the call come from?" the sheriff probes.

"I'm not sure, I assumed it was someone involved in the accident or maybe a passerby."

"You didn't recognize the voice?"

She shakes her head. "Not really. It was a man, and he sounded pretty frantic, said the horses were in bad shape, and hung up before I could ask more questions."

I flip her desk phone around and push a few buttons to check the incoming call list. The last number comes up as unlisted. *Of course it is.*

"What about Logan? Where is he?" I ask, which earns me a warning look from Ewing.

"He's not here yet." She glances at the clock in the waiting room. "He called maybe five minutes ago to let us know he'll be a bit later. Something about his engine stalling, and he's waiting for his dad and a tow truck."

Like fucking hell he is. I'm already halfway to the cruiser when Ewing catches up to me.

"I told her to lock up and wait for a deputy," he tells me as he slides behind the wheel. "I'm gonna have to pull some manpower off the search for Britt."

As much as I hate that, it's the right call to make.

"If he has Janey, my gut says we're already too late for Britt," I suggest.

"Yeah. I'm of the same mind."

He puts a call out to get a cruiser to the clinic, and a few more to meet us up by the Nordic club. We have no idea what we're walking into.

When we drive past the Cabinet View Golf Course, Ewing points out the window.

"Jennifer Wilson, our second victim, was found right there. Not that far from the clinic, or from where we're headed."

"You're thinking that's not a coincidence?"

He shakes his head. "I think the proximity is convenience on his part, not necessarily planned. I think it shows a certain impulsiveness and a lack of planning."

"Then what about the first victim? The one we found near the Swede Mountain Lookout?"

He shoots me a glance before focusing back on the winding road and taking the turnoff toward Flower Lake.

"Phil Jericho's place is on Obsidian Road, right at the turnoff onto Swede Mountain Road," he shares.

I turn my head and look back in the direction of Swede Mountain on the other side of the valley.

"Jericho and Logan's father both sit on the city council," I think out loud, following the same train of thought I had earlier at the search site.

"More than that," Ewing explains. "They're in each other's pocket, politically speaking. They travel in the same circles, play golf together on a regular basis."

"So logically Jericho and Logan would've known each other," I conclude.

I'm trying to remember if I'd seen them interact at any time during the rodeo, but I don't think they ever spoke, at least not in my presence. Which is kind of weird in itself; you'd think they'd at least acknowledge each other. Unless they were trying to avoid anyone knowing.

I'm having trouble wrapping my head around all the possible connections and implications, as I go over some of the events of the past week in my mind.

"It was Logan," I blurt out as Ewing navigates a particularly sharp turn in the narrow road.

"What are you talking about?"

"He's the one who hit me over the head. Earlier, I recalled the last thing I saw when I hit the ground was a pair of boots. Snakeskin boots. The kind he wears."

"That could have been around the time of the attack on Lacey Del Franco. He probably didn't want to be caught hanging around the trailers, and—"

He abruptly cuts off and leans forward, squinting through the windshield.

"Is that Doc's truck?"

I spot the white cover on the back of her truck sticking up from the deep ditch on the side of the dirt road. I have the door open, jump out, and start running before Ewing brings the cruiser to a full stop.

I slide on my ass down the embankment to the front of the truck, which is wedged at the bottom of the ditch, that is thankfully dry. I brace myself and yank the driver's side door open, which gives away easily. Airbags bulge out, and I grab the knife I carry on my belt to deflate them and get them out of my way, so I can see inside.

The truck's cab is empty.

"She's not here!" I call out to Ewing.

Then I notice the gearshift is set in neutral. It's possible that happened as a result of the impact, but my gut tells me no one was in the truck when it went down into the ditch. I find her phone in the footwell of the driver's seat, still powered up but with a cracked screen.

When I scramble back up to the road, Ewing appears to be studying the dirt.

"Looks like the tracks of an ATV, and up ahead it looks like something was parked partially on the grass shoulder."

I follow the ATV tracks to the edge of the road. Where they disappear there is a sharp, deep indentation about four or five feet wide.

"The ATV was loaded onto a trailer," I tell Ewing as I walk up the road a little ways. "The tire tracks go farther up the mountain. What's up there?"

"Not much. Up ahead the road curves back on the other side of Flower Lake where it ends. Not much up there other than a handful of hunting cabins."

I pull out my phone and call Jackson.

"Got her?" he asks right away.

"No. Her truck is in a ditch, but I'm pretty sure she wasn't in there at the time. I need the Matrice here at the

Nordic Ski Club up on Flower Lake Road. We're looking for a truck and trailer, possibly a horse trailer," I add.

It's only a guess, but that's what Janey would've been looking for, since the emergency call that came in was for a pair of horses injured in a vehicle crash. I don't think she'd have gotten out of her truck otherwise.

"Give me fifteen minutes. I need to slap in a fresh battery pack, I'll fly her out from here and we'll follow in the truck."

"We?"

"Yeah. We'll be packing up shortly."

Just then Ewing's radio crackles to life.

"Why?"

I ask the question, but don't really want to know the answer.

"Jillian and Emo found her."

Fuck.

Twenty-Eight

JANEY

"Logan?"

He climbs into the trailer and smiles his familiar charming boy smile; innocent and eager to please. Except, he's not so innocent, is he?

My mind is still sluggish, trying to process all the puzzle pieces that suddenly tumble into place. Flashes of moments in time. Mental screenshots of events, interactions, encounters, all clearer from this new perspective.

I feel ill, suddenly recognizing the friendly smile he shows me as something infinitely darker. More sinister.

"It was time, Janey," he says benevolently.

The fact he's using my first name instead of the customary, "Doc," sends shivers down my spine. It suggests an intimacy that exists only in his mind, and that in itself is terrifying.

"I'm not sure I understand."

If I've learned anything from watching crime shows on

TV, it's to keep your assailant talking. Keep reminding them you're a living, breathing human being. *Christ*, I hope they're right.

"And that's the problem, isn't it?" he says in a gentle voice that fills me with dread. "You don't understand, which is why you've forced me to take extreme measures."

He reaches out and I can't stop myself from flinching as he strokes the raw skin on my wrist with his fingertips.

"Look at what you made me do," he mumbles, almost like he's in a trance.

Then suddenly he grabs for my hair and yanks my head back, his face so close to mine, I can feel his erratic breath on my skin. He looks angry, his eyes almost black with rage as he bores them into mine.

"I admired you, looked up to you. I *trusted* you!" Spit hits my face as his fingers tighten in my hair. "But I should've known better. In the end, you are all the same; dishonest, deceitful sluts pretending to be purer than the driven snow."

Then just as abruptly as he grabbed me, he lets me go, barking out a bitter laugh.

"But we know you're not, don't we? Spreading your legs like a dog in heat for men who aren't worthy of your attention."

He raises his hand, index finger pointed, and slowly taps the tip to my nose.

"You disappointed me, but I'm not ready to give up on you yet."

I freeze when I see him pull a syringe from his pocket, pulling off the cap with his teeth. I have no doubt it's another dose of ketamine.

"Please," I find myself pleading before I can stop myself.

That seems to please him, as that boyish smile creeps back over his face.

"It's a miracle drug. But you know that, don't you? The perfect tool to control animals of all kinds. I learned that in college." The look on his face morphs into something more predatory. "But I've found ingestion takes too long to take effect. Injection gives much better results. Easier to control the dosage, not so messy, and faster."

It's almost like he's seeking my approval, wanting me to acknowledge how smart he is. But I can't bring myself to stroke his ego. I'd rather try and keep him off balance.

"What about Lacey?" I find myself asking.

I remember Ewing mentioning she'd had a piece of a broken needle embedded in her neck, implying she'd been able to struggle. It may not be wise to poke the bear, but I'll try anything to keep him from jabbing that needle into me again.

His face turns beet red.

"What about her?" he snarls.

"She wasn't so easy to control, was she?" I taunt him.

"That wasn't my fault, she showed up on her damn horse. I lost the element of surprise when I had to get her down first."

I almost laugh. It's unbelievable to me he is able to come up with a reason to blame his victim, but I guess that's the earmark of a psychopath; a total lack of responsibility.

Another trait would be the illusion of superiority, a grandiose sense of self. Psychopaths can be prone to boasting, which is something I hope to capitalize on if I can.

All those hours of watching crime shows on TV may come in handy after all.

"What about the first girl?" I have to think hard to remember her name. "Maggie Aldridge?"

He actually chuckles.

"Textbook, but you're wrong if you think she was my first."

My God, how many have there been?

"How did you meet her?"

Almost distracted, I notice him fitting the cap back on the needle as he leans casually against the side of the trailer. As if he's settling in to tell his story.

"At a private party I was dragged to by my parents. She was a server for the caterer. I was bored, so I ended up spending some time talking with the girl. She'd mentioned she liked hiking and was planning to try the trails near the Swede Mountain Lookout. She invited me to come."

Again, he easily shifts the responsibility to his victim. *She* invited him to come, as if what happened to her after was of her own doing.

"I bet she never saw it coming."

His smile is back, as if he's fondly remembering the events.

I suppress a shiver.

"Of course not," he brags. "And if it wasn't for my father's *buddy* walking his dogs and seeing me come down from the trail, no one would've been the wiser."

From the sneer in his voice, I can tell he's not a fan of his father's friend.

"Buddy?" I repeat.

"Phil Jericho," he clarifies, scrutinizing me as I process the shock of hearing that name. "The bastard used it to force me into helping him. How do you think you ended up with the job at the rodeo? You didn't think that was an accident, did you?"

"Me? Why? Why would he want me?"

"You're a woman, you're easier to control," he states

matter-of-factly, shrugging like it's the most obvious thing in the world.

Instantly my hackles go up and I react without thinking.

"I guess you were both wrong then," I snap, regretting it instantly when I see the change in his features.

"The only thing I was wrong about was that asshole tagging along with you," he says through clenched teeth. "He almost caught me trying to get that damn pinto back in the trailer, but I nailed him good."

"And yet he's the one who found Lacey," I remind him, irrationally defensive.

"Right," he drawls, a triumphant smirk on his face. "And isn't that gonna be the death of him when they find his ex-girlfriend murdered and the vial of ketamine she was shot up with at his house."

My stomach clenches painfully at hearing Britt is dead, and it has me lashing out.

"They already did, and guess what? No one believes JD did it. You failed."

In a flash he's on me, yanking the cap off the syringe with his teeth and trying to jab it in my neck. But I'm not going down easy, twisting and kicking, fighting with everything I have.

Sadly, it's not enough, as I feel the needle puncture my skin and my world goes black again.

JD

"You're better off going in on foot."

Jackson's voice fills the cab of Ewing's cruiser.

We followed the road around Flower Lake and are now stopped on the shoulder. Just ahead is the turnoff onto a driveway we waited for the drone to scope out first.

"You're sure the trailer is there?" I ask for confirmation.

"Affirmative. I see two structures, a cabin and some kind of large shelter behind it. It's covered with camouflage netting and branches, but I'm able to see the trailer tongue poke out. A black truck is parked in front of the cabin."

"Any movement?" Ewing asks.

"No."

"We're going in," I announce, running out of patience as I reach for the door.

"Like hell you are," Ewing grumbles, grabbing my arm to hold me back.

"We're two minutes out with all necessary equipment," Jackson reminds me. "Hold off and you can go in properly decked out. You're no good to Janey if you go in blind and he mows you down."

I grind my teeth, hating that he's right. At least if I have earbuds, I can get directions from him through the drone's eyes. The Matrice is relatively silent, and can hover under the cover of trees, remaining virtually invisible.

"Fine," I concede.

Ewing finds a spot to pull his cruiser off into the trees and we both get out of the vehicle to wait for the others to arrive.

"Keep your cool," my father warns me as we trudge through the dense underbrush side by side ten minutes later.

Easier said than done. I can't help think of all the things that could be happening to Janey during these precious minutes that keep slipping through my fingers. I can barely contain the rage flowing through my veins.

Pa, Jonas, Bo, and Jackson showed up in my old truck,

while Sully and Fletch stayed to load up the horses and take them back to the ranch. They brought communication equipment, weapons, ropes, extra batteries for the Matrice, and a medical kit. I hope like hell that last item won't be needed, but I'm grateful Bo brought it, just in case.

I'm lead with Pa, Ewing is right behind us, and Bo and Jackson right behind him. Jonas has taken over control of the drone and is feeding us directions.

It's hard to see where we are in relation to the dirt driveway. It would've been easier to follow it, but there's no way to know if the guy set up a few game cameras by way of surveillance. The military-style netting Jackson saw at least suggests he's taking precautions. Better we stick to the trees, where we can move undetected.

"The cabin about two hundred feet up ahead at eleven o'clock," Jonas warns in our ears. "Go to hand signals."

Pa stops us a little farther along and points up ahead. I catch a glimpse of a roofline.

The plan is to use the trees for cover as we go around the back of the cabin. There we'll split off in two pairs and approach the property from opposite sides. At this point, we don't know whether Janey is kept in the trailer or was moved into the cabin. But Jackson will find a perch in a tree, where he has a good shot at anyone going in or coming out of either structure.

We move even more cautiously now, keeping an eye on the cabin as we circle it.

"Stop!" Jonas suddenly orders. "Movement. Go low."

Pa motions for everyone to get down. I try to maintain a visual of the cabin while staying out of sight.

"He's on the move. Coming around the side now. He's carrying chains."

I'm barely forty feet away, looking at what Jonas is

describing; the kid I'd pegged as harmless, hauling a coil of chains to the shelter at the back of the property. I'm suddenly convinced that's where he's holding her, and the chains give me an odd sense of relief.

You don't chain up dead people.

It also presents me with an opportunity. What's he going to do with his hands full of heavy chains when he's caught by surprise?

I move on instinct, fast but silent, like my grandpa taught me when he took me hunting back when I was a kid. Ignoring Jonas's muffled cursing in my ear, I sense, more than hear, my father right behind me. Still pretty spry and light on his feet for a man his age.

There are fifteen feet of clearing from the edge of the trees to where Logan Osborne is heading toward the trailer. It takes him long enough for me to get within a few feet of him before he hears me coming.

But it's too late, he tries to turn, but I'm already launching myself at him. I catch him mid-turn, tackling him to the ground where he lands face-first. Then I haul my fist back and my mind blanks out.

"You got him, Son. He's down, ease up."

I find myself with my arms pinned to my sides, my father behind me, holding on fast while Ewing slaps the cuffs on Logan, who is not moving.

Then my eyes snap to Bo, who is approaching the shelter.

"Wait!" I yell, wrestling from my father's hold. "Let me go in first."

He holds up until I catch up with him. The ramp is down but the interior is cast in dark shadows. I have to squint to get my eyes adjusted to the dark.

"Damn," Bo mutters beside me.

At the front of the trailer, I see her twisted body, her weight hanging on her arms which are bound to the crossbar above her head. I rush to her side, lifting her to take some of the weight, while Bo pulls out a knife and cuts the zip ties off her wrists.

It's not until she slumps in my arms as my ass hits the floor, I question if she's even alive.

But then her eyes flutter open.

"There you are."

Twenty-Nine

"He's threatening to sue you for assault."

I burst out laughing at the sheriff's warning.

"Let him try."

I tuck my arm tighter around Janey who, so far, has put up with my need to keep her as close as I can at all times these past few days. Although, she did draw the line when I tried to follow her into the bathroom the other day.

The doctor had given Janey a hard time for showing up at the hospital once again, and wasn't enamored with her when she refused to stay the night. She just wanted some normalcy after what she described as being stuck in a spin cycle for a week. It made sense to me, I wasn't going to argue with her, but I *was* going to make sure she was well looked after when the doctor ordered her to take it easy until her follow-up appointment next week.

I immediately shot off a text to Jonas to let him know I'd

be taking some time. His response had been; *I'd assumed as much.*

The hardest part so far for Janey has been to close her clinic for a week. Luckily, Sam Feltner, the other vet in town, offered to take on any emergencies, and Frankie has been shuffling around all the standing appointments.

Still, Janey is going to have her hands full when she's given the all clear by her doctor next week. Her workload hasn't changed, but now she's facing it without the help of an intern.

That's something I still want to talk to her about. Call me selfish, but things have been crazy since she and I got together, and I want to make sure we carve out some time for us. I'm pretty sure she'll be hesitant to take someone else into her trust—given how badly Logan pulled the wool over all our eyes—but she is going to need the help.

"He wouldn't, would he?" Janey asks Junior Ewing, who dropped by to give us an update.

"It won't get far," he assures her. "Osborne Senior is just trying to flex his muscles, now that he's lost all credibility in town. He first tried to get me to file assault charges against you, but I reminded him I was right there on the scene and didn't see any assault take place. Then he tried to claim my incompetence with the mayor, but that didn't go very far either. Now he's threatening with this civil suit. What you're seeing are the last muscle spasms of the man's reputation. It wouldn't surprise me if he was asked to resign. Special Agent Kramer is having a long hard look at his close relationship with Jericho."

Apparently, Jericho had thrown Logan—and by association his father—under the bus, in hopes of securing a deal once he realized there was no escaping the evidence piled up against him.

"Did Jericho end up getting his deal?"

Ewing chuckles and shakes his head.

"Not a chance. Kramer is like a bulldog, she's pulling apart his life thread by thread, determined to dig up every little bit of dirt he's been hiding. Already he's facing something in the range of thirty-five or so federal charges. He's going down, and, if Stephanie has something to say about it, his entire network is going down with him."

I guess Councilman Osborne has good reason to be concerned. He's all but lost all credibility here in town, especially now the full scope of his son's crimes is starting to come to light. His list of victims is growing, with the unsolved rape and murder of two college students in Bozeman now attributed to Logan as well.

The media has gotten a hold of the story and it's been all over the headlines the past couple of days. *Son of Prominent Libby Family a Sick and Depraved Killer*. Fodder for the masses, but no less true.

Logan Osborne is one sick puppy.

He apparently has a type, if you can call it that. All his victims had longer, dark-blond or brown hair, and when you saw their pictures side by side, all looked very similar.

I glance down at Janey, whose brown hair is currently hanging loose down her shoulders, a bit of a departure from her usual braids, a little softer. She fit the profile as well.

But, more intriguingly, all of them look very similar to Megan Osborne, Logan's own mother.

There's been some speculation around that; some reports suggesting his deep-rooted hatred for his mother triggered his deadly spree. But those are just wild guesses, the family certainly isn't supporting those claims.

The kid is a psychopath, I don't know that he needs

much of a justification for his actions. Either way, we may never know the real reason.

What I do know is, he's currently in the custody of the FBI. In my mind, I picture him sitting in a cell next to Jericho's. Wouldn't that be something?

"Is she back in Kalispell? Stephanie?" Janey asks, shifting out of my hold as she gets to her feet and goes to grab the coffeepot.

"She'll be back and forth, I would imagine," Ewing informs her. "At least until she's got both these cases wrapped up." He holds up his hand to stop Janey from topping up his coffee. "I've had enough, thanks. I've had nothing but coffee sloshing around in my stomach for the past week. I'm pretty sure I'm growing an ulcer too."

"You need to take better care of yourself," Janey mutters as she tops up my cup and her own.

"Ha," Ewing barks as he gets up from the table. "Pot meet kettle. I see you haven't exactly been taking it easy."

He indicates the kitchen, which is a bit of a mess right now, since I've started pulling off the cabinet doors and hauling them out back to sand. It's not like me to start a new project when I already have one on the go in Janey's bathroom, but the weather is supposed to be nice for a while and Janey wants to repaint those cabinets to save some money.

"That's all JD's doing," she indicates. "All I've done so far is sit and watch him sweat," she adds with a grin.

Junior shakes his head, grinning before he puts his hat back on.

"On that note, I'm outta here. I'll be in touch."

I walk him out the door and stop on the front step. Glancing back over my shoulder, I see Janey moving around the kitchen.

"Do I need to be concerned about Osborne Senior?" I ask the sheriff in a low voice.

"Nah, he's too much of a coward. Besides, he's already in hot water, lying to law enforcement to cover for his son. I wouldn't worry about him; he'll be too busy dealing with me."

I watch him get in his cruiser and head down the driveway, when my phone rings in my pocket. I grin when I see the name pop up on my screen.

"Ma, I was wondering how long you could hold out."

"Bite me," she snaps. "You two have been holed up long enough. Dinner at the ranch at six."

"Ma—" I start to object, but she doesn't give me a chance.

"Don't be late."

❧

Janey

"I'm so full," I complain.

JD hums beside me, his eyes on the road home, but a smile playing on his lips.

"Forcing a second giant slice of lemon meringue pie down your gullet after eating Ma's taco bake will do that to you," he suggests dryly.

"Well, I could hardly say no," I protest.

His mother had insisted, and I'd been feeling so welcomed by everyone at the large table in the ranch kitchen, I didn't want to ruffle any feathers.

I'd been greeted like a member of the family, and was seated between JD and Thomas on my other side. JD didn't say much—I've noticed he's marginally more talkative one-on-one—but Thomas more than made up for that. I love that old man, he's full of interesting anecdotes, and his ongoing bickering with Ama is highly entertaining.

I've also finally had a chance to get to know Alex, Jonas's wife and Jackson's mother, a little better. It's funny, because Lord knows I've spent enough time here at the ranch, but also at Hart's Rescue, which she owns, but I've only run into her once or twice. I had no idea she went to veterinary school when Jackson was still a baby. He was already an adult when she moved to the Libby area and started up her rescue.

Of course, Jonas and Jackson had been there, and so were Wolff and Jillian, and Sully and Pippa, along with their daughter, Carmi. JD's dad, James, was another quiet presence at the table, a stark contrast to his wife, but I did notice his eyes followed her every move in the kitchen. Makes me wonder if JD looks at me like that.

When I glance over, I catch him side-eyeing me, a warm expression on his face.

"You know you're gonna have to learn to say no to Ma, or she'll continue to force food—and anything else she puts her mind to—on you."

I groan. These are my choices? Say no and risk Ama's wrath, or prepare to burst out of my pants?

"I don't think my pants can handle more padding on my hips," I grumble. "I guess I'll have to offend your mother next time."

He reaches out his hand and gives my knee a squeeze.

"My mother will live, and you can always buy bigger pants. I happen to love your padding."

My knee-jerk reaction would be to reject a comment like

that outright. Most people may tolerate extra weight, but love it?

Oddly enough, I believe JD. When he looks at me—when he touches me—it is with a certain reverence, an appreciation that feels genuine. The few times we've been out in public, he holds my hand or is touching me in some way.

A message to the world we are together, I am his, and he's proud of it.

Proud to be seen with me.

For a larger, and rather plain farmer's daughter, that's a rare experience. But a beautiful one. He doesn't tell me; he doesn't have to. He shows me all the time, and that's a language I understand much better.

We're still considered very new, but in some ways I feel like I've known this man forever. I *know* him, like he knows me. Maybe we met in a previous life. I feel if there is such a thing as reincarnation, this would be at least our second time around, maybe more.

He feels right, and I feel right when I'm with him.

Which is why the words come naturally as he pulls up in front of my house.

"I love you, James Dean," I admit softly, twisting in my seat so I face him.

He doesn't say anything, but a muscle ticks in his jaw, and his knuckles turn white on the steering wheel.

The next moment he's exiting the pickup and stalks around the front to my side, yanking the door open, and grabbing for my hand.

Without a word, he half drags me to the door, where he curses under his breath as he digs through his pockets for the keys he took charge of.

Once inside, he doesn't bother flicking on the lights, but

presses my body against the wall, kicking the door shut behind him with a foot.

Then his hands are on my face, lifting it up, and I find myself looking into the deep pools of swirling emotions.

"You stole my line," he grunts.

I feel a smile spreading on my face.

"You mean, I love you, James Dean?" I tease.

His dark eyes sparkle with humor as he slowly shakes his head.

The next moment his mouth is covering mine, his tongue forcefully spearing between my lips. The hunger in his kiss is an instant aphrodisiac. Then again, I seem to be in a perpetual state of arousal around this man. It doesn't take much to trigger a response.

His hands leave my face and restlessly move down my body, mapping curves and dips, before finally shoving down the back of my pants, grabbing handfuls of my ass. The full length of his body presses against mine, every hard plane and prominent outline imprinting on my flesh. I feel the vibrations of his low growls every time he grinds his cock against me.

I'm not sure how we end up on the couch, but I find myself draped over him, my T-shirt and bra wrapped around my neck, and my pants and underwear tangled around one ankle. He's still mostly dressed, with only his jeans partly shoved down his lean hips. His cock is free, and lightly probing my folds.

He tunnels his fingers into my hair and cups the back of my head, pulling my face within inches of his.

Then, as he surges up inside me, he whispers, "You have my love, Angel."

Thirty

JD

"I'm sorry."

I feel helpless when I glance over and see the tears running down her face.

"No reason to apologize."

She doesn't have a reason, but that doesn't mean I'm not quietly cursing circumstances that left me the only available person to race Sloane to the hospital.

Dan took their daughter, Aspen, to visit his father in Kalispell this morning, Sully and Pippa took Carmi camping at Glacier National Park this week, and the team—along with Jillian—is out on a search for yet another missing hiker. According to Thomas—the only other person left at the ranch—my mother is in town getting her hair done and we weren't able to get hold of her. So, it was down to me.

"I didn't think it was going to move this fast," she laments, before groaning deeply as another contraction takes control of her body. "I think I have to push," she manages.

"Don't do that. Breathe. Five more minutes to the hospital," I remind her.

It's probably closer to ten, even at the breakneck speed I'm driving, but I don't want to discourage her.

I've been at plenty of births, but those were of the animal variety. I'm in foreign territory here, but I'm pretty sure it wouldn't be a good idea to have this baby in the passenger seat of my grandfather's pickup. I'm starting to rethink my decision to drive her to the hospital myself, but I figured it would be faster than waiting around for an ambulance.

She has her eyes closed, lost to the turmoil in her body, when the cell phone she's clasping in her hand starts ringing. She barely even reacts, so I fish it from her fingers and answer.

"It's me," I let Dan know. His name showed up on the screen. "She's having a contraction."

He's the one who called the ranch twenty minutes ago to get someone to check on Sloane after he'd spoken with her.

"Fuck. I'll be at least another forty minutes."

"Head straight for the hospital," I suggest. "Things are moving."

"Fuck!"

In the background I hear Aspen starting to cry.

"Shit, I'm sorry, baby. It's okay. Daddy's not mad," I hear him mutter at her.

"Focus on getting yourself and Aspen here in one piece. I'll handle things on this end until you get here," I assure him with more confidence than I feel.

"Promise. No matter what happens, don't leave her alone," he pleads.

"She won't be. I'll keep trying Ma as well."

"I shouldn't have left her alone so close to her due date," he chastises himself. "But my sister flew in with her kids to visit Dad, and Sloane urged me to go. She told me Aspen was almost two weeks late. We were only going to be gone a couple of hours."

"Is that Dan?"

I glance over at Sloane, who has her eyes open and looks alert and determined. She holds out her hand and I give her the phone.

"Listen to me," she tells him sternly. "This is on me, but I'll be fine. This baby's gonna have to wait until its Daddy gets here, if it means I have to strap my legs together. You keep your damn eyes on the road and stay safe." Then her voice softens. "I love you too. Tell Aspen I'll see her soon."

No sooner has she ended the call, when her face scrunches up as another contraction starts. Her phone slips from her hand and hits the floor at her feet.

I grab my own phone from the console and hit Janey's number. She answers on the second ring.

"Miss me already?"

I can hear the smile in her voice. She does that a lot, and I find I do more than my share of smiling these days as well. She has that effect on me.

"I'm on my way to the hospital with Sloane. She's in labor, and Dan's on his way back from Kalispell."

"Oh shit. How close are her contractions?"

"Close. Where are you?"

"At the feed store picking up a few things. Do you need me?"

"Yes," I admit, feeling instant relief.

"I'll be at the hospital in five."

Don't get me wrong, I'd be honored to step up for my

friend and brother at the birth of his child, and I love Sloane like a sister, but I'm pretty sure they'd both be more comfortable if Janey held her hand in the delivery room instead of me.

She makes it in less, because she's already waiting at the emergency entrance with a wheelchair when I pull up in front.

"I guess that little one is in a hurry," she tells Sloane when she opens the passenger door. "Why don't we get you inside and see what's going on."

Her calm presence instantly changes the dynamic for me. I may appear laid-back or even stoic, but that doesn't always mean I feel that way, and I'm thankful when Janey takes over with confidence.

Growing up with a force of nature like my mother, I don't think I could ever underestimate a woman's strength and resilience, but watching Janey wheel Sloane into the ER is a good reminder why, in many ways, women are definitely the stronger sex.

I'm in the waiting room when Dan comes running in twenty-something minutes later with Aspen on his arm.

"What the hell? You—" he starts when he spots me.

"Janey's in with her," I quickly explain, cutting him off. "Room fourteen. I'll take Aspen."

The little girl isn't too pleased being handed off so abruptly, as her father darts down the hallway, and starts crying.

"Don't cry, little one. Wanna go for a walk?"

I bounce her in the crook of my arm and pace up and down the hallway outside the waiting room. It doesn't take her long to settle down with her thumb in her mouth and her head resting against my shoulder.

I like the weight of her in my arms, and wonder how it would feel to carry a child of my own like this, when I see Janey come through a pair of doors at the end of the hall. She's wearing a bright grin on her face.

"He made it in the nick of time," she whispers when she sees Aspen nodding off in my arms. "The head was already crowning."

I get a flash of a visual I quickly shake off.

"Good. Thank you for dropping everything."

"No need to thank me," she shares. "It was a privilege."

I hook her behind her neck with my free hand, and with a sleeping Aspen between us, drop a kiss on her smiling lips. Then I lead her into the waiting room and pull her down to sit beside me. With my arm around Janey and the baby asleep on my chest, I lean my head back against the wall, close my eyes, and wait for news.

Ma shows up shortly after, asking a ton of specific questions, most of which Janey answers since she'd been in the room with Sloane. She also tried to pluck Aspen from my hold, but the little girl grumbled a protest in her sleep and grabbed on to my shirt with her little fist, so we left her where she was.

Half an hour later Dan walks in, proud as punch with tear tracks on his face, holding the tiniest little bundled-up baby boy in his arms.

Janey

"Hey, Mom."

I hear the sharp inhale on the other end of the line, followed by some muffled rustling.

That would be the sound of my mother pressing the phone against her ample chest. She does that so whoever is on the other line doesn't hear her hollering for my father. It doesn't work, but I'm not about to tell her.

"Father! It's our Janey on the phone!"

I swallow a chuckle. I swear, it's the same every time I call.

My parents aren't even that old, only in their sixties, but you'd swear they were remnants of the fifties by the way they call each other *Mother* and *Father*. I think it may have started as a joke—mimicking my grandparents, who did the same thing—but it stuck somewhere along the line.

The yelling is fairly new though, it started after my dad had his stroke. Not that anything happened to his hearing, as far as I know it's as sharp as it always was, but Mom seems to think since he now struggles with his speech, he must be hard of hearing too.

I can almost see my father rolling his eyes at my mother's foghorn voice. That voice used to come in handy calling Dad in for dinner when he was out on the farm, but it's wasted in the tiny bungalow they call home now.

"I'm putting you on speaker," she informs me next.

"Hey, Dad," I greet my father.

"S-squirt," he mumbles with his unwilling mouth.

Hardly a squirt anymore, but it still makes me feel like a little girl.

It also makes me feel guilty, because I can't really remember the last time I called my parents. Life has been busy, and these past few weeks chaotic, to say the least. I'm not even sure what motivated me to call now, although it may have something to do with the large group of people I just left behind at the hospital.

Family by blood but also by choice, all gathering to greet the newest addition to the High Mountain Trackers clan, little Samuel David Sullivan Blakely. A name way too big for the six pound seven ounce baby who is already loved more than he knows.

Growing up as an only child, we didn't have a big family. Just Mom and Dad, and my father's parents. I never really knew my grandparents on my mother's side, and I know I have a couple of cousins on that side of the family still living in Ireland, but I've never met them.

I'm all my parents have, and I really should include them in my life more.

Which is why I called them as soon as I got in my truck.

"How is everyone doing?"

"Fine," Mom gives her standard chipper response. I don't think she'd tell me if she were on fire. "Your father has joined a card club."

"P-poker," he corrects her.

"*They play for bottle caps*," Mom whispers, as if Dad can't hear her sitting right there.

I hear him make a snorting sound in the background.

"What about you, Mom? Anything new going on with you?"

"Not really. But tell us about you, how are things going at the clinic? Still busy?"

"Yes, I'm actually looking for extra help."

"Didn't you say you had an intern this summer?"

I forgot I'd mentioned Logan, but I'm not about to tell them what happened over the phone, I'd rather fill them in in person.

"Unfortunately, that didn't work out. But I have some other news…"

"What is it?"

"I'm seeing someone."

"Ohh. Did you hear that, Father? Our Janey met a man."

Mom sounds positively gleeful. I know there's nothing she'd love more than to see me happy. I haven't really had any serious relationships worth mentioning, but things with JD feel different. For one, I love him, which is something I want to share with my parents.

Mom asks his name and how we met. Predictably, Dad asks what he does for a living. I field their questions as best I can, and promise to bring him up for a visit soon, making a mental note to check with JD when in the next week or two would work for him.

We say our goodbyes as I pull up to the clinic.

"And?" Frankie asks when I walk in.

"Healthy baby boy. Samuel David Sullivan Blakely."

"What's with all the names?"

"I think they picked Samuel, but David is Dan's father's name, and Sullivan is for Sloane's uncle Sully."

I bend down to scratch Ginger's head and glance at the stack of pink messages on the corner of Frankie's desk.

"Anything urgent?"

"Not really. I told John Findley you'd be by to do the vaccinations tomorrow morning instead. He was fine with that. The messages can wait for morning as well."

"Good. I'll be in the barn unloading the truck for the next ten minutes, and then I'm heading home. Oh, did we get any nibbles on the ad?"

"We got a number. I'll print out the résumés and leave them on your desk."

"Why don't you go over them?" I ask her. "Call the ones you like for a short telephone interview, select your top choices, and schedule them for an interview with me."

If I'm going to have any chance on a life outside of work, I'm going to have to delegate some of the duties.

~

JD's truck is already parked in front of my house by the time I get there.

I'm not surprised. Except when work calls either one of us away, there hasn't been a night we've spent apart this past month. Most of those nights were spent here, and some of JD's clothes and things have slowly made their way into my closet and bathroom.

It's been a natural progression, nothing forced, nobody asked or announced, we've just let things happen organically. It feels right.

Of course, most evenings we end up doing at least some work on the house. Mostly together, but we've had Jackson here a few times, lending a hand. JD has shown me how to tile, and I've been working on the bathroom floor for days. It's slow progress, but I'm being very careful, I don't want to mess it up. It's not like we're in a hurry.

When I walk in, Ginger beelines it to the kitchen, where JD looks to be busy doing something.

"What are you doing?" I ask, after pressing a kiss to his cheek.

"Making us a picnic. It's a beautiful day and it'll be a nice sunset. I thought we'd grab a couple of beers, sit by the creek behind my trailer."

"I'd like that."

Half an hour later, we're sitting in folding chairs at the

edge of the creek. I have a cold beer in hand and am watching the little red-and-white ball on JD's fishing line bob on the water. The sun is already sliding behind the mountains, leaving a warm, golden glow over everything it touches.

"I talked to my parents."

JD turns his head. "Yeah?"

"I told them about you."

He covers my hand on the armrest with his own, slipping his fingers between mine.

"I may have told them I want them to meet you."

"Yeah?" he says again.

I suddenly feel a bit awkward and start backpedaling. "I mean, you don't have to. I—"

"Would love to meet them. Let me know when you wanna drive up."

I lean my head back. "Okay."

It's that easy.

"Exciting day," he states a few moments later.

"It sure was. That little guy was welcomed with such love, so much joy," I observe.

"Hmm. Dan's a lucky bastard."

I glance over at him. "They sure have a beautiful family."

His eyes meet mine.

"Do you ever think about it? Making a family? Having kids?"

"I used to," I share openly. "For the longest time it was something I reserved for later. But life got busy, and to be honest, I never really met anyone I could envision having a family with. I'd almost gotten resigned to the fact a family was probably not in the cards for me. Realizing the window to have children was closing for me was painful, so I tried not to think about it that much anymore. At least I didn't until…"

"Until recently," he finishes for me, a faint smile playing on his lips. "I'm not that different. I think I always wanted a family, but it was more a wish for the future."

"Right," I agree.

He picks up my hand and kisses my knuckles, whispering with his lips against my skin.

"I think my future caught up with me."

Thirty-One

JD

She seems nice.

A total contrast to my sister—who shares my dark coloring—her fiancée, Rachel, is a true California blonde. She's very pretty and smiles a lot, most of the time aimed at Una. It's clear the woman adores my sister, who seems nervous.

"What kinds of apples do you grow?" Janey asks, twisted around in the passenger seat so she can look at her.

"A lot of varieties: Fuji, Granny Smith, Pink Lady, Gala, Jazz, Honey Crisp, Braeburn."

"Honey Crisp and Jazz apples are my favorites," Janey shares. "My mouth waters just thinking of them."

"Harvest will be in full swing by next week and runs well into November. I'll ship you a crate."

That's right too. I hadn't realized we're coming into what is probably the busiest time of year for Rachel, who owns an orchard.

"You don't have to do that," Janey protests.

"But I want to. I ship out a lot. It's part of my business. During harvest months I send out gift boxes with a selection of apples all over the U.S."

"Like jelly of the month," Una explains. "Except only for three months. It's been growing in popularity like crazy."

I glance in the rearview mirror and catch a glimpse of my sister, who looks at Rachel with pride. It's a different side of her. Una has always been such a prominent presence in our family, the center of attention, but here I can see her happily standing on the sidelines, shining a spotlight on her partner.

I hope Ma and Pa get a chance to see her like this as well; happy and in love. It's as obvious as the look on her face.

"Do you favor one apple over another?" Rachel draws me into the conversation.

"I like apples. I'm not a fan of mealy ones, but I like them crisp and juicy. That's all I know," I admit.

"My brother is the least label-conscious person you'll meet," Una shares on my behalf. "If he hadn't picked Janey, I'd say he has no taste at all. I want to bet he doesn't even know the brand of clothes he wears."

"My jeans are Wrangler, which is all I need to know," I fire back.

"Don't all cowboys wear those?" Rachel wants to know.

"All self-respecting ones," Janey contributes.

"Damn right," I mutter under my breath.

When I pull into the driveway of my parents' place, I can almost feel the tension in the back of the truck rising.

"It'll be fine," I tell my sister, catching her eyes in the rearview mirror as I pull up to the house.

Ma and Una have apparently talked quite regularly this

past month, and I'm guessing our mother pushed for this visit. I think my sister might've preferred holding off a little longer, but this weekend was the last chance before Rachel's business would tie her up for the next few months.

Ma seems to have mellowed a bit with both her kids in serious relationships. I know she loves Janey and I have no doubt she's going to love Rachel as well. Ma has a healthy appreciation for strong, independent women.

It's harder to get a read on our father, but I'm guessing as long as his kids and his wife are happy, he's happy. Love is not a word that he uses often, if at all, but we can feel it.

While Janey and I grab the bags from the back of the truck, Ma is already folding Una in a bone-crushing hug on the front step, with Rachel looking on. Then my mother hands my sister off to Pa, and turns to Rachel.

"So," I hear her say in a stern voice, "you're the one who wants to marry my daughter?"

I hold my breath as both Janey and I rush to flank Rachel on each side, just in case. But the pretty woman does not intimidate easily. She lifts her chin, which gains her maybe another half an inch on her petite frame.

"Yes, I am," she states without even blinking. "Next spring at the orchard."

Ma nods, but her face remains impassive.

"Are you gonna make me wear a damn dress?" she snaps, one threatening eyebrow raised.

Rachel bursts out laughing, and immediately returns, "You can wear whatever the hell you want, as long as you show up."

That earns her a barely-there smile. "Fair enough."

"Can we get off the damn porch already?" Pa grumbles.

With Rachel having passed Ma's scrutiny, she's waved inside and everyone else follows behind.

Janey and I are last, but she stops me in the entranceway, placing her hand on my chest and smiling up in my face.

"I love your family."

~

Janey

"Who was that?" JD asks when I join him in the barn.

He's already got Sterling saddled and is working on Red, who is still a little skittish, despite the work JD did with him the past two weekends.

I got waylaid by a phone call just as we were leaving the house so he went ahead.

"Special Agent Shane Wilcox."

"Really? How is he doing?"

Wilcox is the agent who got shot by Mackey, two months ago.

"He's doing well, he called to let us know an arrest warrant has been issued for Osborn Senior."

As expected, the councilman ended up resigning from office last month, and since then, he and his wife disappeared off the radar.

"Apparently, the charges against him are for his involvement in his son's murder spree. I think he said aiding and abetting, obstruction of justice, and accessory after the fact. According to Wilcox, David Osborn stands to face a long time behind bars."

JD hands Sterling's reins to me, and leads Red out of the barn. Sterling is a good girl, and stands perfectly still while I mount, but Red twists and turns, trying to make it difficult for JD to get in the saddle. He bucks half-heartedly when he feels the weight on his back, but JD controls him quite easily and motions for me to go ahead and take the lead.

We steer the horses on a trail that runs into the woods at the back of my property. We discovered it a few weeks ago when we took Ginger—who is fully recovered and loves her exercise—for a long walk. We picked today to pack a lunch and go exploring.

"What about the drug smuggling? Is Kramer still working on that angle?" JD asks from behind me.

"Actually, it sounds like Wilcox has taken over the lead on both cases," I share.

I was a little hurt to have to find that out from him, since Stephanie and I had been in touch over the past few months. When she'd come to town we'd try to meet up over coffee or a meal, and we shared quite a few phone calls. I would've thought she'd be the one to tell me something like that.

"He said Stephanie took a leave of absence."

"Really? Seems odd to walk out on two big cases like that. And didn't you talk to her just last week?" JD reminds me.

"Yeah, I know. Anyway, Shane didn't know or didn't want to tell me what was going on. I tried calling her after I hung up with him, got bumped straight to her voicemail, but apparently the inbox is full. I can't even leave her a message."

"Maybe she needed a break. Took a vacation," JD suggests. "I'm sure she'll be in touch."

I suppose it's possible, and I hope he's right, she'll get in touch at some point, but I shouldn't let it spoil the ride. I've been looking forward to this all week.

It feels good, breathing in the fresh fall air. We're far

enough from the road, you can't even hear traffic noise anymore, just the horses' footfalls and the sounds of nature.

This is not something I would've ever done before meeting JD, taking time for recreational purposes. I've always been all work and no play. Not that it was a hardship at all, I love my job, but there's something to say for taking an occasional day off and doing something for the sole purpose of nourishing your soul.

So I'm capitalizing on the fact Frankie helped me find Suzie Wong, a veterinary technician with a new baby. She wants to work part-time hours for a few years, which works out perfectly for me, since I don't yet have the money for another full-time employee.

I take in my surroundings, occasionally turning my head to point something out to JD or shoot him a smile, as Sterling sets a steady pace up to where the trees grow a little more sparse.

"Let's stop up on that ridge," JD suggests, pointing out a rocky ledge that should offer a nice view of the valley.

We tie the horses to a tree, and JD grabs the backpack he stuffed into Sterling's saddle bag, before we climb the remaining distance to the rocky outcropping. The view from here is amazing. Your eye skips over the busier valley and goes straight for the mountains on the other side. The fall colors are stunning. Maybe not as famous as the ones in the New England states, but no less beautiful.

It's warm for an early October day. I shrug out of my jacket I needed in the shade of the trees, but not sitting here on this rock in the sun. I lean back against JD, whose legs bracket mine.

I'm enjoying the silence we share. Every so often he feeds me a bite of cheese, or a piece of those delicious Honey

Crisp apples Rachel sent us last week. It feels utterly indulgent and blissfully relaxing.

Then suddenly, JD's hand appears in front of my face, instead of food dangling a silver chain with a gorgeously intricate, turquoise-and-silver pendant.

"It's not safe to wear a ring when you're working," he says softly by my ear. "But it would be an honor if you would wear this on your heart, as a sign of my love for you. My shield on your heart and my promise to keep it safe forever."

I tilt my head back and look up to see the love in his eyes.

"The honor is all mine."

~

Thank God for the small wood stove, I'd be freezing otherwise.

Of course, the downside is I have to go outside from time to time to grab some more firewood.

Not so bad during the day, when the temperatures venture into the fifties, but at night—when they dip below freezing—it's still a shock to the system. Hopefully, by the time May comes along, I won't need those extra blankets at night.

Not that I'm sleeping much, I spend most of my nights rewatching episodes of *House*. I'm almost through season seven, which leaves me with just one more season to go. I hope my sleep improves before I run out of episodes, otherwise I'll surely go nuts. The days are already hard enough to get through.

I can't believe I've been hiding out here for close to two weeks already. In some ways it doesn't feel quite that long, and yet, it seems like I left Kalispell ages ago. Maybe it's just that I'm determined to bury the events leading up to my departure deep. Nothing I particularly care to be reminded of, but my mind won't let me forget.

Then to add insult to injury, I was forced to take a leave of absence to *sort myself out*. My boss's words, not mine, but they were delivered in the hospital by my bedside, where I was recovering from what appeared to be a cardiac event.

It wasn't. According to the doctor, what I'd suffered was an anxiety attack. However, they did discover my blood pressure was concerningly high and I was put on medication for that.

When Don Bellinger—my boss at the Kalispell FBI

office—walked into the hospital room the next morning, the serious expression on his face made it clear he didn't come bearing good news. He explained the health scare had been the last in a culmination of reasons he felt it was better for me to take some time off. It hadn't been a question, it was clearly an order, and it couldn't have hit me harder.

The FBI is my life. It has been for the past twelve years, and I don't know anything else. Other than going to the gym regularly, I don't really have anything but my work to keep me occupied. Which is why my life feels like an endless void now that I've been sidelined.

After only one week stuck in my apartment in Kalispell, I'd been climbing the walls. A random phone call from Janey—who I'd remained friends with after she'd found herself at the center of not one, but two intertwined cases I was working on last summer in Libby—gave me the idea a change of scenery might be better for me.

I don't really have many friends outside of my colleagues, mostly because work takes up all of my time, but I connected with Janey. Probably because we're not all that different. She's a veterinarian, but she's also a bit of a workaholic. Anyway, I ended up spilling the beans. I told her the entire sordid story and she immediately offered me a place to stay and lay low for a while.

That's how I ended up in JD Watike's trailer on the banks of Libby Creek.

JD is Janey's man, and although they now live together at her place on the other side of the highway, he still has this trailer sitting on his pretty patch of land. I can see why he wouldn't want to let go, it's a beautiful spot. It definitely offers a better view than I had from my second-story apartment in Kalispell.

It's also lonely though, something I never thought I'd

feel. Other than Janey meeting me here with boxes of groceries when I arrived, I haven't seen anyone. Besides the occasional sighting of wildlife, that is. However, I don't know that I'm ready to face people just yet. I've spent enough time in Libby over the past years since I was transferred to the Kalispell office, I don't think I'd be able to avoid bumping into someone I know. I'm feeling a bit too brittle, still.

Unfortunately, after two weeks here my groceries have dwindled to the point of a limp stalk of celery, a quarter onion, the butt end of my last loaf of bread, and half a jar of peanut butter. Not exactly the sum of a meal. I'm not going to have any choice but to hit up a grocery store once the sun is up, which should be in another half hour or so.

With the quilt wrapped around my shoulders, I get up, shove my feet in my Crocs, grab the bucket by the back door, and slide it open to get to the firewood I chopped and stacked on the deck yesterday afternoon. It actually felt good, doing something physical after weeks of inactivity, staring into space like a couch potato. It was a decent workout I'm still feeling in my arms and shoulders. I groan as I fill my bucket and lift it up.

A rustle draws my attention just as I'm about to step back inside. Swinging around, I squint into the morning's deep shadows, trying to focus in on what I heard. As I scan the faintly visible tree line on the far side of the creek, I hear it again and my eyes snap in the direction of the sound.

Even with only the first faint hint of dawn in the sky, I have no trouble recognizing the large shape of a bear at the edge of the water on the other side of the creek. I can just see him off to my right where the creek bends out of sight. His front legs are in the water as he bends down for a drink, not paying me any attention. This is his domain, after all, and he's at the top of the food chain.

Then suddenly his large head snaps up and he appears focused on something on this side of the creek. I can't see what might've spooked him, but I jump when I hear the snap of a rifle shot.

Instinct has me drop the quilt and the bucket, and I duck inside, where my gun is sitting on the kitchen counter. When I slip back out, brandishing my weapon, I notice the bear is down. A splash of water has me glance to the far right, but I can't see anything. Trees block my view of the creek as it meanders its way south. Careful not to make any noise, I move to the edge of the deck and step down, keeping my eyes peeled and my gun aimed at the spot where I heard the splash.

I stop in my tracks when I see a figure appear, crossing the icy waters of the creek.

~

Jackson

From what I hear, sightings had been piling up this past week.

This isn't an unusual issue for April in these mountains. The animals come out of hibernation and are generally starving for food and water. With a rising population in recent years, food has become more scarce and some of the bolder animals venture closer to populated areas where they can find alternate sources. It's been a growing concern for fish and game wardens because of the danger to the public.

Last week, April fifteenth, the spring hunt on bear

opened, and I've been keeping an eye on this big guy for days now. He was seen on trail cameras along the creek, and has rampaged a few hunting shacks along the way, slowly moving closer to civilization.

I'd set up a few cameras of my own, hoping he'd eventually show up here, and this morning he did. I've been tracking him since the first watery signs of dawn.

This isn't my land, it's my friend JD's, but since he moved in with Janey, he doesn't seem half as interested to join me hunting. I don't blame him; I probably wouldn't want to get out of bed at the ass crack of dawn if I had a fantastic woman like Janey warming my sheets either.

But I don't mind being out here by myself. When it's just me and nature, I don't feel my limitations half as much as when I'm around able-bodied people. Don't get me wrong, I get around pretty well on my prosthesis—most people probably wouldn't even notice much more than a slight limp—but I am all too aware my right leg is missing.

They say it becomes second nature at some point, but the fact is about fifteen percent of the body I was born with is missing, which isn't that easy to adjust to. Every time I catch a glimpse of myself coming out of the shower, I'm still startled at my own reflection. This mental image I have of my former intact body persists, and I'm shocked each time to find part of it gone. Even in my dreams, I still have my right leg.

I went through a really dark phase for a while, especially right after my official medical discharge came through. Special ops had been my dream and I worked my ass off to get there. The training was brutal, my position on my team hard-earned, and our operations were dangerous, but I loved every goddamn minute of my years in service. I was good at my job too; as a sniper I could pick off a moving target at a thousand yards.

But in the end, my excellent marksmanship was irrelevant. We were on our way back to base when we ran into an ambush. Grenades from a Russian GM-94 were launched into the lead vehicle I was in. I don't remember much more than one minute I was looking forward to a shower and a hot meal back at base, and the next there was a scream, right before a blinding flash of light and a loud explosion filled the Humvee. The last thing I remember is the acrid smell of burning flesh.

A sound from across the creek drags me from my slippery slide down memory lane. Lifting my rifle to my shoulder, I squint through my night-vision scope to see the large lumbering shape of the bear moving out of the trees toward the water.

I wait a moment, allowing him to step into the creek for a drink, as I take in a breath and let it out slowly, grounding myself. I place the reticle of my scope right behind the bear's front shoulder, just as the animal raises its large head, blocking my side shot. From across the creek, I swear the animal is looking right at me, but I can't let it unnerve me. If this was just another bear or any other hunt, I might hesitate to pull the trigger, but this bear clearly has no fear and could pose a serious danger to the public.

Determined, I reset my scope, my target now low, between the bear's eyes at the bridge of his snout. The animal still hasn't moved a muscle when I slowly depress the trigger. The crack of the rifle reverberates loudly in the early-morning silence, and the bear drops down instantly.

It's not until I start wading across the creek I detect the smell of a wood fire. Odd, there's not much out here except for JD's vacant trailer. I turn my head and find it just a few hundred yards from where I came out of the trees.

The first thing I notice is the faint glow of light through the small kitchen window and it stops me in my tracks. Next, I catch movement on the bank of the creek, and see the outline of a woman, her arms stretched out in front of her. She's holding a gun in her hands and it's aimed at me.

"You're on private property!" she yells.

Her voice sounds familiar, but at this distance I can't make out her face.

"I'm well aware," I call back, changing direction as I start moving toward her.

Whoever she is, I'm pretty sure she has no business being here or I would've known about it.

"Not another step," she warns me as I approach.

Now that I can see more of her, I have no trouble recognizing her voice. In fact, I'm surprised I didn't recognize her sooner. Although, in my defense, the last person I expected to find camped out here in JD's trailer is Special Agent Stephanie Kramer.

"Easy...it's just me."

I pull off the camo-print balaclava I covered my face with, and see her expression change as she recognizes me. She immediately lowers her gun, but keeps it in her hand by her side, aimed at the ground.

"Jackson. What the hell are you doing here?"

"I should ask you that question," I return. "I live a few miles down the road and this is my friend's land, but you're quite a bit farther from home."

I notice her eyes drifting over my shoulder toward the dead bear. I get the sense she's not eager to share.

Too bad.

"Are you here on another case?" I push. "Does JD know you're using his place?"

Her eyes come back to mine and her shoulders slump visibly.

"Yes, he does, and can you just forget you saw me?"

It sounds more like a plea than a question, and either way, it's a laughable request. Like I'd be able to forget, I've had a hard enough time forcing thoughts of her from my head when she was safely tucked away in Kalispell. There is no way I'd be able to ignore the fact she's camping out right under my nose.

I'm also going to need a serious talk with my so-called friend, who is clearly keeping shit from me.

"Not a chance in hell," I tell her honestly. "So you may as well clue me in. Are you here for work?"

Her gaze drifts again, but this time she answers with a shake of her head.

"I'm on a break. Call it a vacation. I just needed some peace and quiet."

Something doesn't quite ring true. The Stephanie Kramer I met last year does not take breaks or vacations. She struck me as a bit of a workaholic, someone who doesn't have any quit in her and gives her all to the job. I recognized the drive. It's the same one I used to have. I have a strong sense she's not telling me the whole story.

"And you picked Libby?"

She shrugs. "That was Janey's suggestion. She offered JD's trailer which, she assured me, was sitting empty anyway. She was right, this place is peaceful and quiet. At least it was until this morning."

The last is said in a somewhat accusatory tone. It's a challenge I chose to ignore.

"Why did you shoot him?"

"Spring hunt opened last week and this guy was getting a little too comfortable around the more populated areas. Two birds with one stone."

Her eyes are still fixed on the bear's carcass, giving me a chance to take in her appearance in the pale light of dawn. She looks haggard—almost gaunt—with dark circles under her eyes, and I wonder if maybe she's ill. The messy bun, worn sweats, and ridiculous pink Crocs she's wearing are a far cry from the pony-tailed, buttoned-up, suit-wearing agent I know.

Something more is definitely going on and I am determined to find out what.

UP NEXT ARE STEPHANIE AND JACKSON IN HIGH VELOCITY.

GET YOUR COPY HERE.

SHUTTER SPEED

FREEZE FRAME

IDEAL IMAGE

Portland, ME, Series:

FROM DUST

CRUEL WATER

THROUGH FIRE

STILL AIR

LuLLaY (a Christmas novella)

Cedar Tree Series:

SLIM TO NONE

HUNDRED TO ONE

AGAINST ME

CLEAN LINES

UPPER HAND

LIKE ARROWS

HEAD START

Standalones:

WHEN HOPE ENDS

VICTIM OF CIRCUMSTANCE

BONUS KISSES

SECONDS

SNOWBOUND

About the Author

USA Today bestselling author Freya Barker loves writing about ordinary people with extraordinary stories. With 60+ titles to her name, Freya inspires with her stories about 'real' people, perhaps less than perfect, each struggling to find their own slice of happy.

Freya has her hands full with a retired husband, a needy pup, and a growing gaggle of grandbabies, but she continues to spin story after story with an endless supply of bruised and dented characters, vying for attention!

Recipient of the ReadFREE.ly 2019 Best Book We've Read All Year Award for "Covering Ollie, the 2015 RomCon "Reader's Choice" Award for Best First Book, "Slim To None", Finalist for the 2017 Kindle Book Award with "From Dust", and Finalist for the 2020 Kindle Book Award with "When Hope Ends", Freya spins story after story with an endless supply of bruised and dented characters, vying for attention!

www.freyabarker.com

www.ingramcontent.com/pod-product-compliance
Lightning Source LLC
Chambersburg PA
CBHW070406310726
48977CB00003B/586